D0949194

High Stakes

High Stakes

a novel by

JENNIE HANSEN

Covenant Communications, Inc.

Cover photograph © Digital Vision/Getty Images.

Cover design copyrighted 2004 by Covenant Communications, Inc.

Published by Covenant Communications, Inc.
American Fork, Utah

Printed in the United States of America
First Printing: July 2004

12 11 10 09 08 07 06 05 04   10 9 8 7 6 5 4 3

ISBN 1-59156-534-0

This book is dedicated to
Jennie Nell Snowball Smith,
the grandmother I have always loved and admired,
though I never knew her other than through
the stories my father, Jed Smith, shared with me.

PROLOGUE

November 1865

Elizabeth Rose lay still. Rain pounded against the window and beat on the roof. Voices came as from a long distance, though she knew they were in the same room with her. She was tired, so very tired. The pain had stopped, and a heavy silence hung around her like a tangible weight on her chest. There was something she needed to remember, something she waited to hear.

A thin cry reached through the fog surrounding her. For just a moment she thought of the long-haired kitten she'd played with before the war. But the sound didn't come from a kitten. Then she remembered. A baby—her baby. She struggled to brush away the lethargy that held her to her bed, but the dense clouds moved closer, as though the storm had entered the room where she lay.

The baby cried again, calling her back from the storm, and some maternal instinct tried to answer. Her hand fluttered weakly toward the sound. A familiar round face broke through the fog. Chloe held a tightly wrapped bundle before her eyes, then tucked a wailing, red-faced infant beside Elizabeth Rose. The cries subsided to be replaced with a faint smacking sound.

"She a fine one, that girl," Chloe announced. Her voice coaxed Elizabeth Rose to try to open her eyes once more, but the effort was too great.

I have a daughter, Elizabeth Rose thought sleepily. The thought filled her with softness and joy. She wondered if Sean knew and if he'd come home. Briefly she thought of the handsome rogue who had appeared on her doorstep near the end of the war to tell her that Papa wouldn't be coming back and who had stayed to make her his bride and take over the reins of River Belle. Sean knew nothing about running the plantation, but he'd charmed Jim and Chloe into staying— or they had stayed out of loyalty to her and to Papa's memory.

There weren't as many acres under cultivation now as there had been before the war, and expenses were high, but they were surviving—mostly due to the long hours Jim spent in the fields. Sean wasn't like Papa; he didn't enjoy walking the fields or working beside Jim. And the other slaves were gone. Sean had begun spending more and more time in New Orleans, neglecting her and the plantation. It had been almost three weeks since he had last left for New Orleans. Before he left, they had argued. She wished he were here now.

Thunder crashed beyond the mansion's walls. A bright light flickered and was gone. Beside her she heard a faint mewling sound. She attempted to gather the infant closer, but she was so weak her arms wouldn't obey her mind's urging. She'd had only one brief glimpse of her daughter; still her heart swelled with love for the tiny newborn. Barely able to move her lips, she whispered against the baby's ear the words Papa had spoken to her before he rode away to war: "Hold on through all the stormy nights; the sun is always the brightest after the darkest nights."

Somewhere in the fog that seemed to ebb and flow around her, she saw a little girl running across the broad lawns of the plantation, her full skirts billowing around her, while rain pelted her from every side. She tried to reach the little girl to offer her refuge, but it was a man's strong arms that reached the child first. The dream began to fade into nothingness as she felt herself being drawn into a swirling vortex. At the far end she sensed peace and light. She turned toward it, and there was Papa holding out his arms to her.

"Miss Rose! Elizabeth Rose!" She heard Chloe's voice, but she was too tired to answer.

"Elizabeth Rose! Oh, my sweet Rose." Sean had come. She tried to reach her hand toward him, but she couldn't open her heavy eyes. Then Sean's voice faded away as she became aware that Papa was standing at the foot of her bed. He held out his hand once more, and she stepped toward him.

"Papa," she whispered. She glanced back once at the sobbing man kneeling beside the bed and saw her baby's flailing hand catch one of Sean's fingers. She ached to comfort them. Perhaps it was Sean's arms that had caught up the child in her dream. The fog swirled closer, filled with thunder and storm. A heaviness in her heart told her Sean wasn't the one to save her little girl, but the peace that crept closer with the fog seemed to promise that someone would watch over her baby. Without Papa saying a word, she knew she must go with him. *Please, God, after the rain, help her find a brighter tomorrow,* her heart whispered as Papa's hand closed around her own.

CHAPTER ONE

August 1873

Holding the reins steady with one hand, Luke wiped the sweat from his eyes with the back of his arm. His mother passed him the jug of water she kept wrapped in rags on the floor of the buckboard. He took a long swallow and grimaced. The water wasn't even remotely cool anymore. "At least it's wet," he told her as he handed it back. He glanced at her with a question in his eyes. She'd been quiet since they'd started back. It had been her idea to go to Hewitt to hear the traveling preacher. Pa was too busy to leave the ranch, but he'd said Ma could go if Luke would take her. Luke had been more than willing to accept the responsibility. It filled him with pride that Pa thought him man enough to drive Ma to town and look after both her and his finest team of horses.

"We're almost home," his mother said with a smile. "Thank you for taking me to the preaching."

Luke shrugged his shoulders, and one side of his mouth lifted in a slight grin. "Weren't nothin'." After a few moments, he asked, with a hint of curiosity in his voice, "You expect that preacher man is right about us all bein' sinners and how we're all going to burn in hell if'n we don't let him baptize us?" He couldn't remember ever listening to a preacher before, and the time he spent each morning reading verses from Ma's big Bible hadn't prepared him for the singing and shouting they'd just experienced.

"I don't know, son. There aren't any of us that are perfect, that's for sure. But there are so many people in this world that I don't think one preacher can baptize them all. When I was a girl, we went to church every Sunday in a white clapboard chapel with a bell tower. Reverend Jones was a soft-spoken man who spent all week doing good things for people. He never talked much about hell—mostly his sermons were about heaven and being kind and forgiving. He was a good man who encouraged folks to read their Bibles on a regular basis, but somehow I always found something lacking."

"Did you find what you were looking for today?" Luke asked. He glanced sideways at his mother's face and saw her concern.

"No. It wasn't there in all the threats and shouting." She sounded disappointed. They rode for another ten minutes in silence, then just as they topped a hill and saw the ranch spread out before them, she placed her hand on top of his.

"Luke." Her voice held a note he'd never heard before. "God is real. I know it. When you're young and strong you get to feeling like you can take care of yourself and you don't need to think about God. But that's wrong thinking. He helps us—even through the bad times when we get to thinking He's forgotten all about us. I don't know enough about Him to teach you properly, but I do know the preacher back home was closer to the truth than that traveling preacher we listened to in town. Promise me you'll keep looking for His truth."

Luke swallowed hard. He wasn't sure what Ma wanted him to promise, but Pa set store by telling the truth, and he didn't figure it would hurt to agree to what she asked.

"Sure, Ma. I'll look." He slapped the reins across the backs of the horses, urging them to hurry. The new barn was just ahead, and in spite of the Texas sun pouring down from the sky, the pair began to trot.

* * *

April 1874

"Pick up your feet!" Papa's voice was sharp.

"Yes, Papa." Maddie stretched her short legs, trying hard not to step in a hole. Rain earlier in the evening had left the path slippery and filled every low spot with water. She followed Papa down the path that led to the river, clutching the small bag that held the few clothes she had been able to stuff into it in the dark. Trees blocked her view of the sky, causing her to hurry before she lost sight of Papa. The ground was soft under her feet, and she could hear the distant croak of bullfrogs. Each time a trailing strand of moss brushed against her face, she shivered. She'd been foolish to think Papa would want to stay this time. Just because he'd allowed her to attend the one-room school and to play with other children shouldn't have given her cause to think he would stay.

She knew better than to ask where they were going or why they had to leave in the middle of the night. It wasn't the first time Papa had awakened her from a sound sleep to tell her it was time to go. It was the first time, however, that she had questioned their reason for going. She didn't doubt Papa—not really—but snatches of conversation she'd heard during recess the past few days troubled her and made her wonder if they had to leave because Papa cheated at cards.

It wasn't just the possibility that he might cheat at cards that worried her. She wished she knew whether Papa loved her. Sometimes she thought he did because he never left her behind when he suddenly had to go. At least he hadn't yet. But she wondered if he might if taking her along got to be too difficult.

She placed her feet with care on the path. She didn't want to ruin her slippers, and she knew from previous experience that after one of their sudden moves there sometimes wasn't enough money to replace things like worn slippers or items left behind. They had moved so many times, mostly in the middle of the night. She couldn't count how many hotel rooms she and Papa had shared.

She had only vague memories of a big house and a large black lady who had cared for her there. She remembered another house in New Orleans and a lady she had called Aunt Priscilla who smelled nice and who had rocked her to sleep at night and told her stories about visiting Mama on Grandpa's plantation when she and Mama were little girls. Aunt Priscilla had wanted Maddie to stay with her when Papa went away on business, but Papa wouldn't allow it. They had argued, and both had become angry. That was the first time Maddie remembered leaving while it was still dark and everyone else was sleeping.

Until recently, she hadn't questioned the way she and Papa lived, but she was older now and she knew other children lived in the same house year after year. They went to school and they had grandparents and cousins in the same town or on nearby farms. They didn't have to stay in strange rooms all alone while their papas "took care of business." And she suspected other fathers didn't drink as much nasty whiskey as her papa did.

The other children said Papa not only cheated at cards, but he was a drunk too, and he owed somebody a lot of money. She didn't want to believe that the children were right, but she worried that they might be. She wanted to ask Papa about it, but she knew he'd just get angry if she did. She tried not to make Papa angry because when he was angry he sometimes hurt her or threatened to leave without her.

She and Papa reached a small landing on the river's edge, and Papa untied a rowboat while urging her in hoarse whispers to hurry. Placing her hands on the side of the small boat, she felt the way it wobbled and moved away from her when she tried to follow Papa's instructions. At last she swallowed her fear and climbed inside. Papa jumped in after her, causing the boat to dip far to one side before steadying again. She glanced uneasily toward the wide expanse of dark water. It wasn't much of a boat for so much water.

Papa shoved away from shore to where the current picked up the small boat and began to carry it from the cluster of silhouettes that made up the town. Papa stopped rowing from time to time, looking around without speaking. Not until they were several miles downstream did he reach for his portmanteau and the bottle it contained. The river was wide and the current slow, but its expanse seemed to stretch on forever in the darkness.

It was dawn when Papa secured the boat to the rotting dock of an abandoned plantation. They stepped ashore, where Maddie could see the stark outline of a chimney soaring above a pile of rubble at the end of a sweep of overgrown grass and shrubs that was once a lawn. The sight made her sad, but she didn't have time to think about it because Papa wanted her to change into her best dress.

The dress was too small, but with Papa's help, she managed to fasten it. She was small for her age, but she had grown a few inches in the years since Aunt Priscilla had bought the satin and lace dress for her. She'd been enchanted by the feel of the pale rose dress with tiny heart-shaped buttons and row after row of lace. There had been four petticoats, one with a wide hoop, but now only one petticoat remained and the hoop had been left behind a long time ago. She smoothed her hands over the pale satin and wondered if Aunt Priscilla ever thought about her. She didn't think about Aunt Priscilla much anymore except when she put on the dress.

Papa changed his clothes too, putting on a black suit with a ruffled shirt and string tie. He fussed at the wrinkles from their clothing being stuffed in the portmanteau.

Once they were dressed, Papa took her hand and led her to the far side of the derelict mansion to a road he seemed to know would be there. A piercing whistle caused her to jump. Papa grinned and began to move faster. Just around a bend in the road she spied a town. It appeared to be larger than the one they'd recently left, and more prosperous. She could see that the road they'd followed had circled around and come back to the river where a large paddle-wheel boat was easing its way toward a dock. Dozens of people bustled about the dock. Some were carrying boxes and barrels, and some were standing around in small groups. Several wagons clattered by. The boat released another piercing whistle, and Papa took a brush from his pocket and ran it hurriedly through Maddie's pale hair, then slicked back his own locks before easing their way into the crowd waiting for the ferry's arrival.

Moments after the vessel docked and the gangplank was lowered, a few people stepped ashore. Then she and Papa with a dozen or so others made their way aboard the stern-wheeler. She felt a glow of pride that she could read the large letters on the side of the boat proclaiming it the *Delta Queen*. Aunt Priscilla had taught her to read letters, and she'd seized every opportunity to learn more. Her thoughts turned with longing back to the town they'd just left and its small, one-room school.

Papa spoke briefly with a man at the top of the gangplank and handed him some money, then they led Maddie to a narrow room containing two bunks and not much more. Stretching out on one of the beds, Papa was soon asleep. She couldn't unhook her dress by herself, but she was so tired she settled on the other bunk anyway, still dressed in her finery. In spite of her fatigue, sleep came slowly.

When she awoke, she was alone. She found a basin of water and made herself as presentable as possible before venturing out in search of Papa. When she peeked into the dining room, a smiling black man wearing gloves motioned her to a table where she was soon served a large roll and a pink slice of melon. She discovered she was hungry and ate quickly, but when the waiter offered her another roll she declined. She had to find Papa. The waiter pointed to a curved staircase, and when she'd climbed to the top of it and peeked through a red velvet curtain, she saw Papa sitting at a table covered with green cloth. He was scowling at the cards in his hand. She sat quietly for several hours waiting for him to finish, but he never noticed her, and she knew he'd be angry if she interrupted him. At last she returned to their room by herself. With the help of a button hook she found hanging on a nail near the door, she was able to unhook her dress and change it for a simpler one.

Over the next few days, Maddie frequently found herself alone. Meals were taken in the large dining room, and she was free to wander at will around the big floating hotel. Papa spent most of his time playing cards in the smoky room decorated with plush curtains and carpet. She peeked in sometimes to see him sitting at one of the tables with several other men. There were always cards in his hands and a glass in front of him. In the evenings, a man with his shirt-sleeves rolled to his elbows played the piano that was anchored to the floor like most of the furniture on the *Delta Queen*. Making herself as small as possible, she hid behind the red curtain and listened to the music. Sometimes the music carried over into her dreams, and she awoke with the happy tunes scrolling through her mind.

She and Papa seldom left the boat, and Maddie became familiar with the crew and the stops along the way. Sometimes she leaned against the rail and watched villages and farms go by, and sometimes she saw children and dreamed of going to school with them and playing games together until their mothers called them in to supper. Once she and Papa left the boat with a lady who wore a big hat and laughed too loud. They spent the afternoon shopping, and, to Maddie's surprise, Papa bought her two new dresses the lady picked out for her. She didn't like either one, but at least they fit her. He also purchased a new dress and hat for the lady along with a black suit and a ruffled shirt for himself.

Standing at the rail one afternoon, she watched the water churn around the big paddle wheel. After a few minutes, she lifted her eyes to the shore and noticed that the trees were changing color. Most had sported tiny, pale green buds when she and Papa had first boarded the *Delta Queen*. Slowly the trees had become fuller, and their color had deepened to darker shades of green. Now they were changing again to yellows and reds as she and Papa traveled north. She'd heard some of the crew talking about this being the *Delta Queen's* last season and saying that when they returned to Baton Rouge next month the old boat would be converted for hauling freight. It was already carrying more cargo than passengers. She wondered what she and Papa would do and where they would go.

A sound interrupted her thoughts. Someone was singing. Curious, she made her way around a collection of barrels at the stern of the boat. Taking care to make no sound, she moved closer until she could see the coarse leather of a heavy shoe and a bit of blue gingham.

Easing her back against one of the barrels, Maddie listened intently. She'd never heard the song before. It was nothing like the tunes Mr. Joe played on the piano upstairs, but it sounded happy. She shifted further around the barrel until she could see the singer. She stared in amazement at a young girl who looked to be close to her own age. She was dressed in a simple, dark blue dress, and her brown hair trailed down her back in two long braids. Freckles dotted the girl's nose, and her mouth, too large for her face, was open wide as the song poured from somewhere deep inside her. She stopped in midnote when she saw Maddie.

The two girls stared at each other for several minutes before the singer spoke. "I haven't seen you before. Are you going to Deseret? My whole family is going. Owen didn't want to go because Mari isn't going, but he promised to save enough money so he can send for her next year. When we get to St. Louis we'll take the train. Are you traveling by train?"

"No. I don't know," Maddie stammered. The girl spoke funny— not like a Yankee, but not like anyone else she'd ever heard either.

"Well, you probably will. Mam says almost everyone takes the train now. We've been traveling for just forever, and it will be quite nice to have a house again. Did you know there are mountains? Dad says they're nothing like the hills back home. And snow. It rains more than snows close to the ocean where we used to live, but Dad says the snow in the valley lasts and lasts. I think I shall like that; I'm terribly tired of being so warm." She fanned her face to emphasize how warm she found the day. Maddie thought it quite cool on the river.

"I think snow would be nice, though I've never seen any. There's a breeze coming off the water, so it's much cooler here than it would be if we were ashore," she told the strange girl. She paused a moment, then added, "I heard you singing. It was nice."

"I love to sing." The girl smiled a wide, friendly smile. "We all sing, even Dewi, and he's only two. Dad used to play the organ at Capel Seion, but he's not allowed to anymore because he got baptized. He was let go as headmaster at the school as well, and no one wants him to tune or repair their musical instruments any longer. We all were baptized, except Dewi and Ceri—they're too young. When we get to Salt Lake City, Dad says it will be his job to keep the grandest organ of all tuned and in repair. And if President Young will allow it, Dad will play the organ while the Welsh Choir sings."

Maddie knew what an organ was. Aunt Priscilla had taken her to a big church in New Orleans a few times, and she had heard the soaring sound the organ made. *Grand* was a good word for it. But she'd never heard of Capel Seion or Salt Lake City or President Young.

Feeling awkward and shy, she said, "I don't know where we're going. My papa doesn't play organs, just cards. But we go to many different places. If we ever get to your Salt City, I'll ask Papa if I can listen to your dad play the organ."

"I wish you were coming with us now." The girl's voice was wistful. "I don't have anyone to play with except my brothers and little Ceri. But she's only five, almost a baby. Most of the time I have to watch her and Dewi for Mam, but Mam said she is feeling much better today, and she gave me permission to spend the day on deck studying my letters. Owen and Dafydd didn't want me tagging after them, so I found this spot where I can practice on my slate." She looked guiltily at the slate board lying on the deck, then back at Maddie with an impish grin. "I like singing better than practicing my letters." Both girls giggled.

"I like this boat much better than the one we were on before," the dark-haired girl confided. "We planned to be on a different ship with the rest of the Saints when we left for Zion. That ship went to New York and there were lots of Saints on it, but it was already full when we got to the port. Dad said the one to New Orleans would do, and we could take a stern-wheeler from New Orleans to St. Louis, then a train across the prairie. He said it would be a great adventure, but I've been rather lonely."

"Why haven't I seen you on deck before this?"

"Dad says we should stay to ourselves and avoid drawing attention. He's worried because the passengers on this boat are mostly Missourians and he's concerned about our safety."

"Oh, you're perfectly safe on the *Delta Queen*. Papa and I have lived here all summer and nothing has happened to us."

"It's different for us. We're Mormons and many people hate us."

"I don't hate you," Maddie said. The other girl seemed perfectly nice, and she couldn't see any reason why anyone would hate her. But then, lots of people didn't seem to like her and Papa much either, and sometimes they threatened to shoot Papa. "Is Mormon your name?"

"Oh no, my name is Catrin Prosser." Her smile stretched wide and she seemed about to laugh, then her smile disappeared and she became serious. "It's because of Joseph Smith that people hate us. God showed him some gold plates with writing on them that no one else could read. God told him what the marks meant and to write it all down. What he wrote is called the Book of Mormon. Some people got angry because they didn't believe God talked to Joseph Smith and they didn't want to do the things the book said we should do."

"What does the book say we should do?" Maddie puzzled over why anyone would hate someone because of a book, especially if God told this Joseph Smith where to find it.

"Well, first it says we should obey Jesus. We have to make up our minds whether we're on His side or the bad side."

Maddie had a vague recollection of Aunt Priscilla telling her about Jesus. Every night before climbing into her big feather bed, Maddie had said her prayers with Aunt Priscilla's help. Maddie remembered how warm and good those prayers made her feel. She supposed that since Aunt Priscilla talked to Jesus, she must be on His side, and if she were choosing sides she thought she'd like to be on the same side as Aunt Priscilla—and Catrin Prosser.

"Catrin!" a voice called.

"That's Mam," Maddie's new friend sighed. "I suppose she needs me to watch my sister again."

"I could help you," Maddie offered eagerly. Catrin flashed her a wide, grateful smile, and the two girls hastened to find Catrin's mother.

They found her standing in the doorway leading to the cheaper cabins. She was tall and thin with a big belly, and Maddie thought she looked tired. She could see a resemblance to Catrin in the dark hair and wide mouth. Two small children clung to her skirt, and when they saw Catrin they dropped the fabric they clutched and ran eagerly toward her. They stopped when they saw Maddie. The little boy's thumb went into his mouth and he sat down abruptly. The little girl inched closer to her sister, slipping her hand into Catrin's. Maddie swallowed to gather her courage before introducing herself to the woman, and Catrin told her younger brother and sister that Maddie was her new friend and they were all going to play together. The tired woman didn't object, so Maddie followed Catrin and the children clinging to her hands to the space behind the barrels.

Maddie was surprised to find how much fun it was to play with the younger children once they got over their shyness. Catrin taught them songs and told them stories. Many of her stories came from the Bible and the Book of Mormon.

"It's your turn now." Maddie was startled by Catrin's declaration, but then she saw the slate her new friend was extending toward her. She swallowed deeply and accepted it. She looked at it a moment, then began to write.

"This is *A*." She pointed to the letter she had made. Catrin carefully copied the letter, then Ceri wanted a turn. After that, young Dewi grabbed the chalk and attempted to eat it. Catrin rescued the chalk, and Maddie continued to help both Catrin and Ceri with their letters until their mother called them to supper.

Maddie wandered to the dining room to eat her evening meal alone, though she would have much preferred to eat with Catrin and her family.

CHAPTER TWO

Maddie scrambled into her clothes at first light the next morning. She glanced toward Papa's bunk and saw he was sound asleep, snoring loudly, still dressed in his black suit. She wrinkled her nose at the stench of his whiskey breath and unwashed clothing. Today she didn't dwell on his habit of sleeping until well past lunchtime. Instead, she ran a brush quickly over her long, pale hair, wincing at the tangles she never quite managed to remove.

When she was finished, she opened the door and hurried to the dining hall for breakfast, all the while watching carefully for Catrin. She wasn't really hungry, but she had a plan. When the smiling black servant brought her a sweet sticky bun, she wrapped it in her napkin and thrust it into her pocket. Minutes later she was poking around the freight stored on deck. When she located the spot where she'd found Catrin the day before, she settled against a barrel to wait.

She didn't have to wait long. Catrin's lilting voice preceded her to the spot the girls had claimed as their own. Ceri and Dewi were with her, and Catrin was carrying a book.

"Before the elders left for America, they gave us this book," she announced, holding it aloft. "They said it would help us learn English, though we've all been speaking the language from the cradle since Dad decided we would be better off speaking two tongues." She thrust the book toward Maddie.

Maddie cradled it in her hands. Her fingers traced the engraved lettering on the cover. She'd never had a book of her own, and Papa didn't own any.

"Now, you sit here," Catrin indicated a sheltered spot for Ceri. "And Dewi can sit here." She plopped down beside Maddie, pulling her little brother onto her lap. "Will you read to us?" she asked Maddie when she was settled.

Maddie nodded her head and carefully turned the pages until she came to chapter one, then she began, "I, Nephi . . ." It was an exciting adventure, though some of the words were unfamiliar. When she found herself stumbling over the pronunciation, Catrin would help her find the right word. In a short time, Dewi grew restless, and Maddie reached into her pocket for the napkin she'd placed there. Ceri wanted some of the sticky bun too, so Catrin broke it in half for the children to share, then carefully licked the sweet icing from her fingers. Maddie continued to read until the smaller children grew restless again, then Catrin taught them a new song, and they practiced writing on the slate.

Maddie glanced longingly toward the book when Catrin tucked it under her arm and gathered up Dewi and Ceri to return to their mother.

"They're tired and must take naps, but I'll be back in a little while," Catrin promised. "And we can read some more. The missionaries read some and Dad read the rest to us in our own Welsh language, but I want to hear it all in English before we reach Zion."

Maddie didn't always understand what Catrin meant. Some of her words were strange, but she was glad the other girl was willing to share her book and spend time with her. The afternoon passed quickly as the two young girls sat side by side and Maddie pointed to the words she read so Catrin could familiarize herself with them. Sometimes they stopped to talk about what Maddie had just read. She liked reading about the things Nephi and his brothers did, and she found it amazing that Catrin knew so much about Heavenly Father when she herself hadn't even known she had another father besides Papa.

Maddie read about a man who hid in the forest from a wicked king and of a man who stood on a great wall where no stones or arrows could reach him, then Catrin told her about an army of boys who fought in a war and none were injured because their mothers had taught them to trust in God.

They talked about mothers then, and Catrin said she'd be glad when the new baby was born so hers would feel like singing again. Maddie shared her sorrow that she didn't have one.

"You do have a mother," Catrin told her. "She's up there in heaven watching over you. Mam says that once we get to Salt Lake and the temple is finished, we'll go there so we can be together forever and ever. Then, even when Mam gets old and dies, she'll still be our mam."

"How can she be your mother if she's dead?"

"When we get to heaven we aren't dead anymore. In heaven people still care about the people they love here, and after a while, we all die and are together again."

Maddie thought about Catrin's words and hoped they were true. She'd like to think she still had a mother somewhere and that maybe her mother really did love her.

For two more days they read and sang together, then on the third day Maddie stood near the rail with tears on her cheeks, watching Catrin and her family disembark. Catrin turned to wave when she reached the end of the gangplank. Moments later the Prosser family disappeared into the crowd. Maddie watched for a long time, hoping to catch one more glimpse of her friend, but they were gone.

Later that night she tossed and turned on her bunk. She wished Papa would come, though she didn't really expect him until morning. A number of gentlemen had come aboard to spend the evening in the saloon with Papa and the other gamblers aboard the *Delta Queen*. She knew most of them would leave early in the morning before the boat got underway, and Papa would play cards and drink whiskey until the last one left.

Finally she arose from her bed to pull her dress back on. Leaving her shoes behind, she made her way to the stairway leading to the fourth-tier salon. She peeked behind the red curtain to see Papa sitting with his back to her at a table only a few feet away. Seating herself on the top step, she leaned against the wall and felt a little closer to Papa.

She could tell by Papa's slurred voice that he was drinking whiskey. The other voices grew louder and occasionally an argument erupted. She leaned closer to hear better when she heard someone mention the Mormons. Their mean, hateful words made her glad the Prossers were no longer aboard, and she wondered if any of the dreadful stories they told were true. She didn't see how they could be because Catrin and her family were the nicest people she'd ever met.

Being reminded of the friend she'd known so briefly brought tears to her eyes, and she felt terribly alone. Papa didn't even know she was sitting just a few feet from him. Placing one hand on the wall behind her, she stood. Prickles in her feet told her she'd been sitting in one position for too long. It took a few moments before she could walk, then making her way down the stairs and along a corridor, she reached the room she and Papa shared. Slowly she undressed and crawled between the sheets.

She could see a pale, almost blue, sliver of moon through the porthole. She remembered the things Papa's friends had said and decided they weren't true, but it was difficult to put them out of her mind. She tried remembering everything Catrin had ever said, but it was Catrin's last conversation with her that brought her peace. "I'll pray for you, and you must pray for me. We won't see each other anymore, but we'll have the same friend."

"Who is our friend?" Maddie had asked, feeling puzzled by Catrin's words.

"Jesus is our friend. He's Heavenly Father's Son. He loves us both, you know, and we can always talk to Him when we're lonely or afraid. Talking to Him always makes me feel better, and He'll help you too." She had turned quickly to a passage in her book, but instead of reading it, she told Maddie how long ago the earth was dark and people were scared, then Jesus came and it was light again and He blessed everyone, especially the little children. He prayed, and angels and fire circled the children, keeping them safe.

"He promised always to comfort and bless those who believe in him," Catrin concluded. Maddie wished she had Catrin's book. There was something comforting in just holding it, and when she read from it, her heart felt at peace.

Deciding to see if Catrin was right, if Jesus would comfort her even when she didn't have the book, Maddie slid off the bunk and knelt just the way Aunt Priscilla had taught her. Clasping her hands together and screwing her eyes tightly shut, she began, "Dear Jesus . . ."

* * *

June 1874

Luke saw the cow leave the brush, trailed by a spotted calf. Something about the wide sweep of horns caught his attention, and he moved closer for a better look. It was Dolly! She had a healthy calf trailing behind her too. His chest swelled with pride as he watched the cow he'd hand-fed as an orphan calf a few years earlier.

A grin spread across his face. He hadn't been more than nine then and had relished the task of feeding the maverick his father brought in from the range before a predator could reach it. He'd hand-fed a lot of calves since then, but he would always have a soft spot for Dolly.

The cow, now as wild as the other range stock, turned back into the brush, and Luke's eyes widened. The mark on her rump wasn't right! Could he be mistaken? Was this some other cow and not Dolly?

He rode closer, but not close enough that the cow might catch him with her wicked horns. He hadn't made a mistake. The cow was Dolly, but the familiar Calloway brand was no longer displayed on her hide. Instead, burnt hair proclaimed a recent change in ownership.

Digging his heels into his horse's sides, he turned back toward the ranch house. His father needed to know about this. Pa had suspected something wasn't right for several weeks; they'd found few cows with calves at their side this spring, while the neighboring ranch seemed to have more than its quota of calves.

As other ranchers had moved their herds to the area surrounding the Calloway ranch the past couple of years, there had been instances where a few calves had been claimed and branded by the wrong ranch. But this was an honest mistake that happened occasionally when a calf was separated from its mother for one reason or another. Otherwise, changing a brand usually occurred only when breeding stock was sold to another rancher. Luke knew Dolly hadn't been sold, and her new brand wasn't displayed beside the old one, but on top of the old one. The Calloway Cross C had become the Double Bar D.

He didn't recognize the brand as one belonging to any of the neighboring ranches, but this part of Texas was filling up rapidly, and it could belong to any of the newcomers. Then too, it might not even be a legitimate brand. It could be a mark some rustler picked because it was easy to fit over the top of the one his pa used, and it was all the crook needed to start moving a stolen herd north to the new territories.

His horse's hooves stirred up a cloud of dust, and their pounding rhythm seemed to emulate his pounding heart. The only reason he could conceive of for Dolly to be sporting a new brand was if someone were stealing Pa's cattle—but why would a rustler change Dolly's brand, then leave her on the Calloway ranch? It didn't make sense, unless Dolly had somehow escaped the rustlers.

He was almost to the spot where the trail dipped from a higher plateau to the sheltered hollow where Pa had built the ranch buildings. The sharp report of a rifle brought the boy's head up. Several more shots followed in quick succession. The horse beneath him danced nervously as though it sensed something wasn't right. Luke slid soundlessly from the gray's back and, with one hand gripping the reins, moved toward a patch of scrub oak where he could leave the horse concealed. Giving the strips of leather a quick twist around a sturdy branch, he left his mount to make his way on foot to a spot overlooking the house, a place where a few years ago he'd played Indian scout.

Pa had taught him that gunfire always called for caution, so he dropped to his belly to slither his way to the crest of the hill. His heart pounded as he separated a section of thick scrub to provide a view of the ranch buildings.

A thin ribbon of smoke rose from a small fire in the corral. It was the kind of fire he and Pa had built numerous times to heat the branding irons. Squinting his eyes against the sun's glare, he found the corral bustling with activity and a dozen unfamiliar horses hitched to the pole fence that enclosed a small herd of Pa's finest horses. At first the scene below him made no sense. Pa didn't have money to hire men to help him brand. Then as a figure moved closer to a horse several cowboys were holding onto, Luke realized the man was carrying a branding iron. He watched as the two-year-old he now recognized as the offspring of Pa's saddle horse—the one Pa had promised Luke he could break for his own this summer—bucked and screamed as the iron seared its flank.

Anger flared in his chest. Where was Pa? His gaze frantically searched the men gathered around the horse. His father wasn't one of them. His eyes roamed further afield, but he didn't catch sight of his father. If Pa were there, he would stop them, but if Pa was off on the other side of the ranch and hadn't heard the shots, then Luke would have to stop them himself. He was just one boy, and there looked to be about a dozen men clustered around the excited horse that bucked and plunged in protest of the treatment it was being given. He wished Pa would come riding up on his big stallion.

He thought of his mother and wondered if she'd ridden out with Pa. Then he remembered this was wash day. He'd gotten the wash tubs down from their places on the back porch himself that morning. He'd hauled a dozen buckets of water from the spring for her before he'd ridden out. A tremor of fear tightened his grip on his rifle.

A bit of blue near Ma's clothesline almost passed his attention until something made him look again. At first he thought one of Ma's dresses had come loose and fallen to the dirt. A flutter of air revealed a white petticoat beneath the blue. Horror choked him and brought a gasp to his lips. Ma was lying facedown below the clothesline, a dark shadow spreading out from where she lay.

Forgetting the men in the corral or the need for caution, Luke rose to his feet and began running toward the fallen figure, screaming, "Ma! Ma!"

On some level he was aware of a man separating himself from the others, leaping on a horse and starting toward him. He ran on, not seeing his own danger, only focusing on reaching Ma.

Pain shot through his head. He tried to keep running. Ma was hurt. She needed him, but he could feel himself falling. His vision blurred and his eyes stung as he hit the ground.

Gradually he became aware of hoofbeats pounding toward him. He should get up, get out of the horse's way, but his muscles wouldn't obey the orders his head was sending them. Besides, he was too tired, and nighttime had come early. *The night is black. The rider might pass by me in the dark.* It was his last thought before the blackness completely enveloped him.

Frank Haladen reined in his horse, sending a spray of dust over the still figure lying half-way down the slope. Something in his gut twisted. He'd never shot a man before, and this wasn't even a man. Lying facedown in the dirt was a boy, his longish hair still showing the towheaded paleness of childhood. Frank took a lot of teasing from the other men about being a kid—he was just eighteen—but the crumpled figure on the ground looked to be no more than thirteen or fourteen. Nausea threatened and stirred a hint of anger. He hadn't signed on with the Blackwell gang to shoot children!

"Put a bullet in his head! Make certain he's dead!" Jethro's voice drifted to his ears from below. Sweat trickled from beneath Frank's hat, stinging his eyes until he could scarcely see. He raised his rifle, never taking his eyes from the boy on the ground. His hands shook and tears ran down his cheeks. He'd never done anything really bad before. Tom Blackwell's taunts over the past weeks echoed in his ears. "Ye're yeller. Nothin' but a lily-livered, pipsqueak kid. Ain't good fer nuthin' but holdin' horses while real men do the work!"

Frank fought to steady his aim. He'd prove Tom wrong.

A man doesn't have to prove he's a man. That's the work of a boy. He heard his father's words inside his mind, and his gun hand shook. He'd left his father because he'd had his fill of being told what to do. Anger added to his turmoil. He'd had his fill of the Blackwells telling him what to do and of Tom's cruel taunts. The boy was already dead. Another bullet wouldn't matter. He took aim and, at the last second, shifted his sights to fire harmlessly into the ground inches from the boy's head.

Jerking his horse's reins, he wheeled about. Moments later his horse joined a dozen others leaving the ranch at a wild gallop. As soon as he collected his share of the money, he was striking out on his own.

* * *

Luke's mind drifted in and out of consciousness. He had no idea how much time had passed before he became aware of bright sunlight beating down on him and the taste of dirt in his mouth. He had the presence of mind to lie still until awareness returned. Even before he opened his eyes, he knew he was alone. A rider had paused beside him, fired, and missed in the darkness that wasn't night, then had ridden away. At the moment, he wasn't certain whether his survival was a blessing or a curse.

The blackness threatened again as Luke gathered his legs beneath him and prepared to stand. Smoke drifted on the air, faint and far away, an irritation of no significance. First he sat; then, as his vision cleared, his eyes turned involuntarily toward the spot where his mother lay. Sickness rose in his throat, and he stumbled to his feet. Hoarse sobs broke from his throat as he continued his interrupted plunge down the hill.

Minutes later his fears were confirmed as he knelt beside his mother's bullet-riddled body. Tears streamed down his face, and his mind refused to accept what his senses told him. He reached for her as though he would cling to her as he'd done as a small boy when he was afraid. His arms wrapped around her, pulling her close, and he became aware for the first time in his life that his mother was tiny, her stature not much more than that of a child. How could someone who was so large in his life be so small in her person?

Gradually his sobs lessened, and he stood with his mother in his arms. He'd take her inside the house, place her on her bed, then go after Pa. Holding her in his arms, he turned to discover there was no house, only a smoldering pile of rubble. The barn was a similar pile of burning logs. Pa's horses were gone too. He didn't know how long he stood, staring in pain and confusion, until rage awoke him to the need to do something. At last he carried his mother up the hill to the place where he'd left his horse. He struggled to balance her on his saddle, then, giving up, wrapped her in his rain slicker and tied the inert bundle behind the saddle.

He found his father a couple of hours later halfway up the Gorse Creek trail. He'd been shot twice in the back, but it appeared he'd traveled a considerable distance before losing consciousness and slipping from his saddle into the mesquite brush. Luke would have passed him by if he hadn't spotted his riderless horse patiently waiting beside him.

Luke didn't cry when he found his father. He was almost beyond feeling. Kneeling beside the body, he removed his father's watch and slipped it into his own pocket. Then using his hands and the hatchet his father carried in his pack, he scooped out a shallow grave a few feet from where his father lay. After dragging his father into the hole, he returned to his horse for his mother. He placed her beside him, then covered them both with his father's saddle blanket. He filled the hole and piled rocks on top of it. It was the best he could do. At last he sank to his knees beside the pile of stones to whisper, "The Lord is my shepherd; I shall not want. He maketh me to lie down in green pastures: he leadeth me beside the still waters. He restoreth my soul. . . . Yea, though I walk through the valley of the shadow of death, I will fear no evil. . . . Thou preparest a table before me in the presence of mine enemies." He didn't know all the words, and Ma's big Bible was gone. He started again, "Our Father which art in heaven, Hallowed be thy name." Ma had taught him the words, and it seemed more dignified than any words he could think of himself.

Still in a state of numb shock, he rose to his feet, unsaddled his horse, and carried the saddle to a spot near his parents' grave. He moved his few possessions from his saddlebags to his father's and attached a lead rope to his horse before mounting Pa's big stallion. The chestnut was larger and stronger than his gray gelding. His knee brushed the scabbard holding Pa's new Winchester, and he realized that his pa had been ambushed. He hadn't even been given an opportunity to defend himself. He looked back at the pile of stone, and something hardened inside his heart. *Be a man, son,* he thought he heard his father's voice. The wind swept through the mesquite, sounding like his mother crying. He straightened his shoulders. "I'll find them," he vowed.

CHAPTER THREE

It was near sunset when he followed the tracks leading from his burned-out home to a dry wash near the river. An evening breeze coming off the river carried the scents of coffee and tobacco smoke. Ignoring a pounding pain in his temple where the outlaw's bullet had grazed him, he tethered both horses in a stand of willows where they could graze unseen. On foot and carrying the Winchester, he made his way to the campsite he knew he'd find in a sheltered spot cut by the harsh rains of early spring, but dry now in late summer.

As he neared the camp, he bent low and moved silently, the way Pa had taught him to scout deer. There was no sign of a watchman on the ridge above the wash, and as he approached the edge, he dropped to his belly. He didn't want his head suddenly popping into view over the rim. He scooted the last few feet, slithering like a snake, until he could peer over the edge. Below him he could see a dozen men gathered around a campfire eating from tin plates, but there was still no sign of a lookout. A man wearing Pa's best shirt was pouring something from a bottle into a tin cup one of the men held toward him.

Some distance further up the draw, he could make out a herd of horses. He counted twenty-seven. There might have been more in the thick cluster of trees. More than half that number he recognized as his father's. He almost missed seeing a slender, solitary figure sitting on a rock further up the draw from the rest of the encampment, a rifle leaning against his side as he watched over the herd. Turning his attention back to the group around the fire, Luke watched as one of the raiders slipped away from his friends to find a private spot in a clump of brush on the opposite side of the draw. The man wasn't carrying a rifle, and when he began to fumble with his belt, Luke lost interest.

It didn't take long to pick out Jethro Blackwell. Luke had seen wanted posters with the man's likeness, and he'd noticed who seemed to be in charge of the band of outlaws. He was a large man with a drooping mustache who wore a hat with a band of silver medallions around its crown. He also wore his gun on his left hip with the handle facing forward. He was famous for his fast cross-draw. There was no doubt he was the man Luke had seen giving orders back at the ranch as Luke had rushed down the hill toward his mother. Luke sighted down his rifle barrel, taking care to avoid any lingering beams from the setting sun which might alert the gang to his presence.

The jangle of approaching riders turned his attention to the trail leading into the secluded spot. Pulling deeper into cover, he watched for any sign he might have been followed. It soon became apparent the men weren't following any tracks, but were proceeding toward a goal. He felt a tremor of excitement when he recognized the lead rider as the owner of a neighboring ranch.

Big Harrison Duncan and Pa weren't friends, but perhaps the rancher had ridden past the Cross C and had seen what had happened. He'd probably figured that the best way to avoid being the gang's next victim was to go after them. Something held Luke back, making him hesitate to show himself. Instead he watched the riders approach the wash, seemingly without a care for their own safety. He wondered if he should warn them.

He thought about the big rancher who had bought out two neighboring ranches and had his eye on the Calloway ranch because whoever owned the Calloway ranch controlled the water for the whole valley. Pa had seen that right off when he'd selected the land to build his ranch on ten years ago, when there hadn't been any other ranches for a hundred miles around. Warning Duncan seemed like the neighborly thing to do, but there was no way the rancher could miss knowing there was someone in the wash. Most men approach an unknown camp cautiously, but there was nothing cautious in the way Duncan and his riders were riding right into the camp. Duncan's men began to spread out, taking positions around the wash with rifles in hand.

The outlaws greeted Duncan like he was an old friend. He talked and laughed with the men for several minutes, though he didn't dismount. At last he tossed Jethro a small pouch then turned to ride out of the draw. The men didn't watch Duncan ride out; instead they focused on the bag in their leader's hands, each one greedily clamoring for his share.

The outlaw opened the pouch and began to yell that they'd been cheated. Duncan turned from halfway up the trail and fired a single, deadly shot. Jethro immediately fell backward. Luke hadn't even seen Duncan pull his gun. It was already in his hand when he'd turned around.

Pandemonium broke out as a barrage of rifle fire rained down on the outlaws from the concealed riflemen near the top of the draw. Duncan, now partially concealed behind a tree, turned his gun on a man who had attempted to follow him. The riders who had accompanied Duncan to the outlaw camp fired repeatedly at the unprepared outlaws. Some of the outlaws managed to return fire, but the gun battle didn't last long. When the last shot died away, Luke counted a dozen men on the ground. He figured he ought to feel some satisfaction that the gang that killed his parents had paid for their evil deed, but he felt more sick than pleased by what he had witnessed.

He thought about going down and thanking Duncan for avenging his parents' deaths, but something didn't feel quite right. He continued to watch, and his sense of disgust deepened as he watched Duncan reclaim the bag he'd tossed to the outlaw leader. His men spread out to claim the meager possessions of the dead men. Only Duncan and one other man remained on horseback, a little aloof from the others. That was when the significance of the pouch Duncan had tossed Jethro Blackwell sank in.

A flicker of movement caught Luke's attention, and he lifted his eyes to see two horses, riders pressed low against their necks, streak from the far end of the draw. Duncan and his men were too far below the rim to see the riders. He remembered the outlaw who had sat hunched near the horses and the one who had answered nature's call in the bushes behind the camp. The two were escaping, but still he didn't call out to Duncan.

He wanted to pursue the fleeing riders—make them pay too—but something held him anchored to the spot where he lay. Understanding of the day's events crowded into his mind. Harrison Duncan had brought those outlaws here and promised them money to rid him of the Calloways, who stood in the way of his securing the water he coveted. When the outlaws had completed their task, he'd double-crossed them. Harrison Duncan was as guilty of murdering Luke's parents as if he had shot the fatal bullets himself. Hatred, an emotion Luke had never before experienced, drowned out all else.

Luke lifted his rifle once more, steadied it against a notch where two branches separated in the mesquite bush in front of him, then brought the sights to bear on Duncan. For a few seconds he could clearly see the third metal button of Duncan's shirt split by the sights of his rifle, then his vision blurred. The pain in his head intensified. Sweat poured down Luke's face and dampened his shirt. His finger on the trigger turned slippery. He willed his finger to exert the needed pressure. With what was almost a sob, he discovered he couldn't shoot the man.

Berating himself for a coward, he slipped back to the willows where his horses were tied. He spent the night there, neither sleeping nor making plans for the morning, simply staring into the sluggish blackness of the slowly moving river. When morning came, he washed the dried blood from the side of his head, mounted Pa's big stallion once more, and headed toward the settlement. He'd find a lawman in Hewitt.

* * *

The sign over the door said *Sheriff*. It had taken the better part of the day to reach Hewitt, the closest town with a sheriff, and Luke was tired and hungry. He paused, just looking at the sign for several minutes, then swung down from the saddle. After a couple of quick wraps of the reins around the hitching post, he marched to the door and opened it.

There wasn't much light coming in through the dingy window, but he could make out a large man sitting tipped back in a chair balanced on its back legs behind a much-battered desk. He appeared to be sleeping.

As Luke's eyes grew accustomed to the dim light, he became aware of heaps of wanted posters, bottles, and dirty tin plates piled on the desk and on the floor behind the sleeping lawman. The wanted poster lying on top of the stack featured Tom and Jethro Blackwell. Just seeing it made him feel sick. A door with heavy metal bars separated the sheriff's office from a jail that didn't seem to hold any prisoners at the present time.

"Mister." Luke attempted to get the man's attention. When there was no response, he spoke louder. "Sheriff!" The man snorted a couple of times and opened his eyes to mere slits.

"Go away," the man muttered and closed his eyes again.

"Sheriff, you gotta wake up. My ma and pa have been murdered."

"What's this?" The man straightened and glared at Luke.

"The Blackwell gang shot 'em and burned the house."

"The Blackwells?" Luke had the sheriff's attention now. Quickly he launched into an explanation of all that had happened the previous day. When he finished, the sheriff looked at him in a peculiar way without speaking. He appeared both angry and confused.

"It's true. I can take you to where Mr. Duncan ambushed the outlaws." Luke rose to his feet, prepared to ride with the sheriff back the way he'd come.

"Now, boy, if Mr. Duncan and his riders got the drop on those murderin', thievin' Blackwells, it seems we ought to be thankin' him." The sheriff leaned forward, clasping his hands piously in front of him. Luke couldn't believe the lawman didn't understand.

"He paid those outlaws to kill my ma and pa," Luke repeated what he'd already told the sheriff. "Then he double-crossed the dirty crooks."

"Listen here, son." The sheriff straightened in his chair and scowled at him. His words had a hard bite to them. "I can't have you goin' around tellin' folks lies about Mr. Duncan. Harrison Duncan's a fine man, an upstanding citizen. He told me just this morning about your folks leavin' these parts, and I understand how you might be a mite upset over your pa sellin' out and headin' back east, but you got no call to make accusations against Mr. Duncan."

Luke stared at the sheriff in confusion. How could the sheriff believe Pa had sold out? Everyone in town knew his folks were adamant about staying on the ranch they'd built from scratch.

"Pa didn't sell out! Duncan hired the Blackwells to murder him!" Luke lunged forward, waving his arms in frustration. The sheriff lurched to his feet so fast his chair toppled over behind him.

"Your folks weren't murdered." The sheriff emphasized each word. "Mr. Duncan bought your pa's ranch nice and legal. I seen the papers myself. If you hadn't run off, they woulda took you with 'em when they headed out. Fact is, there's still plenty of time for you to ketch up with 'em."

"That's a lie!" Luke narrowed his eyes and wished he were a man. He'd beat the fat fool senseless for siding with Duncan. He was only fourteen, but he could see what Harrison Duncan had done. When Pa wouldn't sell out, he'd hired the Blackwells to kill Pa and his family so he could claim they'd gone back East, then he'd forged a bill of sale. He must have found where Luke had buried his parents and realized Luke was still alive. Claiming Luke had run off accounted for the possibility Luke might show up in town.

The sheriff shifted in his chair and attempted to look concerned, but Luke could tell the fat goat was in fact nervous. He was sweating and casting frequent glances toward the door. Luke wondered who he was expecting.

"Now you best get out of here. I've got work to do," the sheriff said with one more glance toward the door.

"You ain't going to do nothin'?" Luke stared in disbelief at the sheriff.

"I'm going to lock you in my jail if you don't get out of here and stop bothering me." The sheriff moved menacingly toward him.

Luke took a step back, felt the door behind him, and with tears welling in his eyes shouted, "If you ain't going to arrest that murderin' Harrison Duncan, I'll go after him myself—and I'll find them two outlaws that got away and shoot them too." He stepped through the door and with indignation welling in his chest, he strode to his horses, unhitched them, and swung himself onto the back of the nearest one.

He was almost to the end of the dusty row of businesses when a commotion broke out behind him. He turned to see a man run from the bank to leap into the saddle of a horse being held by another mounted rider. A man dressed in a black suit emerged from the bank waving a pistol. Once in the saddle, the first man turned back, firing twice into the doorway of the bank. Luke saw the banker fall forward onto the board planks in front of the bank.

Both riders urged their horses into a run, and Luke dodged into a narrow space between two buildings. They passed him in a cloud of dust and thundered on toward the edge of town. His heart nearly stopped beating in his chest. He knew who those men were. He'd seen them just yesterday when they'd escaped Harrison Duncan's trap. He didn't know the younger man's name, but he recognized Tom Blackwell from the wanted poster he'd seen minutes ago in the sheriff's office. Slowly he urged the stallion forward. It shouldn't be too hard to follow and wait for the outlaws to make camp. His knee pressed against the scabbard where Pa's rifle rested. He'd made a promise over his parents' grave, and he meant to keep it.

He felt a sharp sting and looked down to see blood welling across his forearm. At almost the same moment he realized he'd been shot, he noticed the shooter standing across the street, directing a pistol not toward the fleeing bank robbers, but toward him. His first thought was that someone had mistaken him for one of the outlaws, then he recognized the shooter. Luke ducked low as a second bullet sent shards of brick flying around him. He kicked his horse into a run, and the stallion flew down the street with the gray stretching to keep pace. A spurt of dust kicked up just to his left. The shooter had taken another shot at him, and it slowly sank into his mind that Harrison Duncan intended to kill him and blame his death on the fleeing bank robbers.

A team and buckboard plunged past him, swerving wildly out of control. The driver sawed at the reins and shouted at the horses. Using the commotion as cover, Luke kept the runaway wagon between himself and Duncan as he made his way out of town. When the runaway team began to slow, Luke gave his horses their heads, letting them continue running down the dusty track the outlaws had taken.

Luke had no idea how much time had passed before the horse he rode began to tire and his mind began to function beyond the need to run. Fresh droppings on the trail told him he wasn't far behind the outlaws. His hand crept toward his rifle. He hesitated without lifting it. He couldn't just ride up on the outlaws and start shooting; he had to have a plan. He also needed to think about what the sheriff had said. He wasn't certain whether Duncan had the sheriff fooled or if that sorry excuse for a lawman was in Duncan's pay. Either way there was bound to be a posse following the outlaws, and he wouldn't put it past that thieving, murdering rancher or the sheriff to shoot him if they found him. The pain in his head made it difficult to think clearly and come up with a plan.

Luke slowed and began watching the trail more closely. When he found what he was looking for, he urged his horses off the road onto an outcropping of rock where the horses' hooves wouldn't leave imprints. About a quarter mile off the road the hard surface ended. Luke dismounted to lead his horses to a spot in some thick scrub he could see a short distance away. After tethering the animals where they would be out of sight of the road, he broke off a branch of the brush to wipe away the tracks he had left since leaving the rocky ledge. It might be best to let the posse pass him by and give his horses a chance to rest. He could use the time to allow his wounds to heal and do a little thinking too.

After leaving his horses in a slight draw, he returned to a higher spot where he could watch the road and remain concealed behind a screen of brush. He didn't have long to wait. He counted ten riders moving fast down the wagon track. The sheriff and Harrison Duncan were out in front. He considered riding on, then thought better of it. He suspected the posse wouldn't catch up to the outlaws and the riders would have to return this way. He didn't want to meet them on the return trip.

When night came, Luke made a cold camp and decided to stay put until morning. He estimated it was close to midnight when a distant sound roused him from his blanket and sent him scrambling to check the wagon track. The moon was up now, and from his vantage point in the brush at the top of the hill, he could see the posse making its way back to town. Seeing no spare horses trailing the riders, he figured their hunt had been less than successful. He returned to his blanket and eventually drifted to sleep. His last waking thought was that though the posse had failed, he would not.

* * *

Luke was on the outlaws' trail at daybreak. It disappeared near the river, and Luke figured the outlaws were using the river to hide their tracks. Making certain one end of the lead rope securing the gray was firmly looped around his saddle horn, he rode Pa's big chestnut into the water. He didn't cross, but followed the shoreline. Instinct told him the men he followed hadn't crossed the river. An hour later he still hadn't spotted the place where the fugitives had left the river, and he began to wonder if he'd been wrong to assume they hadn't crossed.

When he paused to check his back trail, he noticed a plume of dust just about where the road should be. There was too much dust for only two riders, which meant the posse was returning to the chase and he'd best make himself scarce. He headed for deeper water. The trailing horse resisted for a moment, then obediently followed the chestnut.

This section of the river was filled with a maze of small islands, circled by shifting channels of water. Even in places where the surface appeared calm, what was underneath could prove treacherous. Pa had told him the region was dangerous and generally avoided by ranchers trailing their herds north because of the numerous quicksand patches and changing river currents.

As he approached one of the islands, he began watching for the telltale quicksand bubbles that denoted danger and gave the stallion his head. Each time he felt the tug of an undertow, he was grateful for the powerful horse beneath him who kicked free and surged ahead. Even so, he couldn't help worrying over whether or not the animal might misjudge a safe spot to leave the water. He also didn't dare look back to see if the posse had reached the riverbank he'd recently left. How he wished Pa were there to advise him.

It was all he could do to hold back tears of relief when he felt the jolt as the horse found solid footing and clambered up a sandy slope onto firm ground. Instead of bursting into tears or whooping with joy, he slid from the horse's back to grasp its bridle and lean his face against the animal's long nose for several minutes before leading the two horses deep into the heart of the island's sparse trees, the one place where they would be concealed from shore. A few trees clustered near the center of the island, but most of the island was covered by long grass and thick shrubs. At least there would be plenty of grass to provide forage for the horses.

Once the horses were tethered in a grassy spot where they could graze, he crept back to the place where his horses had first emerged from the water. When he found a likely spot, he carefully scoured the ground, looking for snakes or scorpions that might have already claimed the spot. Once he deemed it safe, he sprawled on his stomach in the sand behind a twisted bush where he had a view of shore.

He didn't have long to wait before a rider burst through the scrub brush fifty yards or so downstream from the island where Luke hid. He was followed by several other men on horseback. Luke couldn't hear them, but from their gestures he guessed that someone had discovered that the men they followed had left the wagon track. Today's party was smaller than the posse of yesterday, making him wonder if the men had split up in order to follow both the road and the river or if the sheriff had recruited fewer volunteers.

He saw a man gesture toward the river and hoped the posse wouldn't attempt to cross or begin checking the numerous islands. He didn't want to be forced back into the water, becoming a helpless target, fleeing from island to island. He couldn't help but see the irony in his situation—he and the posse were pursuing the same outlaws, but he was in as much danger from the posse as the outlaws were.

More men arrived on the riverbank, and Luke counted fifteen riders, telling him the posse was larger than the day before rather than smaller, as he had first thought. A glint of light on one man's chest identified the sheriff. Luke noticed that the man who seemed to be giving orders was Harrison Duncan and more than half of the posse riders were Duncan's hired thugs. His hand tightened on Pa's Winchester. He knew how to shoot the rifle. Pa had let him practice until he could bring down a deer at a hundred and fifty yards with a single shot. If Duncan moved just a little farther south along the riverbank, he would be in range.

Luke brought the rifle up, sighting along the barrel the way Pa had taught him. He watched the sheriff and Duncan dismount and move away from the other men. Luke followed Duncan's action through his gun sights as the men walked along the river's edge, searching for an indication that the bank robbers they trailed had passed that way. It looked as though Luke might get his wish; Duncan would soon be close enough and clear of the other men.

Think it through, son. He heard Pa's voice in his mind. *If you shoot Duncan, the posse will come after you, and the outlaws will escape. They're close, and if you lose their trail now, it'll go cold.*

His sights leveled on Duncan and he ached to pull the trigger. At the same time he felt sick. He didn't want to kill anyone, not even a man who deserved killing. *Think it through!* Luke's hand was damp, and he felt torn. Slowly he lowered the rifle and watched as Duncan remounted and joined the other men. He watched until the men on horseback became mere dots in the distance.

Luke stayed put for hours after the posse disappeared. Toward evening, he caught a fish for his dinner and searched until he found a few pieces of sun-bleached driftwood he knew would provide a smokeless fire. He baked the fish in the hot coals of the fire, then returned to his lookout point. He didn't have to wait long for the cloud of dust to appear beyond the river's bank, telling him the posse was returning to town.

He wondered if the outlaws had been captured but figured they hadn't been. There were too many places to hide along the river, and the sheriff hadn't appeared to have much knowledge of tracking. His posse was composed of town men and gunfighters. No, the outlaws were still out there. He returned to his horses, rolled up in Pa's bedroll, and slept until the stars began to fade.

CHAPTER FOUR

The sun wasn't up when Luke filled the water bladder and canteen he'd found hooked to Pa's saddle. He filled his own canteen too and wrapped what was left of the fish in a piece of linen Ma had packed Pa's lunch in that fateful morning. He saddled the chestnut once more. After climbing into the saddle, he checked the lead rope attached to the pommel of his saddle and urged his horses into the water. By full light, he was once more scrutinizing the riverbank for signs of the outlaws. At first it was hard going because the posse had trampled over any trail there might have been. It was late afternoon, and he was well beyond the point where the posse had turned back when he found what he was searching for.

He stared down at the single set of shod hoofprints leading from the water. He'd made careful note of the prints each of the outlaw's mounts made over the past few days. These prints belonged to the big buckskin Tom Blackwell rode. There was no mistaking the right front shoe where a nail had begun to work its way loose.

He looked around for a second set of prints, marks almost identical to those made by the horse that trailed behind him on a lead rope. The younger outlaw had been riding one of Pa's horses, another gray gelding Pa had shod himself using a hammer with a slight chip in its surface that he'd dragged home from the Civil War back in '65 before he and Ma had headed west.

Finding no sign of a second horse leaving the water, he wondered if the outlaws might have had a falling out or if they'd split up to confuse the posse following them. It didn't matter to him whether one outlaw lay dead on one of the islands or if he'd escaped into the harsh, uncharted land on the other side of the river. It was Tom Blackwell he wanted. Nudging his horse forward with the heel of his boot, he set out to follow the tracks.

Blackwell was heading west across desolate landscape. He made no attempt to disguise his trail, which showed he figured the posse the same way Luke did—a bunch of townies who wouldn't leave their businesses and homes for more than a couple of days. They hadn't camped either night so as to continue their pursuit with the coming of daylight. No, they wouldn't pursue robbers across the bleak country Blackwell was headed into. But Luke would.

Luke stopped only long enough in the afternoon to rest his horses. He poured a little water into his hat and let the horses take turns drinking. He settled for a swallow of water from his canteen and finished the fish that had also been supper the previous night and breakfast that morning. Once back in the saddle, he kept going as long as he could see the tracks Blackwell's horse left. When night came, he curled up in his bedroll without a hot meal or even a fire to keep him company. He didn't want the outlaw to discover him on his trail.

The next day the tracks that had been heading southwest veered off to the side, and Luke followed cautiously, fearing he might have been spotted. It didn't take long to discover that Blackwell had holed up the previous night in an arroyo near a water hole fed by a small spring but had since moved on. Luke took advantage of the discovery to water his horses and refill his canteens before setting off again across terrain that was becoming increasingly dry and barren.

By the third day he noticed that Blackwell's horse was leaving signs of a loose shoe and appeared to have slowed its pace. Luke sharpened his attention on the landscape ahead. It wouldn't do to suddenly ride up on the outlaw.

By evening he still hadn't caught up to his quarry, and once more he settled for a cold camp. He sucked on the last bit of jerky he'd found in Pa's saddlebags and went to sleep feeling alone and miserable. He dreamed that Ma was standing by the big cast-iron stove deftly flipping flapjacks and insisting he read aloud a chapter from the family Bible while he waited for Pa to join them for breakfast. He woke up wishing he'd worked harder at his lessons—and that he had a stack of Ma's flapjacks to start the day.

Knowing the water skin was nearly empty and his horses hadn't had their fill of water for two days, he started out before daylight while it was still cool. The sun was just coming up when he discovered the kind of wagon track that passed for a road in this part of the country. Peering down its length, he could just pick out a cluster of buildings. As he followed the road, the tracks of several vehicles and quite a few horses merged until he lost the tracks he'd been following. It didn't matter—he figured he knew where Blackwell was headed. He entered Stephenville a little before noon, tired, broke, and half-starved.

He would have preferred to bypass the small town, but it had become clear to him that Blackwell knew the area better than he did and there was a good possibility the outlaw had spent the night in town. He also knew neither he nor his horses could go farther without water and supplies.

Seeing a large sign on a squat building that said *BLACKSMITH,* he reined in under it. Dragging his weary body from the saddle, he led his horses to a nearby pump where he gave the pump handle a few good pulls then watched the animals drink. They gave every indication they were pleased to be tied to a hitching rail next to a full trough of water. Luke couldn't resist rinsing his hands and splashing some of the water on his own face before marching inside.

He approached a large man pumping fire bellows, paused until the man looked up, then inquired whether a rider had brought in a big stallion with a loose shoe the night before or early this morning. He learned that, just as he'd expected, Blackwell had stopped last night to have the shoe replaced, then gone on to the livery stable.

Luke crossed the street to the livery only to learn that Blackwell had only stopped long enough for his horse to empty a feed bag while he visited a nearby café before moving on.

As the proprietor of the livery barn spoke, his gaze returned over and over to Luke's horses. Luke knew the man recognized top horse-flesh—he'd seen that kind of reaction before from men who coveted the animals his father had bred and had meant to use to establish his reputation as the best stockbreeder in Texas. He knew enough to be wary of that look.

"Those are mighty fine horses." The man ran an appreciative hand down the chestnut's withers and along his broad back. Luke knew he was taking note of the Cross C brand on the horse's hip. "You're pretty young to be ownin' this kind of horseflesh."

Luke cast a suspicious glance at the man. He had gray hair and his shoulders were stooped enough to indicate many years of hard work. His hands were wide and calloused. He didn't look like the kind of man who would steal horses, but if nothing else, the events of the past week had taught Luke caution.

"They're my Pa's. He and Ma and the wagons will be through here in a day or two," he lied. "He'll tan my hide for getting so far ahead."

The man wasn't a big man. At first Luke had considered him scrawny, but now he could see that though the man was whiplash-thin, he had the kind of build Ma had called wiry. He could also see something in the man's eyes that made him suspect the older man knew Luke was lying.

"Why don't you step down from that big stallion and bring 'em both inside. I can have them brushed and give them a few oats while you find yourself somethin' to eat. If you like, you can stick around here a few days till your folks catch up."

"I ain't got no money to pay for a livery barn." Luke nudged his horse forward, but the man grasped the horse's bridle.

"Boy, them horses are tired. They're too fine o' animals to treat the way they been treated the last few days. I ain't criticizin' none, and I ain't askin' you to tell me nothing you don't want to be a-tellin', but if you're trailin' that big feller who went through here last night, you need to know it's a six-day ride to the next town and no water holes betwixt here 'n there."

Luke felt sick, and he knew the old man read him right when he went on in a kinder voice. "You can do a few chores for a night's lodgin'. Your horses will be safe in my barn. My name's Baily Patterson, and no customer's ever had cause to regret leavin' his animals in my care. When we're all through here, we'll walk back to the house where my Dory will have a hot meal waitin'."

Luke stared at the man, wondering if he could trust him. When it came right down to it, it seemed he didn't have much choice. The old man was right about his horses. They did deserve better. He also knew he couldn't go on without supplies, and there was only one way to acquire the things he needed. He'd have to sell one of the horses.

Just thinking about parting with one of Pa's horses nearly broke his heart. His steps were slow as he led the horses inside the stable and picked up a fork. But there was nothing slow about the way he pitched into mucking out the stalls. It was something he knew how to do and do well.

Baily Patterson was true to his word. After an afternoon of hard work, he led Luke to a small house set back down a lane behind the livery barn. A large woman met them at the door, and Baily introduced her as his wife, Dory Patterson.

"Land sakes, boy." Dory rested both hands on her ample hips and eyed him critically. "You look like you done fell in the outhouse. Smell that way too. You just take yourself on out to the back porch. There's hot water waitin'. You too, old man." She turned on her husband with a wrinkled nose. She picked up a heavy skillet and waved it at him.

"Now, Dory, that ain't no way to greet a guest." Baily's protest was feeble, and Luke heard him chuckle as he led the way around the house to the back door. A large tin tub sat steaming in the center of the enclosed porch. The old man shucked his clothes and was in and out of the water in two minutes.

"Dory never had no tolerance for dirt, 'specially stable dirt," the old man said with pride in his voice as he climbed into the clean underwear he found folded on a stool near the tub. "You got any clean duds in that bag you're totin'?" He pointed toward the saddlebags Luke had carried with him from the stable.

When Luke shook his head, the old man went on, "Just take your time soakin' off that dirt, and I'll have the missus rustle up a clean pair of britches for you." Before Luke could protest, Baily had disappeared through the kitchen door.

Luke glanced around nervously before obeying the old man's orders to strip and take his turn in the tub. He leaned back until the warm water reached his chin. Spying an untouched bar of soap on the stool beside the tub, he reached for it to lather up his hair and clean the grime from his body. After a liberal application of soap, he dunked himself below the surface of the water to rinse it away. As he raised his head from the tub, he felt a cascade of cold water pour over his head and shoulders.

Startled, he grabbed the sides of the tub and would have stood, but a firm hand pushed him back down. He looked up to see the old man holding a pitcher in his other hand and a broad grin covering his face. "The missus thought you might need a rinse. Clothes are right there." He lifted his hand from Luke's shoulder to point toward the stool.

Luke could only sputter as the old man left the porch, chuckling. He climbed out of the tub and reached for the towel he'd seen Baily use. He was surprised to find a dry one in its place. The clothes he found on the stool fit pretty well—the pant legs and sleeves were only a mite long. Luke figured the clothes belonged to Baily, and since he wasn't a large man and Luke wasn't full-grown yet, they matched up pretty well.

Over supper, Baily brought up the subject of Luke's horses. He offered to buy them both but settled for the gray when Luke wouldn't part with the chestnut. Luke really didn't want to sell either horse, but he knew he had no other means to acquire the supplies he needed for the difficult ride ahead of him. The livery owner handed him the agreed-upon price and offered Luke a real bed for the night to seal the deal. Luke took him up on the offer.

Luke fell asleep the moment his head touched the soft pillow. He wasn't sure what woke him, but he was surprised to discover both his face and his pillow were wet. Then he remembered he'd been dreaming about Ma, and an involuntary sob broke from his lips. How was he going to survive without the parents he'd loved and admired beyond anything?

"Boy, you all right?" A woman's voice came from the doorway.

"Yes'm." He gulped back a sob, trying to hide the way his voice broke.

"No, you ain't." He felt the bed sag as Dory settled on its edge beside him. "You ain't nothin' but a boy and I 'spect you're in bad trouble." Her massive arms surrounded him as she pulled him into an embrace. "You tell Dory all about it. If you've done run away, likely you had good cause. If'n you're missin' your ma and want to go back home, Dory'll help you."

Her sympathy was Luke's undoing. He sobbed as he told her everything that had happened since he'd spotted the cow with a changed brand and discovered his family murdered. The words poured out of his mouth as he explained his frustration with the law and his determination to bring both the outlaws and his murderous, conniving neighbor to justice.

"You can't just shoot those men." She stroked his hair. "Bushwhacking them would bring you down to their level. I 'spect your ma wouldn't like that."

"I'd rather the law hanged them," he admitted. "But the law won't listen to me, and I can't just let them get away with killin' my folks like they was nothing at all."

"I see what you mean," Dory murmured in a soothing voice. "But there's wanted posters out for that Blackwell. I hear he's pretty fast with a gun. If you catch up to him, he might kill you. You need to have a plan so's when you find him you can let a different sheriff or the Rangers know where to find him. That way he'll hang nice and legal."

She made sense, but he wanted to kill the outlaw himself. As though she sensed his thoughts, Dory asked, "Was your ma the Bible-readin' kind?"

"Yeah."

She didn't say any more, but clear as could be, Luke knew she was thinking about that part in the Bible that says "vengeance is mine."

"Ma had a big old black Bible that had been her pa's and his pa's afore that. She set a whole lot of store by that book and every mornin' she made me read a chapter out loud." *I'd read the whole book out loud while my breakfast turns cold and rots away, if it would bring Ma back,* he thought. Dory must have known what he was thinking because of the way he scrubbed at his eyes. "It makes me pure mad to think of Ma's book burning up."

"I know, it would be a comfort to have something she loved to carry with you. There's no way to bring that book back, boy, but the words in that book she loved didn't burn up. They're still in your head, and you can take them out and look at them anytime you like." Saying that seemed to set off the tears again, and Dory held him and rocked him until he fell asleep. He thought he heard her say something about his being welcome to stay with her and Baily until he grew up, but he was too tired to respond.

He awoke at dawn alone in his room. He thought he'd dreamed of Dory comforting him during the night, but his swollen eyes suggested her presence hadn't been a dream. He was surprised to find his own clothes washed and neatly folded at the foot of the bed. He put them on and made his way to the kitchen, feeling self-conscious. Dory didn't say a word about the night before. She shoved a stack of flapjacks and half a dozen eggs in front of him and ordered him to eat.

After breakfast, Baily accompanied him to the mercantile and helped him select the supplies he'd need for his journey. He bought a second water bladder and oats for Pa's chestnut and jerky, beans, bacon, lard, and flour for himself. When they returned to the livery barn for his horse, Dory was there. She handed him a heavy canvas bag filled, she said, with dried apples and bacon sandwiches. He tied the bag to his saddle and went back to say good-bye to the gray. The horse was a favorite, one he'd often ridden since the gray was little more than a colt. It seemed wrong to leave one of Pa's horses behind, but he had to do it. Squaring his shoulders, he walked back to the front of the livery to tell the Pattersons good-bye.

He shook the old man's hand, then turned to the woman. Instead of offering a hand, she wrapped her thick arms around him in a firm hug. "Now you remember, boy," she whispered. "God's watchin' over you, and if you're ever needin' a place to 'bide for a while, old Dory will always have a place for you."

Riding out was harder than he'd expected. He didn't know the Pattersons at all, but they were good people, and they'd offered him the first human kindness he'd tasted since he'd waved farewell to Ma before riding out of the ranch yard that fateful morning. Since he'd had to sell the gray, he was glad Baily Patterson had been the one to buy the animal. He tapped his heels against the chestnut's sides and wondered why Pa had never given his favorite horse a name. He could understand not naming the horses he meant to sell, but Pa had never meant to sell this animal.

Six days later he rode into a ramshackle town. His eyes were red and swollen from blowing sand, and his legs trembled when he slid to the boardwalk in front of a public watering trough. He allowed his horse a few sips, then dipped his hat into the brackish water and poured it over his head. He gave the pump handle a few vigorous pulls, then drank greedily when water shot from it toward the horse trough.

No one questioned his right to be there when he stepped inside a darkened saloon and ordered a plate of stew. When he finished eating, he asked about Blackwell. No one admitted to having seen him.

"You looking for work?" a man at the bar asked.

He nodded his head. The money he'd gotten for the gray wouldn't last forever, and it was beginning to look like he might have a long search ahead of him.

"The Triple A is hiring. The fellow you're looking for might have ridden that way too, if he's looking for work," a cowboy near the end of the bar spoke up.

Luke didn't suppose Blackwell was looking for work—at least not honest work—but the Triple A was as good a direction as any to start searching. He didn't doubt he'd be hired if he applied for the job. There wasn't much he didn't know about horses or cattle. Pa had been a good teacher. Being young wouldn't be a handicap either. Most ranchers preferred cowhands who were thin and wouldn't put too much strain on a horse. Besides, cowboys liked to talk. Eventually he'd hear something about Blackwell—if not at the Triple A, then at the next ranch.

CHAPTER FIVE

As far as her eyes could see, nothing stirred on the vast prairie. The eerie silence was unnerving. She stood where she could see if a wagon should approach along the dirt track where Papa's ramshackle wagon had disappeared sixteen days earlier. Fear made her heart pound faster, and the question she'd avoided from the start wouldn't be denied. *What if Papa didn't return?*

Of course, he would come back. "He'll come back!" She shouted the words as though that would make them true. She detected a faint movement far out on the sea of grass and her hopes rose, only to be dashed when she recognized the ripple of waving grass as a breeze sweeping across the plain ahead of a few distant clouds. The day was so hot she could scarcely breathe. She wished the clouds meant rain, but they were too small and too far away.

She continued to stand until the breeze turned to gusts of wind that tugged at her dress. She turned around at last, despairing that Papa would return today. Already the day was fading, though it seemed too early for nightfall. She debated preparing supper for Papa. He'd be angry if he came and there was no supper waiting, but their supplies were getting low, and she didn't want to prepare food that would be wasted if he didn't come.

She turned her steps toward the sod shanty, dragging her feet as she walked. Even though it was cooler within its dirt walls than on the treeless plain, Maddie hated everything about the sod house. Mostly she hated living like a rodent beneath the earth.

Before taking a step down the steep dirt stairs, she glanced once more at the sky and stood still in shock. Huge black clouds loomed to the west, piled precariously one on top of another. The underbelly of the clouds reflected the green of the prairie. There was something grim and menacing about the dark mass moving toward her.

As she watched, a long finger of whirling blackness stretched from the clouds to the prairie behind the soddie, whirling ever faster toward her. The wind flattened her clothes against her body and whipped the ribbons from the ends of her long braids; then, as though it weren't enough to unravel her braids, it commenced to tear at her hair and sent it swirling about her face.

Scampering down the stairs, she thrust the bar across the door and ran to light the lamp. When her shaking fingers finished the task, she stood still, listening. Overhead a deafening roar sounded like a great locomotive tearing across the prairie. The door rattled, and she wondered if it would hold against the terrific wind. Sudden visions of the door, followed by the table, and even the cookstove, then herself, flying from the dark hole where she cowered made her shake.

She placed the lamp on top of the table and rushed to her cot where she burrowed beneath the single blanket that covered her grass-filled mattress. The storm howled on and on. She clapped her hands over her ears and wished Papa were with her. Then she worried that Papa might be caught by the terrible storm. If anything happened to Papa . . .

A sound pulled her attention to the other side of the room, and she watched as a length of stovepipe tumbled across the iron surface of the stove, then rolled off the edge to continue its journey across the dirt floor, leaving a trail of soot behind it. A hole gaped in the sod roof where the pipe had been. She could only assume that the other pieces of stovepipe were now rolling across the prairie, never to be seen again.

A chunk of dirt slid from the opening, and she gasped when another broke off and flew away, then another. She feared she would soon be without a roof and totally at the mercy of the storm.

"Help me. Please, someone help me," she whimpered. Then she remembered her friend. Only He could help her. He was the only friend she'd had to share her thoughts and fears with for a long time. Papa was gone or passed out on his bed so much that they didn't often talk. Papa was never really there for her, but Jesus always listened to her fears and soothed her aching heart. She'd always be grateful for the little girl who had introduced her to Him. She slid to her knees on the dirt-packed floor.

She didn't know how long she stayed on her knees, but in time she became aware that the howling had ceased and that she was kneeling in mud. She looked around at the dim underground room where Papa had brought her two months ago. The lantern had gone out, but faint light came from the hole in the roof. Rain mixed with balls of ice pelted through a hole as large as the table that sat in the center of the room. Bits of grass and dirt continued to break free from the sides of the hole to splatter the iron stove in their fall.

Climbing back on her cot, she wrapped herself in the blanket. She was cold and wet and more alone than she'd ever been before in her almost thirteen years. Eventually she fell asleep, listening to the rain that gradually decreased in intensity and eventually stopped.

It was morning when she awoke to see sunlight streaming through the hole in the roof. She was surprised to see that any of the roof remained. From her perch on the cot, she looked around at the mud and debris that littered the room she'd struggled for two months to keep livable. She knew she should care more. She should hurry to put it to rights in case Papa should come today, but she continued to sit.

Two days passed with Maddie moving listlessly around the soddie. She occasionally ate a stale biscuit or a spoonful of cold beans. Finally she hauled water from a spring almost a quarter of a mile away to scrub the stove and table. Without a stovepipe she couldn't cook, and she had no idea what to do about the hole. Mostly she sat on a stool she carried outside so she could watch the sky.

Maddie scarcely glanced up when the jingle of harnesses and the clomp of hoofs sounded on the rutted path leading to the soddie. It was a woman's voice that brought her head up.

"Sean Brannigan! You expect me to live in a cellar?"

"Not a cellar, Louise, a soddie. It's surprisingly cool and comfortable." Papa sounded tired and more than a little out of sorts. "Besides, no one said you had to come."

Maddie stood to face the buggy. She used one hand to shade her eyes from the glare of the bright sun and stared openmouthed at the woman who accompanied Papa. She had the brightest red hair Maddie had ever seen and something equally bright covered her mouth. There wasn't anything natural about her eyelashes or the green stuff smeared around her eyes either. Her dress was the shiniest green and, where Maddie took pains to dress so that anyone seeing her wouldn't guess she was beginning to get a bosom, this woman wasn't hiding anything.

"Maddie, come meet Louise," Papa called, and Maddie edged toward the buggy. "Is supper ready?" he went on. He climbed down from the high seat, then helped Louise down. She shook out her skirt, which made a rustling sound, while Papa looked around, seemingly perplexed. The post he usually wrapped the horse's reins around was missing. Thrusting the reins toward Maddie, he stepped forward to take Louise's elbow.

Maddie released the horse from the buggy but hadn't taken ten steps before she heard the woman scream. She stood still, waiting. She didn't have to wait long.

"I can't stay here. Take me back to town right now." Papa wouldn't want to stay either. Maddie didn't doubt he would take the woman back. She only wondered if he would take her too, or if she would have to go on living here by herself.

"Maddie!" It was Papa shouting now. "What happened here? Have you been on the roof?"

"No, Papa." She raised her voice only a little. "It was the wind. I think it's called a tornado."

"What!" Papa looked staggered. "Why, it didn't hardly touch anything in town."

"And you was here all by yourself, girlie?" the woman asked.

Maddie nodded her head, and the woman walked over to her and wrapped her arms around her. "If that don't beat all," she muttered. Maddie found something strangely comforting about the woman's arms and the soft noises she made. She smelled good too.

"Finish watering the horse, Maddie," Papa said. Maddie pulled away from Louise and resumed her trek to the spring. When she returned, Papa and Louise had her and Papa's few belongings piled in the back of the buggy. She climbed over the wheel and found a place for herself on top of Papa's portmanteau.

Maddie fell asleep long before the plodding horses reached town. It was dark when Louise shook her awake and led her through the back door of the hotel and up a narrow flight of stairs. She scarcely glanced at her surroundings before falling asleep again on the bed Louise tucked her into.

It was strange, being tucked into bed. No one had pulled the covers to her chin and stroked her hair as she fell asleep since Aunt Priscilla, and that had been such a long time ago. The gentle touch of a woman's hand went far to ease her troubled mind and soothe her aching heart.

When she awoke, she was alone in the strangest room she'd ever seen. She sat up and looked around. The bed was covered with a red spread, and heavy matching curtains hung above it. Faded red velvet curtains completely shrouded the windows as well, letting in almost no light. A china pitcher of water rested on a chiffonier, and beside it were a china basin and an intriguing array of bottles and jars. An armoire stood open. It held only the green dress Louise had worn the day before. Gold-and-green striped paper covered the walls, and a watercolor sketch of a naked lady who looked a little bit like Louise, with plump arms and red curls, hung on the wall opposite the bed.

Angry voices drifted up the stairs, and she knew Louise had gotten in trouble for bringing her to the hotel. She cowered back down in bed, wondering if Louise would be angry with Maddie for getting her in trouble.

"I don't hire children!" a shrill voice screamed.

"I don't want you to hire her!" Louise sounded both offended and irate. "I only brought her here until her father can find a house for them."

"Bring her back in a couple of years," a man's lazy voice drawled. "I caught a peek at her. She's going to make somebody a lot of money."

"She ain't ever going to work here, and I'm not working here anymore either!" Laughter greeted Louise's angry words.

"I'll just get her, and we'll be out of here." The last voice sounded like Papa, but Papa never got out of bed this early.

"Now you get out of here and find us a place to live!" Louise gave orders to someone. Maddie suspected it was Papa.

Minutes later Louise arrived, wearing a flowered dress that was only a little too small for her. Her face was red, and she moved with quick, choppy steps, revealing her agitation as she gathered up the green dress, the picture, and the jars. She shoved them into a satchel she pulled from the bottom of the armoire. By the time she turned to face Maddie, she seemed more in control, but not wanting Louise to be angry with her, Maddie jumped from the bed and quickly straightened it before reaching for her shoes.

"Oh, leave that!" Louise waved airily toward the bed. "Your papa is finding us a house, and we'll be joining him there as soon as he comes for us." Maddie didn't expect that to be before noon but was surprised when a sharp rap sounded on the door not more than thirty minutes later.

Papa looked tired, and his disposition didn't invite conversation as he drove away from the hotel. Maddie suspected he'd slept in the wagon and hadn't yet had the drink he claimed got him started each morning. He drove toward the edge of town, and just when Maddie had resigned herself to another long trek across the prairie, he turned toward a line of willows. They were almost upon it before she noticed the dugout.

She hated it on sight. It reminded her too much of the soddie. A cave had been dug into one side of the high bank of a small stream, several feet above the trickle of water. The side facing the stream was made of boards, with oiled paper for a window. The floor was tightly packed clay, and the only furniture was a broken-down stove, a rickety table with crates for chairs, and a sagging bedstead in one corner.

Louise took charge, locating a broom which she gave to Maddie to sweep out the hovel and ordering Papa about until all their belongings had been unloaded from the wagon. Papa then disappeared back toward town while Maddie and Louise set about turning the dugout into a home.

Louise sang cheerfully as she turned Papa's packing crates into more furniture and arranged dishes in her makeshift cupboard. She found a tablecloth in one of her boxes and sent Maddie to fetch a bouquet of wild flowers. When Maddie returned, she found brightly colored scarves serving as curtains for the window.

"They're lovely!" Louise sniffed the blossoms Maddie held out to her. She placed them in a blue bottle and set it in the middle of the table. Maddie liked the way they looked. Seeing the flowers on the pretty cloth made her almost forget that the dugout was only a small step from the hated soddie.

There was something exciting about Louise, and as the days blended from summer into fall, Maddie found contentment with her life. Every morning, while Papa still slept, she and Louise would sit outside beneath a willow tree, and Louise would tell her stories about faraway places. Her favorite was about a baby found sleeping in a willow basket in a river, and a princess who rescued him and raised him as her own. Sometimes Louise talked about when she had been a little girl, and she would sigh, remembering a clapboard house and a village church where her papa preached every Sunday.

The days were hot, and Louise joined her in stripping off shoes and stockings to wade in the water. Once Louise encouraged her to pretend she was the princess who found baby Moses, but most days they splashed each other until they collapsed in fits of giggles where the grass grew green and thick beside the stream.

Papa always headed for town by early afternoon. At first, he returned for supper each evening, and while he was gone, Louise and Maddie devoted themselves to cooking and baking. Maddie was impressed by the delicious meals Louise prepared. They were as nice as the food she remembered on the river boat. Then in the evening, Louise tucked her into her improvised bed and told her one more story before kissing her cheek and leaving with Papa to spend the evening in town. The first few nights alone in the dugout, she trembled with each unknown sound that reached her ears, but after a few weeks she grew accustomed to being alone and fell asleep reviewing that day's adventures.

Louise laughed a lot, and the sound of her laughter pleased Maddie. She hoped Louise would stay a long time, but she feared she wouldn't. None of the ladies who came for a week or two ever stayed. Maddie had never wanted any of the others to stay, but Louise was different.

"How did you learn to cook so many good things?" she questioned one day as Louise showed her how to mix biscuits.

"My mamma taught me." She looked wistful for a moment, then smiled. "My mamma knew everything about cooking and cleaning. She worked hard to give Papa and me a good home. I don't think Papa even noticed how hard she worked taking care of us. All he cared about was writing sermons and reading his big, black Bible."

"Did he read his Bible to you?"

"Oh, yes!" There was a bitter edge to the laughter that accompanied her words. "Every morning I had to listen to him read for an hour, and before each meal he read until our dinners grew cold."

"You didn't like his Bible?" Maddie felt disappointed. She had loved reading from Catrin's book and had hoped Louise would share with her stories like those she'd read to her friend.

Louise looked thoughtful for a minute. "I liked the stories Mamma told me. They were from the Bible, but Papa seemed to skip over those. He liked best the parts where he could yell and tell me I was wicked and would be punished."

"I don't think I would like your Papa's Bible. It doesn't sound like a nice book, and I don't want to read it."

"Gracious, child, the Bible is God's book." Louise looked perplexed. "Hasn't your Papa ever told you about Jesus or shown you a Bible?"

Maddie shook her head. "I had a friend once who told me about Jesus. He's my friend, but I don't think Papa knows Him."

Louise placed her hands on her hips as she turned to face her. "Your papa should be ashamed of himself for not teaching you things everyone should know. I ain't done right in my life. I runned off from my folks when I was just a little older than you." Louise paused. In a softer voice, she began again. "After the war I drifted west, always looking for something, but I never found it. I thought maybe I found it when I found you and Sean, but more and more I think I was looking for what I ran away from all those years ago."

One night Maddie awoke to an angry exchange of words between Papa and Louise. She held her breath, waiting for Papa to tell Louise to pack her bags and go, but when Louise was still there in the morning, she felt a ray of hope. Still, she worried as the couple's quarrels became more frequent. Black marks began to appear on Louise's arms and face, and Maddie knew her leaving was inevitable.

Not long after a particularly nasty confrontation, Louise didn't go with Papa to the hotel. She fussed with putting Maddie to bed and spent an extra amount of time telling her a story about Jesus blessing little children. In the morning she began telling Maddie the things a girl should know about becoming a woman. Maddie had the uncomfortable feeling that Louise was getting ready to tell her good-bye.

She awoke early one morning to a strange sound. Tiptoeing to the door, she opened it a crack. Hailstones as big as the end of her thumb were pounding against the ground, turning it white. Her feet turned cold, and she looked down to see a puddle at her feet. Hearing a sound behind her, she turned to see Louise standing with her arm upraised, holding a lantern. By the lantern's light she could see muddy rivulets running down the dugout walls.

Louise woke Papa. He fussed and fumed, then he and Louise set to packing their few belongings. They didn't say much, and Louise never laughed. The hailstorm turned to rain, and when the rain stopped, the muddy water of the small stream reached to within a foot of the front door. They loaded everything into Papa's wagon, and Maddie settled just behind the high seat Papa and Louise shared.

Papa turned away from town, following a muddy rut that led south. They traveled for two days until they came to another town. This town smelled of cattle, and the team bolted at the sound of a steam whistle. After Papa had brought the team under control, he left Louise standing on the train platform with her boxes around her. Maddie climbed onto the high seat beside Papa, and they continued on.

CHAPTER SIX

October 1878

Luke had lost count of the number of bunkhouses where he'd tossed his bedroll. All of his stays had been short. He'd spent more nights sleeping under the stars than under a roof. Finding work had been even easier than he'd expected as he worked his way south. As he'd known from listening to Pa, ranchers were eager to hire youthful cowhands. The ranchers and foremen he approached never asked his age, and he never volunteered any information about himself. Luke came with the additional bonuses of his own sturdy, well-trained horse and a total disinterest in Saturday night celebrations. As long as he did his assigned tasks, no one considered it their business to question why a boy his age was on his own.

The only form of recreation that interested the young cowpuncher was the hours he spent practicing with the six-shooter he'd purchased with his first paycheck. He never went anywhere without the gun tied low on his hip and Pa's Winchester on his saddle. Other cowboys noticed his proficiency with a gun, and gradually he developed a reputation as both a loner and a gunman. In time, many a man who wanted to make a name for himself as a fast gun attempted to goad him into drawing, but Luke couldn't be teased or threatened into doing so and proved indifferent to their taunts.

Without any effort on his part, Luke's reputation as a gunfighter grew. Few knew anything about him, but at the rare times when there was a need for him to draw his weapon, whether in defense of stock or a payroll he'd hired on to guard, his speed and accuracy were stunning. He told no one of his real reason for drifting from one small Texas town to another. Although Luke didn't mean to be mysterious, a legend grew up around him.

He traced Tom Blackwell as far south as the Rio Grande, then after a brief foray into Mexico, lost the trail. But he didn't give up. Blackwell would be back—he felt certain of that. Tom Blackwell wouldn't be able to resist the lure of the little banks springing up all across Texas, and Luke strongly suspected the outlaw was as intent on seeking revenge against the double-crossing rancher who had killed his brother as Luke himself was in evening the score against the man who'd ordered his parents killed.

Luke drifted from one border town to the next, always watching, always listening, waiting for the day when the outlaw would run out of money and return to his old game. It was in Laredo, almost four years after beginning his search for the outlaw, that he first heard of a holdup near Eagle Pass that had all the markings of Blackwell. He saddled the big chestnut and rode west.

The outlaw was gone long before Luke reached Eagle Pass, but rumors abounded that the new Blackwell gang had staged another bold holdup at a small settlement a little farther north. Luke followed the holdups and rumors in a meandering course that crisscrossed west Texas until the day his stallion shied at a newspaper carried by the blowing wind.

It had been months since Luke had seen a newspaper, and his curiosity got the better of him. Dismounting, he caught the paper and stuffed it into his saddlebag. When he made camp that night in a protected draw, he cooked beans and biscuits and, once his hunger was satisfied, he took out the piece of newspaper and studied it. It had been printed in Wallace Creek, not far to the west of where he was camped. He glanced at the headlines, then began to read a story about elections to be held in the fall. Harrison Duncan was running for governor. The thought of the corrupt rancher controlling all of Texas fueled his anger. But it also told him what he needed to know to find Blackwell. Blackwell was headed back to Hewitt. Luke was sure of it. Somehow Blackwell had found out about Duncan's political plans and was working his way toward a showdown.

Lying back against his saddle, he studied the stars as though they were a map. He drew an imaginary line from star to star, seeing each as one of the small settlements between Blackwell's last holdup and the ranch where Luke had buried his parents. He knew this part of Texas, and he knew which towns had banks. A town large enough to accommodate a newspaper would also be large enough for a prosperous bank. His next stop would be Wallace Creek.

* * *

Frank Haladen leaned back in his chair, gave his cards a brief glance, then returned his eyes to the big rancher sitting across from him. Carson was struggling to hang onto his temper and was likely close to depleting his cash supply. Frank had learned during the previous weeks that Carson accepted small losses graciously, but he suspected a major loss would bring an eruption better avoided. He discarded an ace and continued closely watching the other players.

Johnson, who ran the mercantile, played badly even when he held a good hand and never seemed unduly upset when he lost. A fussy little man without a family, he only came to the saloon to play cards for the companionship he found in a few hours at the table. He never played more than a few hands and would soon drop out. He didn't concern Frank.

Two local cowboys had started out the evening joking and amiable, but they were both devoting more attention to the girls who kept their glasses filled than to the game. He wasn't surprised when they both folded and followed the girls upstairs. Frank raked in the pot their distraction had cost them.

The drifter who had joined their game more than an hour ago appeared more interested in keeping his glass full than in winning, though earlier he'd won enough pots to make Frank nervous. He couldn't be sure how old the man was. His hair was gray and slicked back with some kind of grease. His skin had the flushed softness of a habitual drinker. His clothes were shabby but looked as though they might have once belonged to a wealthy gentleman. Sober, he'd played well—suspiciously well—but as his consumption of whiskey increased, his ability began to slip. A belligerent note had crept into the drifter's voice during the last hand. Frank suspected he could win this hand easily, but it might not be wise to do so. He discarded another card.

Taking care to throw in his cards before the stakes grew high, he lost a couple of times to the rancher and once to the drifter, who was now mumbling almost incoherently. If Frank were moving on in the morning, he'd take advantage of the drifter's inebriated state and coax the locals into ever higher stakes; but he was staying, and prudence warned it wouldn't do to pocket any really large winnings. Especially since if all went well, he'd soon end his gambling career and place his stake in Wallace Creek.

He was aware of Bart watching the stranger. Bart kept an eye out for professional gamers who might give his business a bad name, and he and Frank had developed an understanding. As long as Frank made certain the house got its cut and kept his winnings from inciting talk, he was welcome to play at the Golden Garter. Something about the stranger was drawing Bart's attention. Like Frank, the saloon owner likely suspected the old man's winnings weren't entirely dependent on luck and skill.

"That's all for me." Frank tossed his cards onto the table and started to rise. He always made it a point to end participation in any game that appeared headed for trouble. As he did so, he caught part of a phrase, mumbled by the drunken drifter. One word stood out— Blackwell. It had been three months since Amelia, the local newspaper owner and Frank's fiancée, had written a story about the outlaw, and Frank had begun to relax, thinking he'd worried over nothing. Now his fears crowded back.

The old man's fingers clutched at his pant leg. "Y'all give an old man a hand up?" he asked. "My legs aren't what they once were."

"Come on, friend." Frank helped the old man to his feet and steadied him. The old gambler woke Frank to the sobering possibility that if he didn't end his own gambling career, he could end up the same way. "Where are you staying?" He did his best to sound concerned. Truth was, he was concerned, but not only about whether or not the drunk made it to his bed. He needed to know what the man knew about Tom Blackwell. He'd heard a few rumors that Blackwell was back in Texas and that he and a new bunch of desperadoes were holding up banks again. He'd also heard that this time Blackwell wasn't leaving any witnesses alive.

After asking directions from the bartender, he took the old drifter's arm and led him toward the door. Most of the cowboys found something else to look at as he supported the stumbling drunk, but one man deep in the shadows leaned back in his chair as if sleeping. Frank had the uncanny feeling the man saw more than most. The old man staggered and cursed while clinging to Frank with a deathlike grip. As they made their way down the street toward the edge of town, Frank attempted to draw the man into conversation, hoping he could get him to talk about Blackwell. If the old man knew anything about Blackwell, and if the outlaw was anywhere in the vicinity, Frank wanted to know. He had no desire to renew his brief acquaintance with Tom Blackwell. In fact, he would just as soon be as far away as possible should Blackwell show up in this part of the state.

Frank feared his part in the outlaw's exploits might come to light should Blackwell show up and recognize him. And he didn't want his past association with the Blackwell gang to ruin his romance with Amelia. There was also the possibility of going to jail for his part in that long-ago bank robbery that didn't bear thinking about.

Then there was the Calloway boy. Had he killed him? He'd never learned whether or not the boy was still alive. If he were dead and Frank identified as the man who had shot him, he'd hang. He clung to that brief glimpse he'd caught of a boy and two horses in an alley the day he and Blackwell had held up the Hewitt bank. He had to believe the boy he'd seen was the same boy he'd supposedly killed and that he wasn't a murderer after all.

The cool night air served to sober the drifter somewhat, or perhaps he wasn't as drunk as Frank had thought him. His steps became brisker, and he appeared to be in a hurry as they moved toward a crumbling shack on the edge of town. Despite Frank's attempts to draw information about Blackwell from him, the drifter evaded his questions with chatter about the great partnership the two of them could form if Frank would throw in with him.

A lamp flickered in one window of the shack and a shadow flitted briefly on a drawn curtain, alerting Frank that the man didn't live alone. If the man had a wife, he pitied the woman, being married to a drunken gambler. If the man didn't have a wife, then who waited up for his return?

Caution, born of his years alone on the harsh frontier, suggested he might be walking into a trap. Since an attack on the newspaper office, he'd become particularly vigilant.

"I'd best be getting home myself," Frank said, releasing the other man's hold on his arm. "You'll be fine now, so I'll be on my way. My landlady doesn't like me coming in late, disturbing her boys' sleep." He backed up a couple of steps while keeping his eyes alert to any movement in or around the shack.

"Thank 'ee, lad. Would 'ee care to step inside me humble abode for a wee tip of the bottle?" The drifter did an exaggerated imitation of an Irish brogue while clutching at Frank's arms in an attempt to detain him, further raising Frank's hackles. In the saloon, the gambler's drawl had hinted at more than a passing acquaintance with the deep South.

"Not tonight. I've got to be up early tomorrow." He made a hasty excuse and took another step backward to where the shadow of a spindly tree spread itself across the ground. He welcomed the darkness as a shield.

"Me daughter's a lovely lass, and she'd be pleased to meet ya," the old man called after him.

Frank shuddered. He felt naked and exposed until he was safely back on the boardwalk that ran the length of the town. He paused outside the Red Rooster, contemplating another game. He usually didn't play at saloons other than the Golden Garter, but he might make an exception this once. No, he didn't want to test his luck. He couldn't shake the feeling he'd had a close call tonight. Besides, he really did need to be up early tomorrow. He had plans to take Amelia for a drive.

Frank turned toward the opposite end of town. He'd just make a quick check of Amelia's place before turning in. Since the night someone had attempted to burn the office, he'd managed one or more surreptitious strolls past the news office each night, but there had been no repeat of the attack nor any kind of further threat made. Still, tonight he felt uneasy.

* * *

As the morning sun approached its midday peak, Luke watched a man scurry to the alley next to the bank where five horses were concealed, free them, then begin leading the waiting mounts toward the street. He didn't have a clear view of the man whose hat was pulled low, but he could see well enough to know the man's height and way of moving marked him as someone much older than Blackwell. Luke stayed in the shadows of the mercantile, watching as a second man slipped into the alley and moved toward the horses. The second man stopped when he saw the horses, then flattened himself against a wall for a few seconds before stealthily retreating, unnoticed by the man occupied with the outlaws' mounts. For a fleeting moment, Luke found something familiar in the figure of the man leaving the alley—presumably to notify the sheriff—then he forgot all about him.

Excitement hammered through Luke's veins. The man leading the horses wasn't Blackwell, but Luke suspected he was part of the outlaw's gang. He slipped in behind the animals, being careful to keep out of sight. It had taken four years, but he'd soon confront Tom Blackwell.

Shouts erupted from the bank moments after the horses reached the street. Three men burst from the bank's doors, running for their mounts. Luke flattened himself against the side of the bank and held his fire. None of the men dashing from the bank was Blackwell. He heard gunshots but paid no attention to where they came from. He was waiting for Blackwell to burst through those doors. The door opened once more and Luke took aim, and then stopped. He couldn't fire.

Blackwell held a young woman in one arm, using her as a shield. Luke couldn't risk firing a shot for fear he might hit the tiny, auburn-haired woman who was screaming and kicking as she fought to free herself. She wore a blue dress—a blue dress like Ma had worn the day Blackwell and his men had murdered her as she hung the family laundry on the line behind their house. Luke took careful aim once more, cursing the chance that had caused Blackwell to take a hostage.

A man stepped out of the crowd, taking slow deliberate steps toward Blackwell. His hat was low, shielding his face so Luke couldn't see it clearly, but Luke's gut told him it was the same man who had followed one of the outlaws into the alley earlier. Again a nagging suspicion that Luke somehow knew the man crossed his mind. The man was either a hero or a fool to approach Blackwell.

"Let her go, Tom." The outlaw looked startled for only a second, then laughed as he shoved the woman toward the man, catching her rescuer off guard so that he and the woman fell toward the street. A shot came from behind the couple. Luke took his eyes from Blackwell for just a second, long enough to glimpse the retreating back of the old man he'd followed down the alley earlier. He didn't have time to wonder why the man had fired at Blackwell.

With the hostage out of the way, he turned his attention back to the man he'd pursued so long. Blackwell was leaping for his horse, twisting as he did so to send a shot toward the man whom he supposed had fired at him. Shots rang out from two of Blackwell's men. The man on the ground palmed a small-caliber derringer and aimed it at Blackwell. Luke too took careful aim at the man trying to mount his frightened, dancing horse.

The shot from the downed man caught Blackwell in the shoulder, spinning him around to face a man with a tin star on his chest. One blast from the pump-action shotgun the sheriff held pitched Blackwell backward. Luke stood stunned, as though he'd been caught in that shotgun's blast himself. The scene on the street took on an aura of unreality, something like a sepia photograph he'd seen somewhere.

Blackwell and one other man lay facedown in the street. The other man was moving, but Blackwell would clearly never move again. The sheriff's orders, shouted to the men gathered in the street, passed over Luke's head as he struggled to deal with the fact that Blackwell was dead, but he hadn't been the one to shoot him. He hadn't even fired his gun.

Three outlaws sat on their mounts, motionless, with a dozen guns pointed their way. There was no sign of the old man who had brought the outlaws' horses. Taking advantage of the confusion, he had melted into the crowd as someone raced from the bank shouting that the banker was dead. The man who had faced Blackwell continued to sit in the street, holding the woman in his arms as a large, dark stain spread across the back of her blue dress. He stroked the woman's long curls, and tears ran down his cheeks as grief distorted his face. A picture of the old man firing toward Blackwell filled Luke's mind and suddenly made a kind of sense. The old man hadn't been firing at Blackwell, but at the man who had faced the outlaw. When Blackwell had thrust the woman toward the approaching man, the old drifter's bullet had struck her. Luke couldn't watch anymore. Quietly he backed into the alley, slipped into the next street where he'd left his horse, and rode out of town.

His mission wasn't at an end, he reminded himself. Harrison Duncan was still alive. He turned the big stallion toward Hewitt.

CHAPTER SEVEN

Luke drifted slowly toward the Brazos River. When his money ran low he stopped at a ranch, staying only long enough to earn enough to move on to the next town or ranch. He didn't bother to make friends. He did what he was hired to do, then on payday moved on.

Once, as Luke trailed a herd of young stock from one ranch to another, a cougar sprang from hiding toward an unsuspecting heifer. Luke's revolver cut short the cat's flight and fed the rumor that Luke Calloway was a fast gunfighter. A few weeks later, a drunken cowboy went for his gun, and Luke's bullet broke the man's wrist, adding more fuel to the rumor.

The closer Luke drew to the valley he'd once called home, the wilder the stories became, until Luke found that the only ranchers willing to hire him were those looking for a hired gun. Dodging the would-be gunfighters who wished to make names for themselves by calling him out became increasingly difficult.

When he reached Stephenville, he was shocked to see how much the small town had grown. Remembering the kind people who had taken him in and given him a start after his parents' deaths, he made his way to Pattersons' livery stable. It didn't look different, but the old man who met him had changed considerably. His hair was white and his shoulders bent, and his walk had become a shuffle. But there was still strength in his grip as he clasped Luke's shoulder.

"Luke?" Recognition shone in the old man's eyes, and he reached out a hand to clasp Luke's. When Luke took it, Baily Patterson went on, "The missus will be glad to see you, boy. She's fretted about you ever since you left, wonderin' if'n we shoulda tried harder to keep you here with us."

"I wouldn't have stayed," Luke said. "I had to go."

"I reckon we knowed that." The old man shuffled to a stall and held it open for the horse Luke led inside. "See you've still got your pa's horse." He patted the chestnut stallion's shoulder.

Luke smiled. "He's a good horse."

"I'd still like to buy him," the old man admitted with a chuckle. "It's a shame to let him grow old without sirin' a new crop of colts."

"He's still got a few good years." Luke patted the horse with genuine affection and more than a little regret. Pa had planned to build his reputation as a stockbreeder from the colts he'd envisioned being sired by the chestnut stallion. Still, he was glad the horse had been his companion all these years. They'd been through a great deal together.

The stallion's ears perked up, and Luke turned to see a familiar gray head stretched over the pole corral behind the livery. Instead of entering the stall, he led the horse to the waiting gray. He felt like he was greeting an old friend as he stroked the horse's nose. The two animals gave every indication of being happy to see each other, and when Baily swung the gate open, allowing the chestnut access to the corral, he bolted inside.

"You find what you were looking for?" Baily asked.

"In a way," Luke conceded. "I followed Blackwell for four years, then a gambler with a fancy derringer and a sheriff with a shotgun got him first."

"I heard about the shootin' over Wallace Creek way. We wondered if you might come home now."

"I ain't got a home." His words were bleak.

"You always got a home as long as Dory and me are alive." There was a firmness to the old man's words that chipped a piece of ice from the cold lump Luke's heart had become.

He and Baily sneaked around to the back porch of the Patterson house to take baths and change into clean clothes before confronting Dory. When they stepped into her kitchen, the big woman's hand flew to her heart in mock fright.

"Howdy, ma'am." Luke's lips turned up in the first hint of a smile they'd made in a long time.

"Land sakes, boy! If'n it ain't Luke!" Her massive arms nearly crushed him as she pulled him to her. He heard her sniff and felt a lump in his own throat. She pushed him away to get a better look at him. "My, my! You've done grown up. Let me see you." She pursed her lips and stared at him critically. "You've gotten taller, but I declare, you're still needin' fattening up. Now you just sit yourself down to that table, and Dory'll see what she can find to put a little meat on them bones."

Dory placed a roast on the table and began slicing a loaf of bread still warm from the oven. Luke ate until he couldn't hold another mouthful. When Dory continued to urge more food on him, he protested. "I haven't eaten like this since I last sat at your table," he told her. "I've known a few good chuck wagon cooks, and I've had some tasty dinners at out-of-the-way cafés over the years, but there ain't nobody what cooks like Dory Patterson. It's pure pleasure to be sitting at your table again." The old woman took the corner of her apron and wiped her eyes.

After dishes were cleared, they retired to the parlor, where Luke shared some of the experiences he'd faced. At last Dory leaned back in her chair with a stern expression on her face.

"We hear things from time to time," she told him. "There's talk that Duncan feller has big plans to run for governor. And it appears he ain't forgot about you. We been seein' some peculiar flyers makin' their way to this part of the country."

"What she's tellin' you, Luke, is that after that big fracas west of here that left Tom Blackwell dead, a new wanted poster's been printed. It claims you were the other outlaw ridin' with Blackwell when the bank at Hewitt was held up, and it says you were the outlaw that escaped at Wallace Creek."

"I was there that day in Wallace Creek. I saw the outlaw that got away, and he was an old guy. Everything happened awfully fast, but I think he was the one who killed that woman."

"If he was one of the outlaws, why'd he shoot at Blackwell?" Baily asked.

"I don't know. I keep thinking there was something odd about the whole thing," Luke admitted. "I don't think he was aiming at Blackwell. It's more likely he was aiming at the man who confronted Blackwell."

"We've been hearin' stories too, about Kid Calloway, reputed to be the reignin' fast-draw in these parts," Dory added with a disapproving cluck. "'Course we know that's all hogwash, but it makes us a mite worried that if you go after Duncan, you'll be ridin' right into trouble."

Luke leaned forward in his chair, clasping his hands between his knees. "I can't quit. The man needs shootin' just as much today as he did that day he sent a gang of outlaws to kill my folks."

"We ain't saying you got no reason to want justice," Baily continued.

"It's just that laying low for a few years might be a good idea," Dory picked up where Baily left off. "Right now he's scared 'cause of all the rumors about Kid Calloway bein' in on that ambush at Wallace Creek and all that talk about you bein' a gunslinger. He's worrying that you might tell folks what really happened the day your folks got killed, and that could hurt his chances of gettin' elected."

"He's got every kid with a gun who wants to make a name for himself gunnin' for you and every sheriff who wants to stay in office on the lookout for Luke Calloway."

"I wondered where all that gunfighter talk came from." Luke grimaced in disgust.

"Luke, you need to lay low, change your name, and head for the territories for a bit." Dory continued to pursue her point. "Baily here knows a rancher who's putting together a herd to drive north. He plans to take up ranchin' in the Snake River country. He could get you on with him."

Luke didn't reject the plan outright. He wasn't the greenhorn kid he'd been when he set out on Blackwell's trail. His goal hadn't altered, but he could see the reasoning behind dropping out of sight for a time. He agreed to sleep on the proposal. He didn't care a whole lot about whether or not he got killed, but the way he saw things, if some gun-happy sheriff or cowboy got lucky before Luke got to Duncan, there wouldn't be anyone left to see that justice was done.

He wasn't any closer to making a decision when he awoke in the morning. Finally he told the Pattersons he was still thinking and set off for a stroll around town. Dory advised him to keep his gun out of sight and warned him that if anyone asked his name he should tell them he was her nephew, Jeff McCall. He laughed out loud at her worry and headed for the row of false store fronts that lined Main Street.

A piece of paper fluttered from a post directly ahead of him. He stopped to examine it and wasn't too surprised to read a highly exaggerated description of himself. He stared at the picture someone had sketched. It wasn't a good likeness, and the description fit a lot of men drifting across Texas, but anyone who took a careful look at it might recognize him in spite of the slender mustache he now wore and the slightly longer hair that curled against his neck. The face in the picture belonged to the boy who had ridden out after Tom Blackwell, not to the young man who now drifted from town to town with a six-shooter strapped low on his thigh and a rifle always within reach.

After passing the third poster, tacked to the side of the telegraph office, he ducked into a privy behind the milliner's shop and removed his gun belt. He tucked his six-shooter into a pocket and wrapped his gun belt into his jacket, which he flung over one shoulder.

Tomorrow he'd stop shaving. Pa had shaved every morning, and when Luke had discovered the appearance of a few scraggly blond hairs on his chin, he'd bought a razor and commenced the daily task of keeping them shaved off. Now he considered that it might be best to let them grow.

By midafternoon he was feeling restless, and though he'd gotten a few suspicious glances, no one had recognized him. Riding a little further afield might help him gauge the extent of the danger the posters posed. He stopped in at the livery for a chat with Baily before riding out. He didn't tell Dory good-bye—he planned to be back in a day or two.

He rode south, noticing a few ranches and miles of barbed wire. There had been no wire when he'd last traveled this way. Two days later he reined in on a hill overlooking the spring where he'd trailed Blackwell and filled his canteens back when his journey had just begun. He'd passed a handful of homesteads carved from rangeland, with varying numbers of acres where grain and hay struggled with more or less success to survive. A dozen tumbledown shacks sat on the rim of the long wash that ended in freshwater springs.

The sun was setting when he made his way to the spring, where he filled his canteens and searched out a place to tether his horse in the willows surrounding the pool. Once his horse was settled, he set out to study the town. A bright moon hovered on the horizon, providing plenty of light, though he would have preferred darkness. Staying mostly in the shadows, he slipped among the cluster of buildings. It didn't take long to see that the settlement consisted of one tiny general store, two saloons, and a handful of shacks. Not even the telegraph had made it this far.

He wasn't a drinker, but he'd learned that saloons and churches were generally the best places to learn of the happenings and concerns of a community. This place didn't appear to have a church—and it wasn't Sunday—so he headed for the larger of the two saloons. He slipped through the bat-wing doors and made his way to a table in the darkest corner where he could listen and observe.

A poker game was in progress at a table near the bar, the only spot where enough light burned to afford the players a view of the cards they held. Half a dozen men sat hunched around bits of cardboard, and it didn't take long to see that they were playing for higher stakes than most of them could afford.

One after another, three men folded and joined the two at the bar. That left a slender young dandy dressed all in black, a florid-faced farmer, and an old man with his elbows poking through a stained shirt. His gray, unkempt hair and beard, looking as though they'd never been introduced to a comb, stood out wildly from his face. Even so, he looked vaguely familiar, though Luke couldn't place where he might have seen him. After a few minutes, all five men at the bar picked up their glasses and moved to a table between Luke and the three men still playing cards. A few grumbles reached Luke's ears, but he couldn't make out their words.

One of the players called for a refill of his glass. Luke suspected that the empty bottle the barkeep removed from the table had been consumed almost entirely by the old man who had called for the refill.

A movement near the door caught his attention, and he watched two cowboys enter and find a table on the far side of the room. Minutes later a large man, followed by a younger replica of himself, made his way to the bar. The younger cowboy indicated he'd like to join the game and was waved to a seat. Luke watched the ragged old man drain his glass once more.

A noisy group of wranglers came through the door, shoving each other and laughing uproariously at something one of them had said. They made their way to the bar and filled the last two empty tables.

"Gertie!" The barkeep shouted toward the curtain a few feet from the table where Luke sat. "Gertie, get out here." Minutes later a large, sullen-faced girl pushed her way past the curtain and stomped toward the bar. The bartender handed her a tray loaded with bottles and glasses, and she began circulating throughout the room. To avoid drawing attention to himself, Luke took the glass she offered him as she passed his table. She wasn't pleasant or pretty, but that didn't seem to deter the cowboys who attempted to paw her as she passed. Luke hid a sardonic grin as he counted the number of cowboys who would report to work in the morning with bruised shins. He couldn't help thinking that the sharp toe of Gertie's boot served each of them right.

"When you going to replace Maud?" one of the cowboys shouted toward the man behind the bar.

"Why'd she run off to Abilene anyway?" another cowboy whined. "Ain't our money just as good as them railroad boys' money?"

Talk was plentiful now, but most of it centered on stock and weather. From beneath the brim of his lowered hat, Luke's attention traversed the room, stopping once more on the men playing cards. He noted the mounting pile of coins and a few paper bills in front of the dandy dressed in black. Luke had seen his kind before—a professional gambler who drifted across the West earning his living by suckering the men who worked for their slim pay.

The table was almost bare in front of the farmer and completely empty at the old man's place, yet several times Luke noticed an almost imperceptible signal passing between the young gambler and the old man. If he were a betting man, he'd bet the two were in cahoots some way.

The cowboy was knocking back drinks as rapidly as the old man, and the more he drank, the noisier and more quarrelsome he became. He interspersed his drinks with caustic remarks about sodbusters until the farmer placed his cards on the table and rose to his feet. Amid a chorus of catcalls, the big farmer walked out of the saloon.

The cowboy then focused his scorn on the old man, whose trembling fingers pulled a gold locket from his pocket and placed it on the table. The cowboy hooted with laughter.

The gambler picked up the trinket and brought it to his mouth. With a smile he placed it back on the table and raised the ante with a five-dollar gold piece. The cowboy stared at him, then back at the necklace. He glanced at his cards once more before placing his own money on the table.

"I'll see you," he mocked, turning a challenging stare toward the old man. The old man stared at his cards, fumbled with his glass as he raised it to his lips, swallowed deeply, then seemed to gather his courage.

"I'm puttin' up half an hour with my Maddie."

"Who's Maddie?" the cowboy asked, his voice turning to a sneer. "She your old lady?"

"No." The gambler spoke up for the first time, and Luke was drawn to a hard undercurrent beneath his words. "Maddie is a blonde, blue-eyed beauty, cursed to be Mr. Brannigan's daughter." He quietly placed his cards on the table facedown and rose to his feet, leaving the money on the table. There was a dignity to his bearing the others seemed to sense, and they let him pass without remark as he made his way to the doors and slipped outside.

The minute the black-clad figure disappeared, a whir of whispers filled the room and coins began to appear as if by magic in front of the cowboy. Half a dozen laughing cowboys added not only their money but also plenty of lewd advice to spur their comrade on.

"I'll take that bet and call," the cowboy smirked, placing a stack of gold coins on the table and placing his cards right side up for everyone to see. Luke couldn't see the cards, but he understood the cheer that went up. Hands reached for the cowboy, lifting him high in celebration.

"Silence!" a familiar deep voice boomed, and Luke turned toward the swinging doors to see the sheriff who had taken Harrison Duncan's word over his standing in the doorway with his pistol aimed toward the ceiling. Luke slipped lower in his seat, letting his hat drop forward to conceal his face.

"Any you boys seen a rider on a big chestnut stallion in these parts today?" he asked.

A few muttered negative responses floated in the air, but most of the cowboys were in no hurry to provide the sheriff with any kind of answer. Luke suspected more than one had a secret or two he wasn't anxious for the sheriff to discover.

Luke glanced toward the curtain through which Gertie had appeared, wondering if it led to an outside door and whether or not he could make it past the curtain without drawing attention to himself. It was only a matter of time until the sheriff would begin checking the shadowy room a bit closer.

"I got a wire from Stephenville day afore yesterday lettin' me know Luke Calloway was headed this way." The sheriff puffed out his chest with self-importance. A buzz of voices went around the room, and Luke took advantage of the attention focused on the sheriff to drop to the floor. On hands and knees he covered the few feet to the curtain. As he ducked behind the thick swag of fabric, a pair of legs shifted, giving him a quick glimpse of the old gambler, crouched beside the table where the poker game had been played. He was frantically stuffing the money left on the table into his pockets. Something about his furtive movements reminded Luke of the old man back at Wallace Creek who had slipped into the crowd to disappear after shooting the woman. He regretted the circumstances keeping him from following the old thief.

Luke's eyes darted around the small, dark room where he found himself. It looked like somebody's cluttered living quarters. He picked out a dark shape he figured was a cookstove and, to its left, a wooden door. A table and a couple of chairs stood between him and the door. Taking care to step over or weave around the clothing, dishes, and other unidentifiable objects scattered about the room, he made his way to the door, which he eased open, hoping it opened onto the alley and not a cellar. Luck was with him.

Once outside, he sought the shadows as he crept around the building. Tobacco smoke drifted on the air, and he caught sight of a small cluster of men sitting on their horses in front of the saloon. The sheriff hadn't arrived alone. Retracing his steps, he returned to the dark space behind the saloon. From there he crouched low, moving swiftly to the back of the next building.

Something inside his head shouted for him to run, but a more experienced voice deeper inside cautioned him to stay low and avoid silhouetting himself against the night sky. Years of practice had taught him to move soundlessly, and he did so now. When he reached the last of the buildings, he dropped to his belly to wiggle his way over the lip of the gulch, then slid soundlessly toward the willows that hid the spring and his horse.

Regaining his feet, he would have begun running, but the thick stand of willows prevented more than a fast trot. He passed the spring and silently thanked the prompting that had led him to fill his canteens before exploring the town.

A whisper of sound halted his steps. It may have been his horse or a small night animal, but it sent a chill coursing through his blood. It hadn't been the heavy clump of boots or jangle of spurs, but it had sounded like someone clumsily picking their way through the nearby brush. He dropped a hand to his side and raised it again with the six-shooter firmly clasped in it.

Taking care to make no sound, he made his way forward, taking advantage of the soft, muddy ground to muffle his footsteps. The sound came again, and he corrected his direction, peering through each clump of willows before advancing. A shiver of sound, almost a sigh, reached his ears from close at hand. With the tip of his gun barrel, he parted the thick stand of willow stalks before him.

He stifled the exclamation that rose to his lips as he eased the hammer back on his pistol. He could see someone crouched on a grassy hummock, almost concealed by the willows.

"Show yourself!" Though he kept his voice low, he knew no sane person would doubt he meant business. If his voice left any doubt, the business end of the gun he pointed at the figure certainly didn't.

A gasp sounded, and the kneeling figure, losing its balance, pitched forward on the wet grass. He stared in amazement. A woman lay sprawled before him. She turned toward him, and he saw silvery tracks across her cheeks. He noticed, too, that she was more girl than woman. She had been crying, but now her eyes widened in fear. Her lips parted, but before she could scream, he was beside her, his hand clamped over her mouth.

CHAPTER EIGHT

"I ain't going to hurt you," he whispered. Unless he missed his guess, she was the daughter of the drunken gambler who had wagered her in tonight's poker game. "Don't say nothing, and I'll move my hand." When she nodded in agreement, he slowly lifted his hand from her mouth.

"Don't hurt me," the girl whimpered, and he regretted having frightened her.

"I don't plan to hurt you," he whispered. Here was a problem he had no notion how to deal with. He couldn't risk leaving her to raise an alarm, and he couldn't tie her up and stuff something into her mouth to keep her quiet either. Besides, she wasn't in any better spot than he was. It seemed to him she had as much reason to sneak off as he did.

"Please don't tell Papa I ran away. That gambler man in the fancy black suit stopped by the shack where Papa and me been livin'. Papa met him a few weeks ago, and they set up a scheme to beat at cards without anyone knowin' they're workin' together, but the gambler said it didn't work out 'cause Papa drinks too much. He told me what Papa done—that he wagered me—but I can't do it. I just can't." She buried her face in her skirt, and her shoulders shook.

Luke touched her shoulder, feeling awkward. He hadn't had much experience with any young woman, let alone with one who was crying. The pull he felt toward this girl was startling—he hadn't felt much one way or the other for most people since his parents' brutal deaths, except maybe the Pattersons. His instincts told him Pa would have expected him to protect the young girl, but his survival instincts warned that his opportunity to escape the sheriff was quickly slipping away. "Look, miss, we're both in a heap of trouble. I've got to be on my way, and you need to stay clear of your Pa till he sobers up. I suggest we make a pact. I won't tell anyone I saw you, and you keep your mouth shut about seein' me." He rose to his feet, and the girl jumped up to stand beside him.

"Papa won't sober up. He's only less drunk some days than others. I ain't going back—he'll wager me again or outright sell me. He don't care about nothin' 'cept whiskey and cards." The moonlight on her face did strange things to Luke's thinking, even more than her anguished words. She was the prettiest woman he'd ever seen. She had long, pale hair that was almost silver in the moonlight. Her face was heart-shaped, and something about the curve of her mouth made it hard for him to concentrate. He had to go, but he wanted to stay.

"Take me with you." Her desperate plea took him by surprise. He started to protest. It wouldn't be seemly. Her small hands reached out, gripping his shirt with strength born of desperation. His eyes met hers, and he forgot all the reasons why he couldn't take her with him.

"I promise I won't be a bother," she pleaded.

Oh, she'd be a bother all right. He didn't doubt that for a moment, but how could he leave her here at the mercy of men like her father and that cowboy?

A shout came from somewhere above them in the shantytown. He was wasting time. Someone would remember the rider who had sat alone and come after him. The girl's pa would return to his shack for the girl, and the cowboy would expect to be paid.

He made up his mind. He'd take her to Dory. Dory would know what to do with her. "All right, my horse is tied a little way from here. Don't make a sound—don't even whisper until I say you can." He grabbed her hand, pulling her behind him. She didn't hesitate, but ran lightly, matching his steps.

In less than a minute they reached the chestnut horse. Luke placed his hands on the girl's waist and boosted her into the saddle. Toeing the stirrup with his boot, he swung up behind her. It was a tight fit, but there was no time to worry about it.

Luke guided the horse up the draw, staying in the willows until they petered out and the horse began to climb. Before reaching the top of the wash, Luke once more slipped from the horse's back.

"I'll be back," he whispered. The girl nodded her head.

Moving swiftly, but keeping a low profile, Luke climbed to where the ground was level. Nothing appeared to be moving in all the vast land. Taking his time, he turned his attention to the huddle of lights he'd left behind. Neither seeing nor hearing any unusual activity or signs of pursuit, he heaved a sigh of relief. He hadn't been recognized, and the girl hadn't yet been missed. He hurried back to where she waited with his horse.

"Best if we move slowly and keep quiet," he whispered as he settled behind the girl once more. "When we're far enough away, we'll move faster." He tapped his heels against the horse's sides, and powerful muscles surged forward. He was glad the horse had offered no resistance to carrying a second rider. For a fleeting second, he remembered his father riding the horse into the yard and reaching down for his mother to carry her off for a time one bright spring evening. It surprised him that a moment when his parents were alive and happy came to mind. Usually, memories of their deaths wiped out the good memories that came before.

Once the lights of the shantytown disappeared, Luke guided the stallion to the wagon track and urged him into a steady, ground-eating canter. When the horse began to slow, he once more left the track. Walking at a slower pace, Luke sought patches of shrubs and trees in the gullies and hills to conceal their movement.

When their journey began, the girl held herself stiffly erect as though reluctant to touch him; but as the hours passed, her slight body slumped against him, and he found himself holding her in place with one arm, allowing her head to rest against his chest, braced from rolling by the crook of his elbow.

Because he was unaccustomed to riding with someone almost in his lap, the girl at first seemed all sharp elbows and hip bones, but as the hours passed and she relaxed in deep slumber, his burden became soft and pliable. Sometimes he glanced down at her, and seeing her sleeping face filled him with emotions he hadn't ever experienced.

He breathed deeply. The scent of her skin and hair was nothing like that of the women who sometimes leaned close when they served him his dinner or a drink on the rare occasions when he didn't cook his own grub. A memory flickered in the back of his mind, and he thought she smelled a little bit like Ma had when she'd tucked him in bed when he was a boy. He credited thoughts of Ma for arousing protective feelings in him, and he took care to jostle the sleeping girl as little as possible.

Dawn was only hours away when he found a place he remembered from his earlier trek. There was no spring to provide fresh water, but the brush was thick, and a slight depression at the top of a hill provided both a semblance of shelter and a view that would prevent anyone from sneaking up on them.

The girl awoke when the horse stopped. She didn't say anything, but he could tell from her hurried appraisal of their back trail and of him that her fears had returned.

"We're safe for now," he tried to reassure her. He dismounted and reached for her to help her down. She hesitated only a moment before allowing him to lift her from the saddle. He kept his hands at her waist until she felt steady on her feet. As she stepped away, he returned to his horse to remove the saddle.

"If you're hungry, there are biscuits and peaches in that bag." He pointed to the bag he'd placed beside his saddle on the ground. After rubbing down the animal and staking him a short distance away where he would find grass and shelter should rain come before they resumed their journey, Luke walked back to where the girl waited. She'd opened a tin of peaches and was interspersing bites of the sweet, sticky fruit with chunks of three-day-old biscuits. She ate as though it had been some time since she'd last had a meal.

Opening another can of peaches, Luke speared a couple of chunks of fruit from the can, then reached for his bedroll, which he'd left on the ground beside his saddle. He ignored the nervous glances the girl sent his way as he finished eating and rolled out the blankets. Separating the two blankets, he tossed one to her and wrapped himself in the other. The early morning air was warm, which wasn't unusual for late August, but he knew that lying on the ground would bring a chill as they slept.

"You might as well sleep," he told her. "There's walkin'-around room in this little hollow, but don't show yourself up top. We'll have to stay put here once it gets light, then when it's dark again, we've got some hard riding ahead of us." He didn't wait for her response. He closed his eyes and slept. He'd learned not to waste any of the precious time that could be given to sleep.

When he awoke, the sun was high overhead. He took his time examining the hollow and testing the air for any sounds that didn't belong. The girl sat a few feet away with her skirt wrapped tightly around her drawn-up legs. Her worn, much-patched blue dress brought a pang to his heart, reminding him of his mother and of the girl shot down in the street at Wallace Creek. The protective tug he'd felt in his heart the night before as he'd held her returned in greater force.

He raised his eyes to see long, blonde hair flowing down the front of her dress. He'd never seen such hair. Ma's hair had been a rich honey color, acquiring golden streaks when she worked in the sun, but this girl's hair was like the cobwebs that glittered in early morning sunlight. Her nimble fingers moved deftly, twisting it into a long, pale braid. When she reached the end, she tied it off with a bit of string and began winding it like a crown atop her head. He felt a pang of regret as the mane of sunshine-colored hair disappeared. His attention finally focused on her face. She was even more beautiful than she'd been the night before with moonlight highlighting the tear stains on her cheeks.

He found himself memorizing the soft curve of her cheeks, the slender bow of her mouth, and the rich blue of her eyes surrounded by lashes the color of oat straw. A sprinkle of tiny freckles spread across her bit of a nose. If the cowboy who had wagered his pay and that of his friends to have her had actually seen her, Luke could have understood his determination to win her. But just thinking of the crude lout laying a hand on the girl brought a swell of fury almost as great as that he'd experienced that long-ago day seeing his mother lying dead beneath her clothesline.

"I suppose it might be handy to know each other's names." The girl jumped at the sound of Luke's voice. She blushed, and he could tell she wouldn't have plaited her hair in front of him if she'd known he was watching her.

"My mama named me Madeline Elizabeth Brannigan, but no one ever called me all that. I'm just Maddie." She ducked her head as though waiting for a snicker or some sort of criticism.

"It's a pretty name, something special you ought to keep for special times. I like Maddie too. It sounds kind of spunky, like a girl brave enough to set out on her own." He gave her one of his rare smiles.

"I know who you are." She looked down at her shabby shoes and fiddled with the hem of her skirt. "At first I didn't, but there's been a lot of talk about Kid Calloway all summer. Pa said the sheriff from over Hewitt way came by a couple of weeks ago to warn folks you was headed this way. He said you held up the bank there five years ago and you threatened to kill Harrison Duncan." She held her breath as she waited for him to confirm or deny her guess.

Luke snorted with derision. "Kid Calloway is a name old Duncan invented to make folks think I'm some kind of outlaw. I'm not, and I never held up no bank. Duncan hired some outlaws to kill my folks so he could steal our ranch, then he double-crossed 'em. The couple outlaws that escaped were so mad they held up the bank in Hewitt. I saw it happen, and so did Duncan. The weasel took a couple of shots at me, figurin' if I was dead, I couldn't tell what he done."

Maddie trailed the fingertips of one hand in the dirt for several minutes without looking up. At last she slanted her head so she could see his face. "You don't act like the kind of man who might do all those awful things I heard about, and you've been good to me, so I reckon I believe you. I'm sorry about your folks. Is your name really Calloway?"

"It is. Luke Calloway." He hesitated, then went on, "An awful smart lady suggested I change it. From now on I'll be goin' by Luke McCall."

"Luke's a good name. I'm glad you're keeping that part." She ducked her head again.

Luke rose to his feet, stretched a bit, then wandered off to check on his horse. When he got back, he found a couple more tins of peaches. They sat in the shade of a low juniper, picking the fruit out of the tins with their fingers, then drinking the juice. They talked, and Luke was surprised how easy it was to talk to Maddie. It wasn't like the bunkhouse talk he'd shared with other cowboys, but more like being with the Pattersons or his own family before all the trouble started.

He liked the way Maddie checked for snakes before sitting down and took care to stay low when she moved around without making any big fuss about it. She didn't complain about the heat or dirt or the limited amount of water Luke allowed each of them. He could tell by the careful way she moved that she was sore from last night's ride, but she didn't complain. He suspected the high pommel of the saddle, combined with little or no experience riding astride, accounted for her tenderness. He wished he had some of the ointment Ma used to give him when he was little and sometimes stayed in the saddle longer than he should have.

When the sun was almost out of sight, Luke saddled his horse. He spread his bedroll behind the high cantle to create a cushioned seat for Maddie behind him and tied it in place to keep it from sliding. He mounted first near a chalky lump of dirt, then slipped his boot out of the near stirrup. He held out his hand to Maddie and she took it.

"Step into the stirrup," he instructed. She did so and, lifted by his strong arm, she swung up behind him. He saw her wince, but she didn't say anything when she settled onto the blankets he'd prepared.

"Keep hold of my belt or wrap your arms around my waist," he told her. "We'll be moving fast, and I don't want to worry about you sliding off if we have to make a quick turn or run for it."

The big horse again didn't seem bothered by the additional weight of a second rider and seemed anxious to stretch his legs. Luke held him to a fast walk until they once again reached the road, then he gave him his head. When the horse began to tire, Luke reined him in to a gentle lope, then eventually slowed to a walk.

Once the horse's ears pricked and he snorted a warning in time for Luke to leave the road and find a spot where they could stay out of sight behind a gentle hill. Luke leaped from the horse, hissing a warning for Maddie to duck low. He slithered on his stomach to the top of the hill, where he could part the long prairie grass and watch as a buckboard pulled by four mules with jingling harnesses plodded by. Two men sat on the wagon box. Before they were out of sight, a command rang through the air, and he watched in alarm as the mule skinner halted his animals. He relaxed when he realized the men were only making camp.

Sliding backward, he was soon beside Maddie again. "It's all right," he whispered. " But we'll need to stay low for a while." He helped her to the ground, then took the chestnut's reins and led the stallion for nearly a mile, trudging side by side with Maddie until he deemed it safe to climb back onto the horse.

Toward dawn he could tell Maddie was barely hanging on. Stephenville was another six hours' ride, and it would be full light before they reached it. He couldn't openly ride into town with Maddie. It was unlikely anyone would recognize her, but she would attract attention and be remembered, especially if someone recognized him.

He began looking for a place to stop and was chagrined to see how many ranches and farms dotted the land. Several dark spots caught his eye, but they were only small washes or gullies. None was large enough to protect them from prying eyes should anyone ride past. He needed to find a place to hole up before they reached the stretch he remembered as miles of barbed wire which would hold them to the road.

They passed a cluster of farm buildings that were closer than he liked. On the journey out from Stephenville, he'd found the windmill and acres of plowed ground points of interest. Now each sign of the presence of people was a potential threat. A line of farm clothes hung limply between two posts behind the house, giving him an idea. He began to search for one of the shallow gullies.

"Maddie," he whispered when he found one and rode into the brush that lined its sides. "We'll camp here for a few hours, and you can sleep."

As he'd hoped, she was too tired to notice that he didn't unsaddle the horse but left him tied to a sturdy root, exposed by an earlier gully washer. He glanced toward the sky and was pleased to see a canopy of stars. He wouldn't want to leave Maddie alone in a gully if rain were likely. He spread the blanket on the ground, and she sank down onto it. She was asleep almost the moment her head touched the blanket. With unfamiliar tenderness, he spread the other blanket over her.

He lost no time scrambling out of the gully, and his steps turned to a fast trot as he hurried back the way they'd come. He slowed when he neared the ranch house. Separating the strands of barbed wire so he could step between them, he circled the house in a wide arc to reach a side yard he'd noticed earlier from the road. Just past the privy, he spotted what he'd been looking for. Stepping into the open, he snatched a couple of pairs of overalls from the line, quickly stuffing them inside his shirt. He turned to go, then a pang of conscience sent him back to place a dollar in the pocket of one of the remaining pairs of overalls.

Maddie was still sleeping when he returned to the gully. He judged he'd been gone no more than an hour, and an hour of sleep was little to go on, but he didn't dare delay putting his plan into action. They needed to be on their way before the sun came up. Already he could detect the grayness that precedes dawn.

"Maddie." He crouched beside her, giving her shoulder a shake. Even in the dark, he could see and feel the fear that brought her instantly awake.

"It's all right, Maddie. It's me, Luke." He kept his voice low and imbued it with all the kindness he could. "We have to be on our way."

When Maddie sat up and appeared to have all her faculties about her, he handed her one pair of the overalls he'd taken and took his spare shirt from his saddlebag.

"Put these on," he said. "You can wear my hat. It'll cover your braid and help you to look like a boy. I'll turn my back." Once he'd turned around, he pulled the second pair of overalls over his own clothes and snapped up the shoulder straps.

Hearing a giggle, he asked, "You decent?"

"I think so." She giggled again, and he turned around to see by the rapidly lightening sky a boy a few inches shorter than himself in a pair of overalls several sizes too large. Maddie was rolling the sleeves back to free her hands, and Luke knelt to turn a cuff on the overalls. He removed his hat, poked his hand up the crown to alter its shape, then plunked it down on her head. It helped, but she was still too pretty. Stooping, he picked up a handful of dirt and moistened it with water from his canteen. He wiped it on both of their faces, then took his handkerchief to wipe most of it off. Satisfied, he stepped back.

Maddie reached for his handkerchief, rolled it, and tied it around his head as she'd seen some of the farmers in the many places she'd lived do. By the time she'd picked up her dress and petticoat and Luke had stuffed them in his saddlebag, the sun was sending the first pink tinges of morning over the horizon.

Luke made no effort to conceal their movements as they rode openly toward Stephenville. He couldn't avoid tensing whenever they passed another rider on horseback, but when no one challenged them, they continued on.

It was past noon and his stomach was growling when they rode into the small town. He picked a route that led to the back of the livery stable. Once he was sure no one had noticed them, he dismounted and helped Maddie down. It took only a few minutes to strip his gear from the chestnut and open the gate to the pasture where the gray and a few other horses grazed. The big animal joyfully rolled a few times in the dirt before trotting toward the other horses.

Picking up his gear, Luke led the way to the back door of the livery. The interior of the barn was dark after the bright sunlight, and it took a moment for their eyes to adjust. Hearing angry voices coming from the front of the barn, Luke tossed his gear inside an empty stall and told Maddie to wait in the stall with his gear until he found Baily.

Fishing his gun out of the overalls, he held it in his hand as he crept toward the voices. Ducking into an open stall, he peered through the board slats at a man wearing a fancy vest and shiny boots that didn't look like they'd been worn a whole lot. A black leather gun belt rode low on the man's hips and was tied off above the man's knee. A black, wide-brimmed felt hat hid the upper half of his face. Luke recognized his kind. He was a gunfighter, most likely one who had read a few too many dime novels and decided he was fast enough to take Kid Calloway.

An angry voice was shouting at Baily, demanding to know whether the old man had put up Kid Calloway's big chestnut horse when he'd come through and how many days it had been since the Kid left for Hewitt. The would-be gunfighter's hand clenched and relaxed over and over above his gun like he was getting ready to draw. Luke eased the hammer back on his own gun.

"I heard you befriended the Kid right after he held up the Hewitt bank," the gunfighter snarled. "Answer my questions or you're a dead man," he threatened. He landed a punch to the old man's midsection, and Luke took careful aim.

"Enough!" a voice roared. Luke had missed the blacksmith's arrival as surely as the gunfighter had.

"This is none of your business." The gunman turned, his hand once more hovering near his gun.

"This makes it my business." The brawny man sighted down the barrel of an old Sharps, such as the buffalo hunters used. Luke grinned, until he remembered he was in the line of fire too. If the blacksmith let go, the shot would go right through the gunfighter and on through him as well, blowing them both and half the barn to kingdom come. He considered showing himself and getting the gunman outside, but fortunately the would-be gunfighter backed off when challenged by the blacksmith, leaving with a volley of curses and threats.

Baily thanked the blacksmith and they talked briefly before the big man made his way back across the street. Luke considered adding his thanks, then thought better of it. The fewer people who knew he was in town the better.

"Baily," Luke called softly, not wanting to frighten his friend.

"Luke? That you?" The elderly man turned with a smile spreading across his face, then he sobered. "You've got to leave here pronto. Town's full of gunmen looking for you. Even that lazy sheriff we've got stopped by to ask if I'd seen you."

"I'm planning to take you up on that Oscarson trail boss who's trailing a herd of cattle north. Only problem is, I met somebody east of here who's in a worse fix than me. I gave my word I'd help out." He led the way to the far stall where he'd left Maddie.

Maddie looked as though she were poised to run when Baily and Luke peered inside the stall.

"This is Baily Patterson," Luke made a hasty introduction. "You don't need to fear him any."

Baily stared suspiciously at the slight figure occupying one of his stalls, then stepped forward, extending his hand.

"Well, young feller, if Luke vouches for you, you're fine by me." His hand closed around Maddie's and the old man jumped back as though he'd been stung. His eyes widened and he whispered, "You ain't no fella. You're a girl!"

CHAPTER NINE

Luke and Maddie hid out at the livery barn until after dark before creeping to the back door of the Pattersons' house.

Baily and Dory were waiting alongside a tub of hot water. Dory whisked Maddie into the kitchen, while Luke cheerfully shucked his clothes and stepped into the steaming water.

While he bathed, he told Baily about the events of the past few days, including how he came across Maddie.

"I couldn't leave her there. I'd always feel responsible for her becoming what her pa had in mind for her," he finished.

"You did right, son, but it does complicate things. I 'spect you'll want to be on your way as soon as you're rested up, and I can't blame you none," the old man said. "But what about the girl? What do you plan to do with her?"

"I was hoping I could leave her here. She could help out and be company for Dory while you're at the livery." Luke stepped out of the tub and reached for the towel Dory always left on a nearby chair.

"Dory'd like nothin' better, I'm sure. We always wanted young'uns, but the good Lord never saw fit to send us any. You're as close to a son as we'll ever have, and it's going to be hard seein' you ride off again." Baily stared down at his clasped hands and swallowed a time or two. "Problem is, Maddie wouldn't be safe here. That feller what come into the stable today knew about us bein' friends. More yahoos just like him will come along, and they'll be knowin' the same thing. Sooner or later one of 'em will spread the word about Maddie, and her pa will come lookin' for her here."

Luke was quiet. What Baily said made sense. What would become of Maddie when he left? He worried the problem over in his head while he dressed but got no answers.

Dory tapped on the door and told them to hurry. They each picked up a handle at either end of the big tub and carried it to the garden, where they upended it over one of Dory's rosebushes. When they entered the kitchen, they found a second tub needing to be emptied. Once that was taken care of, they trooped into the kitchen once more, and Luke stared in amazement.

Maddie hovered uncertainly in the doorway leading to the spare room that had been his bedroom the two times he'd stayed at the Pattersons' home. Her hair glistened in the lamplight in one long braid that disappeared behind her back. Her cheeks were rosy, and she wore a deep emerald-colored dress with a wide collar of white lace at her throat. He caught a faint whiff of mothballs, telling him Dory had opened a long-closed trunk of things she'd worn herself a long time ago.

They sat down to a dinner of roast beef, freshly baked bread, rice and beans, and yellow squash. When he felt full to bursting, Dory placed the biggest slab of pie he'd ever tried to get his tongue around in front of him and set a pitcher of cream on the table. While they ate, he retold his and Maddie's adventure to Dory.

"Land sakes!" Dory exclaimed when he finished. "It's a good thing you got this poor girl away from there." She turned her attention to Maddie and, seeing the girl was almost asleep with a forkful of pie halfway to her mouth, she took charge of getting Maddie a nightie to wear and hustling her into bed in the spare room.

"I can help you with the dishes first," Maddie objected, struggling to her feet and attempting to gather up their plates.

"I'll not have anyone falling asleep in my dishpan. You just get between the covers right this minute." She placed her arm around the girl's shoulders and propelled her toward the door of the bedroom, pulling it shut behind her once Maddie stepped inside.

Luke wondered for a moment where he would sleep. He could have slept this afternoon in an unused stall, but he'd been too on edge. Maddie hadn't slept either, though she was exhausted and had enjoyed little more than an hour's rest in more than twenty-four hours. Dory spread a pile of quilts on the parlor floor and insisted he make use of them. He wasted no time pulling off his boots and settling himself in the makeshift bed. He fell asleep listening to the murmur of Baily and Dory's voices in the kitchen. He knew Baily was filling his wife in on the problem of finding a place for Maddie where she would be safe from her pa. He knew he should give more thought to the problem, but he was so tired, his brain refused to do any more thinking.

* * *

"Luke, you best be wakin' up." The voice crept into his consciousness as though coming from a long way off. "Luke!" There was a hint of impatience in the voice now. His eyes popped open, and he noticed two things right away. Baily Patterson was leaning over him with straw in his hair and a faint odor of the stable clinging to his clothes. The second thing was daylight creeping under and around the closed curtain of Dory's parlor.

He sat straight up, his hand snaking toward his weapon. He couldn't remember the last time he'd slept so late.

"You don't need that, son. Least not yet." Baily snagged one of Dory's fine parlor chairs and pulled it forward. "There's a posse in town lookin' for you. The sheriff from Hewitt is heading it up, and it looks to me like he scoured every saloon between that place and here for hired guns and outlaws to make up his posse."

"I'll go." Luke rose to his feet, quickly stepping into his pants and reaching for his shirt. "I don't want any trouble coming to you and Dory."

"What about the girl? Rumor is you stole her against her will."

"He didn't." Maddie stepped into the room with Dory right behind her. Luke fastened his shirt in record time. "I begged him to help me escape."

"We believe you," Baily turned to assure her. Luke sat on the horsehair sofa to pull his boots on. "But that posse's gonna believe what they want to. They're makin' a lot of loud talk about hangin' Luke and takin' you back to your pa."

Luke looked up to see Maddie's face turn pale. "They won't hang me, and Maddie's not going back to a pa who thinks more highly of gambling and boozing than of her. I'm leaving and taking her with me."

Dory gasped. "It ain't fittin'. You can't be ridin' around the country with a young woman. It'd ruin her reputation."

"We'll get hitched, then no one can say nothin'." Luke went on fastening his gun belt and tying the holster low on his right hip. He heard both Maddie and Dory gasp but didn't look up to see Maddie's face. For some reason, looking at Maddie at that moment scared him more than facing the posse.

"Well, then, we'd best be makin' some plans." There was a note of glee in the old man's voice. "I already hid that big horse of yours where nobody's goin' to find him right off, and the gray too. We'll just have to keep the pair of you out of sight till nightfall."

"I'll get Reverend Mink over here, and don't you worry none, Luke. He's a man what knows when to keep his mouth shut. Maddie can wear my weddin' dress. It's been folded up so many years, it'll take a mite of work to get the wrinkles out. And vittles. I best get started packin' some grub for you to take along."

He listened to Dory prattle on, but he hadn't heard Maddie say one word. Gathering his courage, he raised his eyes and met Maddie's straight on. He wasn't sure what he saw there—fear, hurt, but something more. It was that something more that led him to take a couple of steps toward her. He reached for her hand and was surprised by how small and perfect her capable hand felt in his.

"It's the only way." He kept his voice soft. "I promise I'll make you a good husband, and you won't ever have to worry about being hit or not having enough to eat—and I don't drink. We got on well enough on the trip here, and I figure we can manage fine being hitched. If you just can't bear marrying me, I'll do my best to think of something else. I'll see that you get away from your pa, no matter what you decide."

"I'll marry you." She didn't stammer or act skittish, just said it straight out.

Passing the time without drawing attention to themselves or the Pattersons was the hardest thing he had to do all day. Maddie kept busy helping Dory prepare dinner, and the women spent a lot of time in Baily and Dory's bedroom, presumably fixing up something for Maddie to get married in. Baily returned to his livery barn since folks might wonder if he stayed away. Luke wished he could have gone with him. Forking hay to the horses and cleaning stalls would have been easier than doing nothing.

Out of desperation for something to do, he cleaned and oiled both his six-shooter and the rifle that had belonged to his pa. He paced the floor and wished he could talk to Ma about Maddie. Sometimes he talked to her in his mind, but he recalled how much store his mother had always set by the old Bible that had been in her family for generations. It had been the textbook by which she'd taught him to read. Ma believed in praying too, though Luke hadn't done much of that on his own. It seemed perfectly logical to him that a woman like Ma would be in heaven, and he wondered if he asked God to let her know he was marrying a good woman, if God would see that Ma got the message.

He made his way to the spare bedroom and knelt beside the bed the way he'd seen Ma do. He wasn't sure what to say or if God would even listen to someone who'd carried vengeance in his heart so many years. He'd gone to church a few times, but it was to gain information about Blackwell's possible movements, not to listen to the various preachers. He wondered if God would hold that against him. Most of the preachers hadn't impressed him any more than the traveling preacher he'd taken Ma to hear all those years ago.

Gathering up his courage, he began to speak. "God, I never learned much about prayin', and I'm sorry to be botherin' ya now, but I'd like my ma to know I'm marryin' Maddie. She ain't been done by proper and her pa is a danger to her, but she's a fine girl, and I think Ma would like her. I ain't forgot about what Harrison Duncan did to my folks, but there ain't nothin' I can do about that right now, and Maddie needs my help. And God, I ain't askin' for anything for myself, but if you could sort of help me look after Maddie, I'd appreciate it. Amen."

He stayed on his knees, thinking, for a long time. His thoughts gradually shifted from worrying about getting married to planning the route they should take to catch up to the Oscarson herd. Based on what Baily had said, the herd should be a few days out from Indian territory by the time they reached it.

A sound outside the house drew his attention. He stood and, taking care not to cross in front of the window, peeked around the side of the curtain. Two men wearing stars on their chests stood outside the Pattersons' front gate, arguing. One was the sheriff from Hewitt. He pointed at the house several times, and each time the Stephenville sheriff shook his head.

Backing away from the window, Luke gathered up his and Maddie's meager belongings before slipping down the hall to tap on Dory's door.

"There are a couple of lawmen at the front gate," he whispered. Dory opened the door at once, a pair of scissors still clutched in her hand, and ushered him inside. Pressing her finger to her lips, she motioned him forward and pointed to a table beside the bed. He caught a glimpse of Maddie closing a large trunk. Dory beckoned for her to come closer, then, lifting one side of the table, she motioned for Luke to lift the other. Puzzled, Luke did as she indicated.

Once the table was removed, Dory kicked aside a thick, braided rug and then knelt to press one blade of the scissors into a small crack in the floorboards. To his amazement, an entire section of flooring lifted up. The sudden pounding on the front door caused Luke to rush forward and help Dory open the trapdoor.

"Baily built this hidey-hole when we first moved here and were afraid of Indian attacks," Dory whispered as she urged them to climb down into the dark recess. Luke scrambled down a wooden ladder, then held up his arms to support Maddie as she joined him. Dory passed him his rifle and saddlebags before closing the trapdoor. The total darkness was almost overwhelming. He stood still, listening as Dory pushed the table back into place. When that sound ceased, there was silence.

He felt Maddie's hand on his arm and knew she was afraid. Placing one arm around her, he drew her to his side. With his other arm outstretched, he explored the small space they found themselves in. They stood on a plank floor in an approximately eight-by-eight-foot room. The walls were timbered to prevent their collapse, and a shelf held a number of cans and bottles.

There was nothing to do but wait, so Luke spread his bedroll on the planks and helped Maddie to sit with her back propped against a wall. He folded his legs and sat beside her, keeping his arm around her shoulders. They didn't speak, not even a whisper.

Footsteps overhead had them both holding their breaths. A few minutes later, the scraping sound of the table being moved came again. Luke reached for his gun. Holding it pointed toward the spot where light was beginning to show, he drew back the hammer.

"Everything's fine. They're gone." Dory's voice reached them before the trapdoor opened enough to reveal her kneeling at the top of the ladder. Luke eased the hammer back and stood to give Dory a hand lifting the heavy door. Minutes later, Maddie and Dory were hugging each other and Dory was telling how the Stephenville sheriff was put out with the Hewitt sheriff for thinking he could push the good citizens of Stephenville around.

It was early evening and not quite dark yet when Baily tapped on the back door and stepped hurriedly inside. Following quickly on his heels was a slender, middle-aged man wearing a black suit and carrying a Bible.

Luke's stomach clenched, though he did his best to act like he wasn't the least bit concerned about getting married. Wearing his best pair of jeans and a shirt he'd paid two dollars for, he stood beside the preacher and waited for Maddie and Dory to come out of Baily and Dory's bedroom. It was an odd time to be thinking about it, but he suddenly recalled he wasn't yet twenty years old. Somewhere in the back of his mind he supposed he'd planned on marrying someday, but he hadn't actively considered it. He certainly hadn't given any thought to marrying a girl he wasn't sure had passed her sixteenth birthday— a girl he knew almost nothing about.

The bedroom door creaked, and it took all the self-discipline he'd mastered to keep from bolting from the room. A rustling sound preceded the women, drawing Luke's attention back to the doorway. He couldn't resist looking. His mouth dropped open, and his knees went weak.

Maddie stood in the doorway. At least, he thought it was Maddie. She looked like an angel standing there in a pale blue satin gown that shimmered like moonlight on a mountain pool. Her hair was caught up on one side by an ivory clip and fell in silvery curls to her shoulders. A piece of lace a foot wide circled the bottom of her skirt, which was too wide to pass through the doorway on her first try. She had to turn sideways and bunch up her skirt with her hands to get through.

Her skirt made a whispering sound as she walked toward him. He swallowed audibly and slowly held out his hand to the vision approaching him.

She took it, and he felt her fingers tremble. It was strange, but knowing she was scared too served to wipe away his own fears. He drew her closer, then turned her until they were both facing Reverend Mink.

The words were a blur, and he felt like he was standing outside himself, watching a young cowboy make solemn promises to a princess from one of the stories Ma had told him when he was a child. He should have been too tongue-tied to speak or even to stammer his responses, but he knew he'd somehow said the right things at the right time because the preacher was telling him to kiss his bride. That brought a return of that panicky feeling. While concentrating on keeping his hands from trembling, he leaned his head forward. Her lips pressed back with just the slightest pressure. He knew then that just one lifetime with this angel would not be enough.

He straightened, feeling a warm flush on his ears. Baily put one arm around his shoulders and thumped him on the back. Next Dory hugged him, while huge tears ran down her cheeks. Maddie got her share of hugs and good wishes too, though Luke didn't dare look at her. Reverend Mink slipped out the back door, leaving the four of them to continue their preparations.

Dory accompanied Maddie back to the bedroom to remove her finery before they sat down to the dinner that had been simmering in Dory's oven all afternoon. Baily cleared his throat and looked uncomfortable once the ladies were out of sight.

"Sit down, son." The old man indicated one of the straight-backed kitchen chairs. Still feeling slightly dazed, Luke did as he was asked. Baily paced the floor for a couple of minutes, then drew up another chair facing Luke.

"Seein' as your pa ain't here," he started, and Luke hid a smile. He should have guessed Baily would take his role as surrogate father a step further.

"I know what happens 'twixt a man and a lady," he told the old man with a lot more confidence than he felt. He'd been hanging around saloons and listening to bunkhouse talk for enough years to have learned a few things.

"Do you?" Baily asked, and there was a hint of skepticism in his voice that made Luke flush.

"Well, I ain't done it," he admitted, "but . . ."

"Son, I've lived a lot of years, and I've heard and seen the same things you have, and they ain't right. Those fellas you've heard— braggin' about all they done—don't know the first thing about lovin' a woman. You just worry about keepin' Maddie happy, and you'll be happy. She's young and scared and probably don't expect much. She's kind of like those young horses you and your pa used to raise. If you pet 'em and brush 'em real gentle-like and let 'em get used to you a little bit at a time, they gets to be right good horses. But if you set out to show 'em who's boss and break 'em like wild mustangs, they's ruined and has no spirit at all."

"I don't think Maddie would like being compared to a horse." Luke found he didn't like that comparison either. Deep inside, he knew there would forever be a picture of Maddie, his bride, more ethereal angel than woman, tucked away in a private place in his heart.

Baily started to walk away, then turned back. "Luke, I meant no insult to Maddie. You're a good man, but it's been a long time since you had much that's good in your life, and I'm not sure Maddie has ever had any consideration. She's special, and I think you know that. But I'm hopin' you'll come to share with that gal the rare kind of lovin' me and Dory has knowed all these years. Take your time at the beginnin' if you mean to build something that's gonna last."

* * *

Luke closed the door behind him and swallowed hard. His bride was sitting up in the middle of the old iron bed. By the light of the lantern that sat on the bureau a few feet from the bed, he could see her eyes were wide and she looked as skittish as a coyote pup. She was wearing a white nightgown many sizes too large, cinched up to her neck, and her long, pale hair flowed like a mountain stream down her back and over her shoulders. He felt an almost physical ache to run his fingers through the shining strands. She was lovely, and he supposed he wouldn't be a man if he didn't feel certain things just looking at her, but he was surprised by an emotion even stronger. He walked toward her and sat down on the side of the bed.

Pulling off his boots, he placed them carefully beside the bed, then reached for the buttons on his shirt. Once it was removed, he turned to look at Maddie. He saw the slight tremble of her bottom lip, reminding him that she was scared. Baily's words came back to him, but this time he heard the message the old man had tried to share with him.

"Maddie." He reached for her hands. "You don't need to be scared. I'll not do anything until you let me know you're ready. We only have a few hours until we have to be on our way, then we have a long ride ahead of us. It's best if we both get as much sleep as we can. I'm going to blow out the lantern before I shuck my britches and climb in that bed beside you. All I'm askin' of you is to let me hold you until we both fall asleep. We've got a whole lifetime to learn about being a husband and wife."

There was relief—and perhaps a bit of skepticism—in her eyes as she moved over to make room for him. He turned to blow out the lantern, let his pants fall to the floor, then lifted one corner of the quilt to slip beneath it. For just a moment he felt as clumsy as a newborn colt. He had no idea how to go about gathering Maddie in his arms. He only knew that he wanted to feel her close beside him. Even more, he wanted to be the one she turned to through all the years to come. A tentative hand touched his and he clasped it in his own rough hand and felt a rapid flutter in her wrist. He gave it a gentle squeeze, then whispered, "Go to sleep." After what seemed a long time, he heard her breathing become relaxed and even. Cautiously, so as not to wake her, he slid his arm around her. His hand brushed her hair, and unable to resist, he stroked its satiny length. She sighed and snuggled closer. That was when he knew everything would be all right.

CHAPTER TEN

Luke awoke when a soft rap sounded on the bedroom door. For just a moment he felt disoriented by Maddie's weight across his arm and her slight body curled against his side. She sat up quickly, and he felt her long hair sweep across his chest, filling him with regret that they must be on their way.

"We're awake," he called softly.

"Everything's ready." Baily's low voice came through the wood panel.

Luke's hold on Maddie tightened for just a moment, and he felt her slender arms return the pressure. His lips brushed her cheek before whispering, "We have to go." She didn't answer but slowly withdrew her arms from around his neck, and he knew she understood. He too relaxed his hold and rolled away from her.

He stepped out of bed and into his pants before lighting the lantern. He kept the wick low in spite of knowing that Dory had covered the window earlier so they wouldn't have to dress in the dark when it was time to leave. He averted his face to avoid embarrassing Maddie when the rustle of bedclothes told him she had slipped out of the opposite side of the bed. It only took a moment to grab his shirt and pick up his boots and chaps.

At the door, he paused with his back to her to say, "I'll check our supplies. Meet me in the kitchen when you're ready."

"I'll only be a moment. Dory laid out clothes for me earlier."

* * *

The door made a soft click, and she was alone. Reaching for the hem of the voluminous nightgown she wore, she quickly pulled it over her head. She didn't want to keep Luke waiting. She stopped before reaching for the pair of britches lying on a chair beside her. Her reasons for not keeping Luke waiting were nothing like her life-long concern for not keeping Papa waiting. She wasn't afraid of Luke, even if he was a famous gunfighter.

She examined that thought as she dressed. She'd always been a little afraid of Papa, though Papa prided himself on being a southern gentleman. In her heart, she guessed she'd always known he wasn't really a gentleman. It hadn't taken Louise's warning that men weren't always what they seemed to be to keep her away from the men who played cards with Papa. Some instinct had warned her early that those men would only hurt her. Perhaps it was that same instinct that allowed her to trust Luke—and it hadn't let her down. He was a good man. A quiet place near her heart told her she wouldn't regret marrying him.

Her fingers flew as she finished fastening buttons. When she finished, she looked around the room to see if she'd forgotten anything. The nightgown lay at her feet. She picked it up, folded it, and left it on the chair, then took a moment to straighten the bed, feeling her face grow hot as she remembered lying beside Luke. She'd never been so close to a man before, and it hadn't been terrible, as she'd always supposed it would be. He hadn't . . . She turned away. She supposed there would be more, and perhaps Louise was right about that too. Letting a man love her wouldn't be bad, if he were the right man.

She felt a sudden urge to be on their way. Dory had been kind to her, almost like the mother she sometimes dreamed waited for her in heaven, but Luke was in danger. He needed to be far from here, and she wanted to be by his side—not only as he rode north, but all his life.

* * *

Luke entered the kitchen to find his saddlebags lying on the table. Beside them lay a second set of leather bags that appeared to be well used, and he remembered that Baily had promised to find gear for Maddie. A brief glance assured him that his extra set of clothes was neatly folded inside his bag, along with a new bar of soap, extra ammunition, several pairs of socks, and his shaving gear. The few clothes and toiletries in the second set of bags were almost identical to his own. Two bedrolls and two flour sacks with bulging sides completed all they would carry with them.

"I'm ready," Maddie spoke from behind Luke. He turned to see the slight, boyish figure that had ridden into Stephenville with him. Gone was the satin and lace dress she'd worn to wed him, and gone was the demure white gown she'd worn to bed. In their place were baggy denim pants and a flannel shirt with a loose jacket. On her feet were sturdy boots. Only her long, pale hair proclaimed her female.

He saw she wasn't speaking to him but to Dory. As his gaze shifted to Dory, he sucked in his breath at the sight of scissors in her hand. His first impulse was to protest, but even as he opened his mouth he knew it had to be. Maddie couldn't masquerade as his brother and accompany a trail herd with all that hair bunched under her hat. It had to go. The knowledge nearly choked him.

The first snip of the scissors sounded much too loud and brought unexpected pain to his chest. He couldn't watch. He turned his back, and only when he heard a small sob did he whirl back around to see Maddie standing with slumped shoulders in the center of a pool of shining locks. He looked at the mound of hair on the floor and felt like crying too. Slowly he lifted his eyes until he could see Maddie's tear-stained face. Heedless of where he stepped, he reached for her and pulled her to him.

"Don't cry," he whispered into her ear. "You're still beautiful, and your hair will grow back. Someday we'll have a little place of our own, and I'll buy you a pretty dress and ribbons for your hair."

"I'm sorry. I don't mean to act like a child." She sniffed and tried to smile.

"It's a shame, that's what it is," Dory sniffed and reached for her broom. Luke wasn't certain whether she was mourning Maddie's hair, as they were, or if it was the necessity of their leaving that brought her to the brink of tears. Before her broom reached the pile of hair on the floor, Luke reached down to claim a silky strand. He wound it tightly on one finger before opening the back of his pa's pocket watch and tucking the coiled lock inside. He didn't dare look at anyone for fear he'd see amusement on their faces because of his sentimental gesture.

"I found an old pair of chaps that look like they might fit Maddie," Baily spoke almost apologetically. "I figured they might help her feel more like she was wearin' a skirt. 'Sides, with ridin' fast at night and chasin' cows out of the brush once you catch up to Oscarson, she'll need the protection." He handed her a folded pile of leather. Carefully she unfolded the chaps, and Dory helped her buckle them in place. Luke noticed they also served to hide the feminine curve of her hips. He supposed that was a good thing.

"Best be on your way," Baily reminded them. He cleared his throat, then went on in a gruffer voice. "The horses are saddled and waiting at the far end of the pasture beyond that little grove of trees where I've kept them out of sight."

"I owe you." Luke reached inside his jacket for a small leather bag that held the wages he'd accumulated. It wasn't a lot, but he could buy the gray back and pay for Maddie's saddle and gear.

"No, son," Baily protested. "I've been paid. That stallion of yours hasn't been just eating grass in that pasture. Come spring, I'll have a couple of fine colts." He blew out the lamp and added, "I'm sure going to miss you young folks."

Dory gave them each a swift hug, then propelled them toward the door. "Take care of each other," were her parting words.

"Come on, Maddie," Luke whispered as he led the way.

"Best you start calling 'er Matt," Baily reminded Luke, giving his hand a final farewell clasp before stepping back to allow them to pass.

Luke paused on the threshold. Rain streamed from the sky in a steady deluge. He'd been so absorbed in their departure and the loss of Maddie's hair that he'd been unaware of the storm. The blackness of the stormy night rivaled the darkness of the cellar where they'd taken refuge earlier. A loud growl of thunder rumbled in the distance, and Maddie moved closer, just touching the arm that held his rifle.

"Gracious!" Dory exclaimed, snatching rain slickers for them from pegs on the wall. "Put these on before you're soaked to the skin." They stepped back from the door and did as she told them.

"I'm sorry." Luke turned to Maddie as they both fastened the long coats and reached once more for their packs. "I'll find shelter as soon as it's safe."

"A little rain won't hurt me." She smiled back at him, and his heart swelled at the courage he heard in her words.

"The rain may be a good thing," Baily told them. "It'll likely keep anyone from snooping around looking for you tonight. Besides, a good rain during the night leaves the world fresh and clean the next morning. It'll clear the air so you can ride a lot farther before the heat sets in again."

After good-byes were repeated, Luke slung his pack over one shoulder, freeing a hand to hold Maddie's. Together they stepped into the rain. Leading her through the darkness, he tried to avoid puddles, but in the blackness they were hard to spot. At last they reached the pasture, where they could follow the fence and tread on grass.

The horses were right where Baily had said they would be. Luke secured both bedrolls and draped the saddlebags and supplies behind the saddles. Next he returned his rifle to its scabbard and turned to assist Maddie to mount the gray.

They moved quietly at first, feeling their way slowly beyond the small town. Once they reached open range, they rode faster. They didn't talk much and frequently paused on hills to look back, checking for anyone following, though there was little that could be seen in the driving rain.

Once Maddie leaned forward to ask, "What are the horses' names?"

"Pa never gave 'em names." He turned his head to answer.

"Why not? I never heard of horses not having names."

"Pa raised horses to sell. He said it was easier to let them go if he didn't give them names. 'Sides, he figured the cowboys and ranchers who bought them ought to have the honor of naming them."

"But what do you call them?" She patted the gray's neck, and he could tell she'd taken to the horse. Truth be told, he was glad to have the gray back. The gelding had been his favorite mount before all the trouble began, but when he had to sell one, it had made sense to keep the more powerful stallion.

"I don't know what Baily called the one you're riding, but I just call this old boy Horse." He patted the animal's rain-soaked neck.

"That's awful." Maddie laughed softly. "You can go on calling that one Horse if you want to, but I'm naming this one Prince."

"I suppose that will do."

She was silent for a bit, then she asked in a more tentative voice, "You don't mind if I give him a name, do you?"

"Mind? 'Course not. You've got as much right to name him as I do. You're my wife, and what's mine is yours." He kind of liked saying she was his wife. He thought a lot about what that meant as they rode on through the night. He hadn't had a lot to do with married people in a long time, but he remembered Pa doing nice things for Ma and saying a man had a responsibility to take care of his wife and children. The thought of someday having children with Maddie occupied his mind for some time. It was both a pleasant and a frightening dream.

The sky was beginning to lighten and the storm had blown past when Luke began looking for a place to rest where they would be out of sight. He needed to be mindful too, of protection from the sun or a surprise flash flood while they slept. Finding a creek bed flush with runoff, they followed it until he found what he was seeking in thick brush that overlooked a sandy cut in the creek bank. Taking only enough time to care for their horses and eat a few bites of the thick beef sandwiches Dory had packed for them, they spread out their bedrolls side by side.

Maddie stretched out on her blankets and gazed at the array of colors spreading across the landscape. She inhaled the clean morning air and gave a little laugh.

"What's funny?" Luke asked as he finished wiping down the wet horses before seeking his own bedroll, inches from hers.

"It's not anything funny, really," she told him. "I was just thinking I'm tired, wet, and sore, but this is the happiest I've ever been. My old life is behind me, washed away with the rain, and today my new life begins."

Luke reached across the narrow space between them and took her hand. As he lay gazing up at the sky between the thick branches of a bush nearly large enough to be called a tree, he realized with a start that he felt happier and lighter too, than he had in a long time. He looked up at the brilliant streaks of morning color spreading across the vast sky and felt the first peace he'd known in almost five years. It was almost as though his parents were telling him to be happy, and a quiet thought came to his mind, telling him his parents approved of Maddie and his plans to begin a new life with her. He rolled over until he was lying close beside her. She welcomed him with the gentle touch of her lips against his throat.

When they awoke, the sun was beginning to set. Luke scouted the area while Maddie prepared a quick, cold supper. When Luke returned, they ate and were on their way as soon as darkness fell. Feeling it safe to relax their vigil some, Luke rode beside Maddie. He hadn't had much experience talking to a woman—the dance hall and saloon women he'd encountered made him uncomfortable, and the ranchers' wives and daughters hadn't had time to spend chatting with a drifter. Maddie was different, and he found himself telling her about his long quest to bring his parents' murderers to justice. Maddie was initially quiet and reserved, but she seemed to gain confidence as she told him of early memories of a big house in Louisiana, a river boat on the Mississippi, and the increasingly shabby houses she'd lived in as she'd moved west with her father.

"I don't remember my mother," she told Luke. "She died when I was born. Papa was ill for a long time after Mama died. I was nearly ten before I realized his illness was the kind that comes in a bottle. When I was five he sold Mama's plantation, and we went to live with a cousin in New Orleans. We didn't stay long. Papa had a falling out with Mama's cousins, and after that we moved around a lot. At first I blamed the war and Mama's death for his drinking, and I thought someday he'd change. Every new town seemed like a new beginning, and I always hoped we'd be like other families."

Following a slight pause, she went on in a slightly embarrassed voice, "Sometimes Papa had lady friends who came to stay with us for a while. We would eat better, but they always ended up fighting with Papa, and he would send them away. It wasn't until I was about twelve that I finally understood he wasn't like other fathers and he wouldn't ever be. By that time, his money was gone and Mama's few things had all been sold. His only income was what he won at the gaming tables. The past few years he hasn't won enough to keep food on the table—though he always seems to have enough for another bottle."

"How did you manage?" Luke asked. He felt sick thinking of Maddie going to bed at night without enough to eat.

"Sometimes Papa tried to work, but he couldn't keep a job. Sometimes I did odd jobs and cleaned houses for ladies in the towns where we lived . . . and I learned to empty Papa's pockets when he came home at night, leaving just enough coins so he wouldn't know." She looked down, embarrassed. "I suppose that was really stealing."

"I'm not sure you should call it that." Luke wrinkled his brow as he thought about what she'd done. "It sounds to me like you were trying to keep the both of you alive. Besides, to my way of thinking, your pa was stealing from you when he bought liquor instead of food, leaving you hungry."

"Luke, you're my husband now, and I promised Dory I'd do my best to be a good wife to you, and she said there shouldn't be any secrets between us. That's why I'm telling you about Papa, though it shames me." She was quiet so long he wondered if she were through talking about her childhood. When she began speaking again, it was in a quiet, more subdued voice. "After a while, I wasn't a little girl anymore, and that brought other changes."

"What other changes?" He tried not to let the suspicions her words conjured enter his voice.

"Well . . . Papa never did pay much attention to me, and he mostly slept when he wasn't drinking or playing cards. But a couple of years ago he started staying away for longer periods of time. He'd been mean to me before when he was drunk—hit me and things like that—but he started talking meaner. Once he brought home a red dress and said I should put it on and go to the roadhouse with him. I wouldn't do it, and that made him awful mad. He said it was my fault we didn't have any money or decent clothes. He said I should . . . do things." Her voice dropped to a strained whisper, and she looked away, too embarrassed to meet Luke's eyes.

Luke felt a surge of anger. "He was wrong!" The words exploded from his mouth. "He had no business blaming you or making that kind of suggestion."

"I didn't do it, Luke. I didn't think he meant it, but when that gambler told me Papa had lost me in a game of cards to some cowboy, all I could think of was to run away." She burst into tears. Luke brought his horse to a stop, and the gelding stopped too. Luke reached for Maddie, and without hesitation, she leaned her head against his shoulder and cried for all the hurt and loneliness of her childhood, and especially for the final insult her father had dealt her.

"What would you have done if I hadn't been running too?" Luke recognized how much harder it would have been for a girl to strike out on her own than it was for him—a boy who was big for his age.

"I don't know. A voice inside my head seemed to be saying, *Run,* so I just ran. I didn't stop to take any food or even a blanket," she admitted.

"I'm glad you obeyed that voice." Luke smiled and leaned closer to her, gently dropping a hand to her knee for a brief moment. "We've got some tough times ahead of us, but in a couple of weeks we'll be out of Texas. It's not likely anyone will follow us into Indian territory. Then neither your pa or Duncan will be able to find us once we reach the Snake River country up north."

"Are the Indians hostile?" Maddie straightened, a note of fear creeping into her voice.

"No. Probably the only Indians we'll encounter will be a few right after we reach Red River Station. The trail boss will give them a few head of cattle for a toll, and we'll pass through without trouble."

He nudged the stallion to begin moving again, and the gray followed. They rode without talking for several miles while they each mulled over in their minds what they had learned of the other. Maddie was the first to break the silence.

"Do you believe in God?" she asked.

"Ma believed in God. For a long time I thought she had been mistaken." Luke realized the question was important to Maddie, and he determined to answer as honestly as he could. "I couldn't see how God could have let my folks die and Duncan go free. Then, as I got older, I figured it wasn't God that did it, and I shouldn't hold Him responsible. 'Course, He could have stopped it, some part of me argued, but I figured Ma would say He had His reasons for not interferin'. Yesterday, a little bit before we got married, I kneeled down by the bed in the Pattersons' back bedroom and prayed. It was the first time I had prayed since the day I buried my folks."

"I pray 'most every day." Maddie looked down for a moment, then lifted her chin and looked directly at him. "For a short time, I had a friend who knew a lot about God. She taught me how to pray and promised me that Jesus would always be my friend and that He would watch over me if I asked for His help. That's what I was doing when you found me."

Luke didn't know what to say, so he said nothing. He recalled his first sight of her kneeling behind some willows and how he'd thought someone was set to ambush him. Her words filled him with warmth and gave him a great deal to ponder as they rode on.

It took four more days of hard riding and four nights of sleeping in each other's arms beneath a canopy of stars before they caught up to Oscarson's herd. By that time they were almost to the Red River, where they would cross into Indian territory. It was late in the afternoon when they topped a rise to see a long, low cloud of dust moving toward the river. With only about fifteen hundred head, Mr. Oscarson's herd was smaller than the great herds that had been driven north when the trails were first established. Luke had been told the herd included cows and young heifers Mr. Oscarson planned to retain for breeding stock and that the man intended to sell the other part of his herd at a railhead. The cattle he meant to keep would be trailed on to his new ranch in the Snake River valley.

Neither Luke nor Maddie said anything for several minutes as they sat atop the hill surveying the slowly moving herd. Luke was glad they'd reached the herd, yet he felt a lingering sadness that their short time alone was at an end. He'd miss the long hours he and Maddie had spent discussing their lives. He felt the tips of his ears grow hot as he admitted he'd miss the star-filled nights when they lay in each other's arms too.

At last he spurred the stallion on. Maddie followed on the gray, and she looked the way he felt—full of regret that their time alone was over. From now on Maddie would be Matt, and he'd have to remember she was his brother, not his wife.

They followed at a distance until they could see the drovers were settling the cattle for the night, and the men were taking turns approaching the chuck wagon. Taking care not to disturb the long-horned beasts, he and Maddie approached the herd slowly and from an angle as they looked for the man who was ramrodding the outfit. Riding well to the right of the herd, they moved toward a tall, thin man standing at one end of the chuck wagon, which was parked almost half a mile ahead of the herd. He fit the description of the man Baily had said was in charge of the outfit. A few feet away, Luke dismounted, and Maddie followed his lead.

"Mr. Oscarson?" Luke addressed the man who had turned to watch them ride in. "A friend of mine, Baily Patterson back in Stephenville, said you were looking for a few more men to trail your herd north."

The man gave Luke a quick appraisal and seemed to like what he saw, but he raised a skeptical brow when his gaze lit on Maddie. "I don't hire children."

"Matt's my brother. He's sixteen, and I promised Ma afore she died I'd take care of him. He's tougher than he looks." Luke knew that most of the men who trailed the great herds or worked the ranches as cowboys were young and that boys younger than sixteen often hired on, but Maddie in her boy's costume looked a lot younger than sixteen.

"All right. I'm shorthanded, or I'd send you packing. The boy can help Cookie." He jerked his head in the direction of a short, bald man wearing a leather apron while dishing beans from a cast-iron pot.

"Get yourselves some grub and turn in. I'll send someone to wake you when it's your turn to watch the herd. We cross the river at first light." Oscarson took a few strides away, then turned back. "What do I call you?"

"Luke. Luke McCall, and my brother's Matt."

Luke had never had a brother, but he didn't figure any brother of his would have dished up his beans for him, so he didn't allow Maddie to fill his plate. He could tell she was just a little fearful of the rough, dirty men who surrounded them when they found a spot near the fire. She sat a little closer to him than he figured a brother would do, but he didn't widen the space. He figured she'd do all right once she got used to this new way of life. He was glad she'd be helping the cook and staying a good distance away from the temperamental longhorn cattle.

He coughed to hide a grin when Maddie attempted to bite into a biscuit that was both hard and tasteless. She pulled it from her mouth and gave it an indignant look. Having her be Cookie's helper might not be a bad thing in more ways than one. Each morning of their ride from Stephenville, she'd made biscuits that matched Dory's for lightness and flavor.

A dusty cowboy settled on his other side and began shoveling beans into his mouth with one of the hard biscuits. He introduced himself as Bill. Luke told him their names, and Bill eyed the mostly untouched food on Maddie's plate.

"You best eat that, kid," Bill said. "Breakfast will be worse. Old Cookie ain't usually this bad, though he ain't ever real good. He's just lettin' Oscarson know he's put out 'cause the boss can't spare a man to drive his wagon or scout for buffalo chips."

"He'll have help tomorrow," Maddie muttered, keeping her voice pitched low. She picked up her plate and walked toward the little man who was now scouring his pots with sand.

"Kind of young for a trail drive," Bill commented as Maddie walked away.

"He doesn't have anybody but me." Luke told him the story he'd told Oscarson. When he looked back at Maddie, she was gathering up supplies and returning them to the chuck wagon. She seemed to be doing fine, so he took care of their horses and brought their bedrolls closer to the fire. He didn't want to be too close since he figured Maddie needed as much privacy as he could give her, but being too far from the other men would make them appear standoffish.

He was unrolling their blankets next to their saddles when a commotion broke out behind him. He turned in time to see a rough, unshaved man with beans down the front of his shirt raise his fist as if to strike Maddie. He was larger than most cowboys, and he had her backed against the chuck wagon, clutching an iron kettle between them. Luke dropped the blankets and took off running. Instinctively his hand moved toward the gun on his hip.

"Back off, Compton," a man's voice snarled. Cookie stood at the back of the wagon, a shotgun aimed at the trail hand. "That boy's mine, but he won't be no use to me if you go knockin' him around. If you expect to eat, you'll keep your hands off 'im."

Luke hung back, but his hand stayed on the butt of his Colt, waiting to see if Compton would walk away. Slowly the man lowered his fist, snarled something only Maddie could hear, then walked away. Luke reached Maddie's side in time to hear Cookie tell her to set a fresh pot of coffee on the fire, then turn in. "If you ain't here by four to start fixin' breakfast, I'll come roll you out of your blankets," he warned.

Luke didn't fall asleep easily when he and Maddie crawled into their blankets. He wanted to scoot their bedrolls together and hold her as he'd done each time they'd slept since leaving the Pattersons. It didn't seem right not to hold her and soothe away her fear of the angry cowboy and any nervousness she might feel about her changed circumstances. He considered leaving the herd and riding on by themselves, but they needed both the protection the group provided and the provisions they'd earn for their hard work. The money at the end of the drive, along with the meager savings he'd accumulated over the years, would help them establish the home they planned to have someday. He was glad Cookie was protective of his helper. He just hoped the old man wouldn't work Maddie to death.

When his inner clock woke him, telling him it was time to saddle his horse and begin circling the herd, Maddie awoke too, and he walked her to the chuck wagon before joining two other shadows headed for the line where their horses were picketed. He found it harder than he'd expected to walk away from her.

CHAPTER ELEVEN

Luke was among the last of the cowboys to come in for breakfast, and he couldn't help feeling proud of Maddie when he heard the surprised grunts and positive exclamations as the men forked flapjacks into their mouths. He savored each morsel for the few minutes he had until he had to return to the herd.

The minute he set his tin plate down, Cookie snatched it up and thrust it into a wooden box to wash later. "We have to cross the river first, Matt. We'll set up the wagon again two or three miles the other side," he explained to his new helper as he directed her to fetch the team. Luke groaned, wondering if Maddie knew how to harness the draft horses. He'd somehow have to get them harnessed for her. He hurried toward the remuda, only to find he needn't have worried. Not only was the team in harness, but he found that his own saddle had been switched to the gray and a young cowboy not much older than Maddie was checking the buckles and straps on the team's harnesses. The horses were some of the best he'd seen since Pa's herd, and he was glad to find himself working for a man who was not only a good judge of horseflesh but who believed in properly looking after the sixty or seventy horses in the outfit's remuda.

It took most of the morning to swim the herd across the river, even though it was a relatively easy crossing. This late in the season, the water was at its lowest, and earlier herds had beat the shifting, sandy bottom to a firm bed. A few contrary cows bolted downriver, and Luke spent hours alongside Bill, roping and dragging them back to the main herd. But for the most part, the cattle were cooperative. He was glad to discover that the gray had forgotten nothing of its earlier training. It was dark when he at last slipped off his boots and slid into his blankets. Maddie was already asleep.

One day blended into the next, and it seemed the only time he could be with Maddie was when he walked her to the chuck wagon each morning well before dawn. Sometimes when he rode flank, he caught glimpses of her picking up dried cattle or buffalo chips for the fire. He figured she gathered a few wild onions and other herbs on these expeditions too, since a few tasty herbs added to the chow appeared to be a welcome surprise to most of the men.

All but Compton treated Matt with deference, knowing full well that Cookie's young assistant was responsible for the improvement in their chow, and Luke was relieved that for some reason Maddie didn't have to undergo the harassment inflicted on most new cowhands.

* * *

Maddie looked forward to the mornings when Cookie sent her hunting for buffalo chips and bits of wood for the cook fire. He'd devised a sling for her to carry the precious fuel in, and she carried a small bag to which she added edible roots and leaves. Just this morning she'd found a clump of onions. She hadn't needed Cookie's warning to keep the herd or chuck wagon in sight. The memory of a nightmare summer she'd spent almost entirely alone on the prairie, far to the east of where she now found herself, was all the warning she needed to keep her from straying too far afield.

This morning she was particularly grateful to escape camp. She needed a few minutes to think by herself and to pray. It was difficult to pray in a camp full of men who didn't give much thought to God, but she needed His help. Her knees still smarted from being tripped as she'd returned the coffeepot to the fire after serving Compton a second cup this morning. She wanted to ask Luke to help her deal with the cowboy, but if she told him Compton was making a practice of waylaying her and causing her grief, there would be trouble, and she didn't want trouble. She didn't want Luke to fight Compton. Luke was much too quick to go for his gun. So far no one had guessed his identity, but a gunfight might make the other cowboys suspicious. And what if Mr. Oscarson sent them away? Somehow she had to find a way to avoid Compton.

She'd been aware that Mr. Oscarson was gradually shifting the herd to the western edge of the twenty-mile-wide swath cut by herds moving north through the summer. This shift made her job easier and the sling heavier. Reaching the top of a hill, she set her heavy load down and gazed back over the herd a mile or more behind her. She attempted to pick out Luke, but there wasn't much difference in color between Horse and the plodding cattle.

Seating herself atop the canvas sling, she turned to stare toward the distant Colorado peaks. The prairie seemed to go on forever, and she wasn't certain it was possible to even see the mountains, but each day she looked. Today she saw that the hill she sat on dipped away sharply to a hollow filled with big, brown boulders and long, yellowing grass. A single stunted tree hinted that a spring had flowed there earlier in the season.

Luke had told her they would cross the mountains on their way to the Snake River country. She looked forward eagerly to the day when she and Luke would build a little cabin on the far side of those mountains. She didn't mind traveling with Mr. Oscarson's herd, though many of the rough cowboys had at first frightened her, and Compton still did. She had to work hard, but she had always worked hard, and she liked Cookie. He wasn't as critical as Papa. But she wanted to be alone with Luke again. She saw him only when he walked her to the chuck wagon each morning and when she dished up his meals. She missed the nights when he'd held her and whispered words filled with happy dreams in her ear, and she missed riding beside him, their stirrups almost touching.

One of the boulders moved in the yellowing grass below. She froze. Her heart began to pound. Before her eyes, the boulder rose to its feet to become a great, shaggy beast. One by one, more of the brown lumps joined their leader until twenty of the animals stood in the hollow.

"Buffalo," she breathed the word in awe. Slowly she stood, never taking her eyes from the animals. Fearing they might charge her if she moved suddenly, she took her time gathering her load of chips and twigs. She backed up, taking tiny, careful steps down the hill until she could no longer see the animals. Once she thought there was enough distance between herself and the small buffalo herd, she whirled

about and began to run. The sling banged against her side, but she
didn't slow her steps until she reached the chuck wagon.

"Boy! What's got into you?" Cookie scowled as she slid to a stop
beside the pot of beans he was stirring, sending a cloud of dust
swirling toward the pot.

"Buffalo!" she panted.

"Where?" The old man rose to his feet, a look of excitement on
his face.

Between gasps for breath, she told him.

"Stay here and finish dinner," he commanded. She dropped to a
crouch to stir the beans that were beginning to scorch. As she stirred,
she watched Cookie gather up a large canvas, his best knife, and the
biggest gun she'd ever seen. Minutes later he rode out on a gray mule
toward the hill where she'd seen the buffalo. That night the men cele-
brated over buffalo steaks. Neither she nor Cookie mentioned her
role in the feast, but when Luke reached for a second steak, she found
herself feeling smugly pleased with herself.

* * *

They'd been on the trail a little over two weeks when Bill pulled
his horse up beside Luke's and leaned over to whisper, "It appears
Compton has some kind of grudge against your brother. I overheard
Cookie telling the boss that at first he thought the kid was just
clumsy because on several occasions he returned to camp covered in
dust or mud after gathering chips or drawing a bucket of water from
one of the shallow streams. But this morning he spotted Compton
sneaking away from a place by the dry streambed where he'd sent
Matt to scrub out the pans with sand. A few minutes later Matt came
limping back to the wagon with sand in his hair and scratches on his
face. When Cookie questioned him, he said he fell, but Cookie thinks
that Compton roughed him up a bit."

Luke's eyes narrowed, and he dug his heels into his horse's side. Bill
grabbed his bridle, stopping him from going after Compton. "Don't
do it," he warned. "Oscarson will fire you if you desert the herd."

Bill was right, but Luke ached to punch Compton. He couldn't
allow the bully to pick on or injure Maddie. He'd got Maddie into

this, and he meant to take care of her. He struggled to check his anger and made up his mind to get Maddie alone so he could find out what was going on. His chance finally came that evening when Mr. Oscarson sent him to scout ahead for grass. Being one of the last herds through for the season, they were finding everything close to the trail grazed to the point the cattle were wallowing in dust. If he could find feed within a few miles of the trail, they would allow the cattle to graze for a day before moving on. He stopped at the chuck wagon to request permission for Matt to ride along.

After assuring himself that supper was almost ready and the biscuits were browning nicely on a bed of coals, Cookie told Matt to run along. She strapped on the chaps she wore when searching for cow chips in thick brush. When she finished with the buckles, Luke removed his foot from the stirrup and pulled Maddie up behind him.

"Keep an eye out for greens," Cookie called after them.

They rode in silence at first, with Luke enjoying the feel of Maddie's arms around his waist. Once out of sight of the herd, she leaned her face against the back of his shirt and, without words, he knew she too missed the closeness of the week following their departure from Stephenville.

"Maddie," he said at last, having made up his mind to ask her straight out. "Has Compton been bothering you?" She was quiet for so long, he knew the answer was yes. "Why didn't you tell me?"

"I was afraid," she admitted.

"Afraid?" he asked incredulously. "Didn't you think I could handle him? I've been taking care of myself a long time, and it hasn't been by backing off from bullies like Compton. He has thirty pounds on me, but I'm just as tall, and I know how to fight. If he'd rather shoot, you'll recall folks didn't start calling me Kid Calloway just because of Duncan's vendetta against me."

"Luke, it wasn't any of those things. I'm just afraid the men will make fun of me if my big brother has to protect me. Besides, Compton's mean. I've seen his kind before. If you whip him, he'll find a way to get us both back. I can stand it a few more weeks until we get to the railhead. Promise me you won't do anything to make him mad."

Luke didn't like it. He'd noticed that bullies who went unchecked went on to take greater liberties, but Maddie had a point too. He couldn't be with her every minute, and if he whipped Compton, there was no telling what he'd do to Maddie the first time he found her alone.

"Promise me?" Maddie persisted.

"I won't start a fight," he gave her a reluctant half-promise. "But I'll be watching." He didn't tell her he intended to have a word with Cookie, perhaps Bill as well. He would make certain someone was always around to keep an eye on Maddie.

They found what they were looking for about dusk. It would take the slower moving herd until about midday the following day to reach it. They dismounted and stood admiring the rolling waves of drying grass for several minutes. In the center of the bowl-like depression, they could see a thin line of willows outlining a creek bed. It would be dry this time of year, but if they were lucky, there would still be enough water in a few holes to tide the herd over until they reached the Cimarron River. The cattle would have plenty of feed, and it would be good to stay put for a day.

As was his habit, Luke examined the sky. Faint whiffs of clouds were scuttling across the blue expanse. Behind them were rapidly building storm clouds. As they watched, the clouds piled one on top of another to become towering monsters rolling toward them. Lightning flashed, and they heard the slow grumble of thunder.

Maddie gasped and clutched him tighter, burying her face against his shirt. Having heard about her experience in the soddie during a tornado, Luke understood her fear and put an arm around her to offer reassurance.

"It's going to rain. We'd better head back to camp," Luke announced. He hated for their short interlude together to end, but the clouds building dark towers to the north, bringing on early darkness, told him they didn't have a lot of time.

The wind picked up, and Luke urged the stallion to a faster pace. Lightning split the sky, and they heard the restless bellowing of the cattle before they saw them. A second flash of lightning silhouetted the chuck wagon and, beyond it, the herd. A loud clap of thunder rumbled like cannon shot across the prairie, followed by the hoarse cry of a man.

"Stampede!"

"Cover your face!" Luke thrust his kerchief toward Maddie. She pushed his hand away and jerked her own kerchief over her mouth and nose, leaving his to cover his own face.

"Hang on!" Luke shouted and immediately felt Maddie's hands tighten around his waist. It momentarily crossed his mind to be glad they both wore thick, heavy chaps to protect their legs, then his whole focus was on the stampeding cattle. He bent low, giving his horse a swift kick. They flew over the prairie straight for the front of the bawling, charging herd.

Whipping the ends of his reins against the stallion's neck, Luke urged the horse to greater speed. It occurred to him to wish that Maddie weren't with him and that his horse weren't weighted down by two riders. Then he remembered that brief flash of illumination when he'd seen the herd moving toward the chuck wagon and was glad she hadn't been near the wagon tending to last-minute supper details.

The sounds of thunder and clashing horns melded with the pounding hooves of the bawling cattle running in frenzied madness. Dust nearly obliterated the churning mass of animals, forcing him to squint as he came alongside the longhorn matriarch who led the wild-eyed herd. Matching the stallion's strides to the rangy cow's, he reached for his Colt, firing it twice to gain her attention so he could push her into a wide turn. Experience had taught him that turning the herd on itself—forcing a mill—was the only way to slow a crazed, stampeding herd and gradually bring it to a stop. He became faintly aware of another rider a short distance behind him, pressing the herd in the direction he'd turned the leader, and doubled his efforts. Together they might keep the herd from scattering.

Huge horns rattled, and the bellow of cattle continued to match the drum rolls of thunder. Each time the leader bolted for open range, Luke turned her back toward the herd. Sometimes she swept nearly seven feet of deadly horns his direction, and he thanked a Higher Power for the nimble-footed horse he rode. Maddie's grip on his belt seemed to slacken, then tighten.

"Hang on, Maddie," he shouted as the horse leaped and dodged, even though he knew she couldn't hear the sound of his voice over the tumult of thunder and stampeding cattle. He couldn't bear thinking of what those horns and the thundering mass of animals behind the cow would do to Maddie if his horse stumbled or failed to swerve in time.

The sky opened and rain poured down, drenching men and beasts. With the rain, the herd began to slow, revolving like a spiral until the cattle stood, restlessly stomping an occasional hoof. It was over. The drovers circled the herd, moving slowly now, their voices soothing as the animals hunched wearily and gradually settled.

"Well done." Luke turned to see who had ridden up behind him. Reed Oscarson slumped wearily in his saddle, looking both exhausted and pleased. "I don't think we lost many head, and all of the men seem to be accounted for now that I see young Matt is with you. It was like an answer to prayer when I saw that big stallion of yours streaking toward the front of the herd. My horse was giving his all, but I knew I wouldn't make it to the front before the herd scattered. You saved us days of gathering up the herd and the possible loss of a significant number of cattle."

"Cookie? Is he safe?" Maddie asked. Luke noticed that her hands still held him in a death grip. He'd probably have to pry her fingers from the leather circling his waist.

"Yeah. Cookie said the first of the herd parted like the Red Sea to go around the chuck wagon," Oscarson chuckled. "It was the last few stragglers who tipped it over. Cookie's already yelling for you to get back and help him get hot coffee going for the men."

"I'll drop Matt off at camp, then get back to the herd." Luke wheeled the horse about but didn't push the exhausted animal to a trot. Instead, he let it take its time returning to where the chuck wagon lay on its side. Sparing Horse was only an excuse. In fact, he was in no hurry to set Maddie down to resume her chores. He needed her small body pressed against his back as assurance that she was alive and well. He let the stallion pick his way back to camp while he questioned Maddie to make certain she was all right. He noticed she was soaked from the rain with her shirt plastered to her skin. Fortunately she was wearing her thick chaps. A suggestion that she don his leather vest brought a blush and quick acquiescence.

The cook already had a fire going by the time they reached the chuck wagon. Maddie wasted no time sliding from Luke's horse and stumbling her way to Cookie's side. *She has grit, but this ain't no place for a woman. From what I know of women, most would have been screaming or weeping at the sight of that rampaging herd, but not my Maddie.* Emotion overwhelmed Luke, and he felt his hands shake as he thought of how easily one misstep this night could have taken her from him. He'd lost enough in his brief life, but at that moment he knew the one thing he must never lose was Maddie. If needing Maddie as much as he needed breath was love, then there was no doubt he was in love with his wife.

CHAPTER TWELVE

The showdown with Compton came sooner than Luke expected. He'd been keeping an eye on the bully for several days when he saw the man stick a foot out to trip Maddie as she carried a bucket of water toward the tub where tin plates and cups waited to be scoured. When she stumbled, sending the precious water spilling across the dirt, Compton jumped to his feet.

"Clumsy fool!" he shouted. "We don't have water to waste. Somebody needs to teach you a lesson." He balled up a fist and stalked toward her. Maddie backed up, and Luke could see she was in danger of stumbling into the fire pit.

"It won't be you." Luke grasped the man's shoulder and whirled him around. His other fist landed deep in the man's belly. As Compton launched a retaliatory swing, Luke landed a left to the man's chin, sending him crashing to the ground. He came up swinging, and Luke calmly dodged his flying fists, landing one calculated blow after another that wasn't hard enough to stun the man but slowly backed him until his boot heels teetered against the rocks circling the pit and the heat of the campfire warmed the back of his jeans. A dangerous smile was the only warning Luke gave the bully. One more punch would push Compton into the fire he'd attempted to crowd Maddie into.

Compton realized his predicament about the same time both Mr. Oscarson and Bill grabbed Luke's arms, preventing him from landing the blow that would have toppled him onto the red coals. Luke roared in anger and struggled to free himself. Seeing Luke restrained, Compton leaped toward him, but he stopped short when Cookie's shotgun nudged his ribs.

"He was trying to kill me," Compton screamed.

"Shut your mouth," Oscarson ordered. "If you start those cows running, I'll leave you afoot out here. You think I don't know what's going on. You torment that kid every chance you get. And I'm calling a halt to it. Now get on your horse and take the first watch."

"That kid's the best helper I've ever had. If anything happens to him, I'll come after you," Cookie threatened as he reluctantly let Compton walk away.

Luke's eyes met Maddie's, and he read the fear and misery in them. He ached to go to her, to hold her and soothe away that look. He hated feeling helpless to care for her the way he wanted to, the way he figured Pa would have kept his ma safe. He had a hunch Maddie was right about what she'd said earlier too. Compton wouldn't let it go. He wasn't the kind of man who could admit he'd deserved the beating Luke had given him or the dressing-down the boss had handed out in front of the other men. There would be trouble before the ride was through.

* * *

Luke avoided further confrontation with Compton during the weeks after their fight, though he caught a few malevolent glares from the other man. That didn't concern him, but more than once he intercepted a dark look directed toward Maddie that made him uneasy. Luke began counting the days until they would reach the rail-head, and he found himself reverting back to the prayers Maddie had shared with him during those few days they had traveled alone. Late at night when he lay in his blankets staring up at the stars or during the lonely hours that he rode alone beside the herd, he began fashioning prayers like those Maddie had prayed.

They were beyond Indian territory and well into Colorado when Oscarson rode up beside him while he was riding swing and said they needed to talk. Luke paced his horse to walk beside the boss's horse.

"We'll reach Cheyenne Wells in Colorado in three days," Oscarson began. "I want you to ride ahead and secure holding pens. I'll be selling most of the cattle, but I intend to hold back three hundred young cows to trail on to the Snake River country. Find a holding pen or a place outside of town where we can hold the smaller herd until spring. It's too late in the season to reach my ranch before winter sets in that far north."

"I'd like to take Matt with me." He made the request as casually as possible. He didn't want Oscarson to know how important it was to him that his "brother" not be left behind. There was no way he could ride off for several days, leaving Maddie defenseless.

Oscarson sighed. "Cookie won't be happy, but it's likely for the best." He hesitated, riding silently beside Luke as though he wished to say more but didn't know how to go about it.

"I'll be letting most of the men go after I sell the larger herd," Oscarson said at last. "With the small herd, I won't need as many riders. The hands I'll be keeping are men who want to stay on to help me start the ranch." Luke's heart sank. He'd been counting on staying with the drive until they reached the ranch Oscarson was building, then looking for land in the Idaho country he and Maddie could homestead themselves.

Oscarson wasn't through speaking, and he appeared almost nervous. "Compton will be among the hands I let go. He knows that, and I expect trouble before he goes. That's why I want you on your way now."

"I'll get Matt." He touched his heels to his mount's side, but Oscarson leaned forward to catch the horse's reins just below Luke's hand. "I think you need to know Compton has his suspicions about Matt. Cookie figured it out right after that big stampede and spoke to me. I'd already guessed but figured as long as the men didn't know, it wouldn't be a problem—but . . . well, we aren't the only ones who figured out Matt isn't your brother. Matt isn't even a he. I don't know what that gal is to you, but Compton means to have her."

"She's my wife." Luke's mouth set in a firm line. He wasn't really surprised Oscarson had guessed, and in a way he was almost glad to have Maddie's identity out in the open.

"I was hoping that was the case," Oscarson said. He looked away but didn't release his grasp on Horse's reins. Luke didn't say any more, but he had a pretty good idea Oscarson knew what he would do to Compton if he laid a hand on Maddie, and he wanted to avoid trouble.

"When you get to Cheyenne Wells, I want you to make arrangements for the herd, then give this letter to Marcus Murphy at the bank." Oscaron handed an envelope to Luke. "Murphy'll pay you your wages. In addition, he'll give you enough cash to pay for tickets to Ogden, Utah. As soon as arrangements are made, ride north until you reach the transcontinental railroad line in Nebraska. You could wait for a train going east that would connect to another line that travels north and eventually meets the westbound transcontinental, but it would take a lot longer and cost more. You'll need to move along as fast as you can. Every indication points to an early winter, and I don't want a snowstorm to catch the two of you alone out there on the prairie. Once you reach Utah, I'd like you to wait for a shipment I have coming—that is, if you'd like to continue working for me until you get your own place going."

"I'd like that, sir." Luke felt almost overwhelming relief that Oscarson wasn't cutting him loose.

"I sent to England for a couple of bulls," Oscarson continued his explanation. "They're heavier and nowhere near as cantankerous as these Texas longhorns. I mean to breed a line of cattle that are as tough as these beasts but easier to handle and a whole lot easier to chew. I need a man in Utah before December first to take receipt of those bulls. You'll have to winter over there and come on in the spring. Interested?"

"Yes, sir."

"Get your gear together and head on out. Oh, and one more thing," he added before releasing the stallion's bridle. "I've made arrangements for a man and the bulls to winter over with Ian McBride a day's ride north of Ogden. He has room for both of you. McBride's a Mormon, but he's a good man. If you're still interested in starting your own place when you get those bulls to my ranch, I'll pay your wages in young stock." Oscarson extended his hand and Luke took it.

"You've got a deal." Luke waited until he was out of sight of the other man before letting a wide grin spread across his face. It was all he and Maddie could want—a chance to acquire land and build a place of their own. They'd raise cattle at first, but eventually he wanted to breed and train horses, just like Pa had done.

Thinking of Pa brought a twinge of sadness, and he wondered if he'd made the right choice and how long it would be before he could return to Texas to keep his vow to kill the man who'd had his folks shot down. "I haven't forgotten," he muttered under his breath as he dug his heels into Horse's side.

When he reached the chuck wagon, which was halted several miles ahead of the herd beside an almost dry water hole, he looked around for Maddie. Seeing only Cookie, he rode up beside the man.

"Where's Matt?" he called.

"I sent him to get water," the man retorted. "I knowed you'd be coming after the young'un, so I figured to put him to work filling the wash water barrel before the herd gets here muddying up the hole."

"Thanks, Cookie." He wheeled his horse and started toward the water. A scream rent the air, followed by silence. Luke slid from the chestnut's back and charged into the brush, drawing his Colt as he ran. Maddie may have been surprised by a rattler, but he suspected he'd find a two-legged snake. Compton should have been riding right flank, but Luke hadn't seen him as he'd ridden toward camp.

Making as little noise as possible, he slipped through the last of the brush and reeds surrounding the water hole to find Maddie struggling to free herself from Compton's grasp. With one hand over her mouth, he was tearing at her shirt with the other. Maddie delivered a couple of ineffective kicks, and Luke suspected the hand across her mouth was depriving her of air, weakening her ability to fight. But even if her air weren't being cut off, she was half the size of Compton.

"Let her go!" Luke stepped into the clear, where Compton could see the Colt. His action had the desired effect of startling the man into releasing his stranglehold on Maddie's mouth. She drew in a couple of deep, gasping breaths before Compton's beefy arm tightened around her throat as he used her for a shield.

"I said let her go." Luke's voice dropped to a menacing low.

"Thought you could get away with keepin' her all to yourself," Compton sneered. "You ain't man enough to take her back."

"A man hiding behind a woman says a whole lot about who's the coward here. You're not man enough to fight me fair."

"Put that gun away, and we'll see who's afraid to fight," Compton laughed.

Luke called the other man's bluff, carefully holstering his gun and waiting like the gunfighter Duncan and so many others had branded him. He didn't doubt he could draw it again before Compton could reach his own gun. As he had hoped, the other man released his hold on Maddie in order to grab for his own weapon, but he gave Maddie a shove that sent her stumbling forward directly between him and Luke.

Luke's Colt was instantly back in his hand, but he couldn't fire for fear he'd hit Maddie. His hesitation cost him the advantage. Compton fired and Luke felt the bullet breeze past his face, telling him all he needed to know. Like many men who carried a gun, Compton had learned a fast draw, but his accuracy didn't match his speed.

Maddie dropped to the ground, and Luke took aim. No one could fault his accuracy. He'd honed his skill over the long, lonely years when he'd trusted in nothing but his own abilities. Compton became the outlaws, the crooked sheriff, the greedy rancher, everyone who had stolen his youth and all he loved. God had given him a second chance with Maddie, and he meant to keep her. This time he wasn't a helpless boy unable to defend what he loved.

"Hold it right there!" Cookie's voice boomed from the sidelines. Luke hesitated, but Compton didn't. He let loose another shot, but in his hurry to fire, the bullet went wild. Cookie discharged a barrel of his shotgun into the air. He then pointed the shotgun straight at the man. "I still got one barrel," he threatened. Slowly Compton lowered his gun, and Maddie crawled toward Luke. He caught her to him with one hand, keeping the one holding his Colt steady as he continued to watch Compton.

"You two get your things and get going," Cookie told them.

"It's my fight. I can take care of Maddie," Luke argued.

"Please, Luke." The quaver in Maddie's voice told him she was near the breaking point. Cookie was right—she didn't need to see any more. Taking her with him, he backed toward the brush. In his concern for Maddie, he almost missed that split second when Compton raised his gun. Luke threw himself in front of Maddie just as the shotgun boomed and Compton's shot dug into the ground harmlessly beside Luke and Maddie. Pulling Maddie to her feet, Luke ran with her through the brush toward the chestnut stallion. Tossing her into the saddle, he told her where to find Oscarson.

"Circle wide of the herd, so you don't startle them into running," he warned her.

"Don't go back." She clutched at his shoulder.

"I have to. Cookie fired both barrels. If Compton isn't dead, I can't leave Cookie at his mercy." Luke slapped the stallion on the rump, sending Maddie after the trail boss.

When Luke got back to the water hole he found Cookie kneeling on the ground beside Compton with Compton's six-shooter in his hand. He saw at a glance that Cookie hadn't aimed at the man, or Compton would have been cut to shreds. As it was, he would be picking buckshot out of his hide for some time to come. Seeing that the man who had tormented Maddie and attempted to force her was still alive, Luke drew back the hammer on his six-shooter. He'd end this now. Too many enemies had eluded him—this one would die.

"Don't do it." Cookie didn't lift his head, but he'd heard him draw back the hammer. "I figure God makes allowance for killin' when there ain't no choice, but when He gives a man a chance to walk away, he ought to do it. You ain't a killer. Don't let this piece of cow dung turn you into one. 'Sides, if'n you shoot him now, you'll likely hang, and come spring there'll be a babe with no pa to teach him the things a boy needs to know to become a man."

Luke rocked back on his heels, stopped by Cookie's words. He was going to be a pa? His own pa materialized in his mind, and the old ache of loneliness nearly sent him to his knees.

Warmth spread through his chest. Cookie was right. He couldn't kill Compton. He stared at the man on the ground and saw the fear in his eyes. Knowing what he'd planned to do to Maddie brought his anger surging again, but he couldn't let his and Maddie's baby have a killer for a pa. Slowly he lowered his gun, replaced it in its holster, and turned away.

As soon as Oscarson arrived, Luke said good-bye to the men and left Cookie to explain what had happened. He saddled Prince and helped Maddie into the saddle. Cookie came running with a bag of supplies he'd prepared before Compton's attack on Maddie. She looked back once to wave to Cookie and the mournful group of men gathered around him. Luke wasn't sure whether they would miss him, but he knew the cowboys would miss Maddie's biscuits.

* * *

They arrived at their destination two days later and took a room at a hotel in town. Maddie hung back, shuffling her feet when Luke registered them as Mr. and Mrs. Luke McCall. She blushed when the clerk peered at her more closely and turned back to his book without comment.

"We'll want hot water," Luke told the man as he handed them keys to their room.

The room was on the second floor and looked out over the town's main thoroughfare. It was plain, boasting only an iron bed, a low chest holding a pitcher and basin, and a row of hooks on one wall. Maddie sat down on one side of the bed and jumped back up, blushing scarlet when the springs groaned. Luke laughed and placed an arm around her. Tipping her chin up so she had to look at him, he brushed a light kiss across her mouth just as a knock sounded at their door.

"That will be our bath," he told her. With a show of reluctance, he released her to answer the knock.

After luxuriating in hot baths, the two of them headed out, Luke to make arrangements for Oscarson's herd and Maddie to go shopping. He'd given her money and instructed her to buy a dress. When he returned, he found a new pair of pants and a thick, warm shirt lying on the bed, but the best surprise was the sight of Maddie in a blue gingham dress, her freshly washed hair framing her face in soft curls. The dress was a little too large, and she'd tied the sash behind her back to take up the slack. It wasn't as fancy as the satin dress she'd worn when she married him, but it left him just as awed by the sight of her in it.

"You look beautiful," he told her. She smoothed the front of her dress in a self-conscious gesture.

"It cost too much."

"It's worth every penny you spent."

"I'll still have to wear pants when we ride north, but I wanted to . . . to look . . ." She paused, uncertain how to go on.

"Pretty," he finished for her, pleased that she'd wanted to wear the dress for him.

"There's something I . . . should tell you." She bowed her head and twisted her hands together. "I think . . . I don't know much about . . . but . . ." Her voice trailed off, and Luke hid a smile. He figured Maddie was trying to tell him about the baby, and he understood there was more to the dress she wore than an attempt to please him. A rush of tender feelings had him placing an arm around her and gently leading her to the bed where he seated her before sitting down beside her and taking her hand.

"I'm going to have a baby." The words suddenly rushed from her mouth, and her eyes sought his. Wanting to reassure her, he placed a hand on either side of her face and smiled into her eyes.

"We'll be good parents," he promised. "This baby will have all we missed growing up. Maybe not too much of the trappings money buys at first, but he'll have all of the things that matter most."

CHAPTER THIRTEEN

Luke finished the arrangements for Mr. Oscarson's herd as quickly as possible. He wanted Maddie to be able to stay at the hotel longer, but September was gone, and he remembered Oscarson's warning. They needed to meet the train before they were trapped by early snow. Two days after checking into the hotel they were checking out again, heading north on a hundred-and-fifty-mile ride through desolate prairie.

The nights were cold, and a chill wind seemed to blow from the north without interruption. Even so, Luke enjoyed riding beside Maddie. He hadn't known how much he missed having someone to talk to during the lonely years he'd pursued Blackwell. And Maddie wasn't just anyone. She was bright and observant and had visited many interesting places. Besides, she had the ability to make him think and feel things he'd nearly forgotten. Occasionally, they came to a homestead where they were invited to spend the night and visit with folks starved for a bit of company, but most nights they slept along the trail. More mornings than not, they found a thin layer of ice on the streams near their camps, and they kept blankets around their shoulders until almost noon as they rode.

Each time they camped, Luke tethered the horses where they could reach water and grass. He also took time to check the animals' condition and rub them down. Without fail, Maddie had supper waiting when he returned to their campfire. She never complained about the cold, but he noticed she'd started wrapping herself in a blanket when she knelt beside their bedroll each night. Once she caught him watching her as she finished her prayer, and she asked in a halting voice if he'd like to pray with her. Feeling a little foolish, he nevertheless nodded his head. Maddie's simple prayer left him feeling sort of the way he felt when he soaked in Dory Pattersons' bathtub.

They saw quite a few rabbits and an occasional fleet-footed antelope, but Luke didn't take time to hunt. They had enough supplies to last them through their journey, and he didn't want any delays. Two mornings in a row, Maddie was sick, which worried Luke, but she said that was one of the few things she knew about having a baby. Catrin's mam had been sick every day, and Catrin had confided that it was because her mam was expecting another baby.

Luke didn't dare ride too hard because of Maddie's condition, but when clouds began to form one afternoon, hanging low over the trail, he worried about a norther catching them without shelter on the plains, and he pushed on a little further than usual. He knew Maddie was afraid of storms on the open prairie, and knowing they should soon be reaching the railroad, he found himself saying a prayer of his own that they would reach it before the storm hit.

He was almost ready to call a halt to the day's ride and look for shelter when he spotted a black line in the distance. They rode on and finally reached the tracks, following them to a water tower where the train would have to stop. Even though he was tired from the long hours in the saddle, he couldn't rest until he had settled Maddie in an impression sheltered from the wind and watered the horses.

Maddie stared at the cross beams that supported the elevated water tank and felt disappointment. She was glad they had finally reached the tracks but felt let down that there was no town surrounding the water tower where they might have found shelter from the pending storm. Luke hadn't said anything, but she knew he was worried about snow. Even though they'd reached the tracks, they couldn't be sure snow wouldn't halt the train before it reached them or block the mountain pass, stranding them before they reached their destination.

A few railroad ties littered the ground near the tower. Luke dragged them near the slight depression in the ground to form a windbreak for their camp that night. He refused to allow Maddie to help move the heavy beams, so she set about starting a cook fire and preparing a hot meal for them.

Bits of ice drifted in the wind, stinging their faces as they finished their supper. Still she delayed seeking the shelter Luke had arranged.

"What's wrong?" Luke knelt in front of her, the concern in his eyes making her feel guilty.

"I'm fine. It's nothing," she tried to reassure him. She didn't know how to tell him his shelter brought back unhappy memories. She knew she was being foolish. She rose to her feet and let Luke lead her to the earth-and-timber windbreak. There they crawled into their joined bedrolls. Luke wrapped his arms around her and drew her close. He fell instantly asleep, but she lay cradled in his arms, listening to the wind howl. She thought about the wind that had come while she was alone on the prairie a few years earlier, and her thoughts turned to the dugout where she'd been content—until a storm came. This time she wasn't afraid. Luke would protect her. She burrowed closer, seeking his warmth. She trusted him as she'd never trusted anyone but God before in her life.

Life hadn't been easy since she and Luke had met so unexpectedly, but she was happier than she ever remembered being. She suspected her Friend had been responsible for placing Luke in that shantytown when she'd needed him, and once more she thanked Him for both Luke and the little girl who had introduced her to Jesus. She was grateful too for a sad, painted lady who had stayed with her and Papa for a time long ago, a lady who had tucked Maddie into bed at night with stories about Jesus.

Luke made a faint whistling sound as he slept, and she snuggled closer, placing one of her hands on her abdomen in an unconscious attempt to pass on Luke's warmth and comfort to their child. His arm tightened around her, and she slept. When she awoke, it was to a world of whiteness. A thin coating of snow covered their quilts and lent a surreal quality to the nearby water tower and the endless prairie. The wind had stopped blowing, and the snow was no longer falling, but black clouds still hovered menacingly from horizon to horizon. The temperature seemed to have dropped dramatically.

She dressed quickly, then went to stand beside Luke, who already had a fire going and water heating. He handed her a tin mug, and she felt welcome heat from it seep into her hands. Perhaps it was an odd time and place to feel a pang of regret—regret that this time together was ending. She was anxious to move forward, to obtain land of their own, and to welcome the arrival of their baby, but she never wanted to lose the closeness and joy she'd felt on this journey with only Luke.

Luck was with them, and they had to wait only a day. It was midafternoon and the major snowstorm was still holding off when they saw the plume of smoke in the distance and watched as what began as a black speck grew larger and larger. By the time they could hear the engine and count the cars trailing behind it, the horses were already dancing with nervous, mincing steps. Two long blasts of the train whistle sent them lunging and rearing, attempting to escape the noisy monster rushing toward them. Luke grasped both animals' bridles and held on until the train stopped and the horses stood trembling and rolling their eyes. He couldn't leave the animals, so Maddie took charge of arranging their passage. It took all of Luke's powers of persuasion and brute strength to load the animals into a boxcar.

Luke felt almost as skittish as the horses about boarding the train, but Maddie seemed relieved to find a seat where she could sit near a window and alternate between watching the endless miles go by and sleeping. She'd ridden trains with her pa before they had gone to Texas, so the experience wasn't as new to her as it was to him. She took a cloth from her bag to wipe the seat and the window ledge before sitting down and settling in next to Luke. He worried that the illness that seemed to strike her every morning would be aggravated by the rocking motion of the railcar and the constant haze of smoke, but they proved more bothersome to him than to her.

The train carried them swiftly toward the mountains, where Maddie stared in wonder at the towering peaks and the ever-deepening drifts of snow. In all her and Papa's travels, she'd never seen snow before, and it quite fascinated her. Each time the drifts blocked the tracks, making passage impossible, Luke joined the other men who were issued shovels and assisted in clearing the track. Maddie watched with her nose pressed against the car window. She discovered that if she breathed on the glass, the ice covering would soften so she could scrape a small, round hole with her fingernail to peer through. When the men returned to the train car, their faces and ears were bright red with cold. After stomping off as much snow as possible, they huddled around a small, inadequate stove at one end of the car. Once Luke returned to his seat beside her, he welcomed the blanket she had ready to wrap around him until the next time the engine was forced to stop.

Though she enjoyed the trip in a strange way, she wasn't accustomed to sitting for so many hours or having nothing to do. Sometimes she walked back and forth in the aisle of the train to keep her muscles from cramping, but the lurching movements of the train caused Luke to worry that she might fall. They each sighed with relief when the train left the mountains to wind its way into Ogden.

Maddie knew she must be looking pale and wan by the time they reached the frontier railroad town because of the concerned glances of the other travelers. It was a tremendous relief when the engine huffed into a station in the first town she'd seen in months. Her legs trembled with weakness as Luke helped her down from the train car. She looked around and wasn't tremendously impressed by the shacklike buildings that surrounded the train depot or the layer of soot that seemed to cover everything in sight.

Luke asked around about a place to stable his horses and quickly located one only a few blocks away. It didn't take long to unload the horses and lead them to their temporary home. Before leaving them, Maddie patted both Horse's and Prince's noses and guessed that the animals were as pleased to stop traveling for a time as she was.

There was no snow in the valley, and as she and Luke left the stable to walk toward the main part of town, she found Ogden to be more appealing than she'd first thought. They passed a number of large, attractive homes and discovered several streets of businesses. Large numbers of people, including women wearing huge hats and full skirts, were wandering in and out of the stores. Everything from fancy buggies to lumbering wagons traversed the streets, and a general aura of busyness wafted in the air. She wanted to look around the bustling town, but Luke was anxious to find comfortable lodging for the night and hurried his steps. At last he spotted a hotel that looked respectable but not too expensive.

Their room overlooked a busy street, and Maddie was pleased to find it neat and clean. It was slightly larger than the one where they had stayed in Colorado, and the bedspread and drapes were in better repair. The room even boasted a small table, two chairs, and an armoire.

Maddie wanted to do little more than sleep the first few days after their arrival, but still she joined Luke at least once each day for a stroll around town. The part of town near their hotel was wild and noisy at night, which made them both uncomfortable. Luke had taken off his gun before boarding the train, hoping to leave his reputation behind him, but now he took to carrying it again, concealed in his coat pocket.

About two weeks after their arrival, Luke took Maddie shopping for a heavy cloak and a warm dress and stockings. He purchased a heavy coat for himself as well. If they were going to live in this part of the country, they needed warmer clothing. The days were getting cold and the nights even colder. Besides, it was time for Maddie to begin dressing like a woman again, and the dress she'd purchased in Kansas and kept folded in her saddlebag as they rode north had been her only dress.

Carrying their purchases, they wandered down to the telegraph office to check for a message from Oscarson. Luke had wired the trail boss in Cheyenne Wells as soon as they'd arrived, but he hadn't yet received a response. Though he checked at the rail yard daily, there had been no sign of the bulls yet either.

The telegraph operator looked up from his desk as they walked through the door. "Message just came for you," he announced, handing Luke a sheet of paper. Luke read the message carefully, then read it again.

Finally Maddie asked, "Well, are they still in Cheyenne Wells?"

"Yes. He says he received word the bulls have been delayed and won't arrive here before May. He wants us to go on to McBride's place." Luke wasn't sure how he felt about the news. He was glad Maddie wouldn't have to continue staying in the hotel or resume traveling until after the baby arrived. It was also good that when her time came there would be a woman to help her, yet he felt nervous about meeting McBride.

They didn't talk much as they returned to the hotel. Both their minds, it seemed, were filled with questions they were reluctant to voice. When they reached their room, Maddie removed her new cloak, smoothing it with her hands after hanging it from one of the wooden pegs on the wall. She unlaced her shoes and placed them near the foot of the bed, then lay down. After a few minutes, Luke noticed she hadn't fallen asleep as she'd done each afternoon since arriving in Ogden. Instead she twisted one way, then turned back, adjusted her pillow, then turned over again.

"Are you all right?" he finally asked. "If you're sick, I'll ask the desk clerk to send for a doctor."

"I'm not sick." She gave up trying to sleep and sat up. "I just don't know what to expect when we get to the McBrides'. Before Papa and I got to Texas, he gambled on riverboats for a few months. After he thought I was asleep, he went upstairs to the bar. Sometimes I crept up and hid behind a curtain where I could see him. One night, he was sitting at a table with some other men, and they were talking about the Mormon problem. If even half of what those men said was true, it might be dangerous for us to stay with the McBrides."

"I thought you said you had a Mormon friend when you were a child." Luke seemed puzzled by her concern.

"I did, but I remember her whole family had to be careful that none of the men on the boat found out they were Mormons. Being a child, I didn't understand why they were hated, but I knew they were. That time in Arkansas wasn't the only time I heard bad things about the Mormons or heard men talk of the violence that seems to follow them."

"Maddie, I never even heard much about Mormons until Mr. Oscarson told me about Mr. McBride, so I figured I wouldn't judge the man until I meet him."

"Those men in Arkansas said that Mormon men steal other men's wives and daughters and lock them up in Salt Lake until they agree to marry them." Her lip trembled, and tears began to well up in her eyes. Luke sat down beside her and put his arms around her.

"Mr. Oscarson says McBride is a good man, and I've come to think right highly of Mr. Oscarson. I don't think he'd send us there if he thought you'd be in any kind of danger. I've heard a few wild tales since arriving here as well, but you needn't worry." He flashed her a cocky grin. "You're married to Kid Calloway, the fastest shootist in the West. I ain't going to let any man steal my wife."

"You said you were through with that life, that you'd never be mistaken for a gunfighter again." She sat up and wrapped her arms around him.

"I won't go looking for a fight," he promised. "But I'll never hesitate to defend you or our baby. You're my life now, and I'll do whatever I have to, to keep you safe. I won't allow Mormons or outlaws or anyone else to hurt you."

CHAPTER FOURTEEN

Fat flakes of snow fluttered to the ground from leaden skies as Luke and Maddie turned their horses up a winding lane leading to a large two-story house almost hidden in a grove of trees. The snow and accompanying drop in temperature made Luke glad that he and Maddie weren't continuing their journey to the Snake River country just yet.

They heard the shouts of children before they saw them—two small boys racing toward the house to announce their arrival. A dog barked, and a woman emerged from the house to stand on the wide veranda-style porch to watch their approach.

"Hello," Luke called once they were within hailing distance. "Is this where Ian McBride lives?"

The woman nodded, and as they rode closer, Luke could see she was a pretty woman in her middle thirties with light brown hair wound atop her head in an intricate style.

"We're the McCalls. I work for Reed Oscarson, and he directed us to come here." Luke didn't know how much he should explain to the woman. She was nothing like he'd expected, though he wasn't sure exactly what he'd expected. If he'd considered the woman at all, he supposed his imagination had veered between a downtrodden, slave-like creature to a brazen saloon woman wearing satin and rouge. The woman smiling at him from the porch wore a faded calico dress, much like his mother had worn, and her apron was clean and crisp. She didn't fit the lurid tales a few men had been eager to share with him when he'd arrived in Ogden and began asking questions concerning the town and the people who had settled the area.

"Ian rode over to the Palmers' this morning. Brother Palmer has a horse he's thinking of selling, and Ian wanted a look at it. I'm sure he'll be back before supper," the woman explained. "You're welcome to come inside and wait." She turned to call through the door. "Jacob! Joseph!" As she turned, Luke saw that her apron did little to conceal her approaching motherhood.

Two lads, appearing to be about nine or ten, scrambled onto the porch as though they'd been waiting on the other side of the door. Their freckled faces were alight with anticipation. They were followed by several other children with varying shades of red hair who stared at him and Maddie. There was a great deal of giggling and whispering among the children.

"Take the McCalls' horses to the barn," the woman told the boys. "Give the horses a good rubdown and a measure of oats," she added. Then she waved a hand toward the other children. "Shoo! Get back in the house. It's too chilly to be out here without your coats. Besides, you're letting all of the heat out of the house, leaving the door open like that." They ran back inside, closing the door firmly behind them.

Luke helped Maddie down from Prince and was pleased to see she was more curious about the woman and children than afraid, though the slight tremble in her hand told him she wasn't completely over her fear.

"Will you be all right?" he whispered to her. "I think I'd best unsaddle the stallion myself." She nodded her head and followed the woman into the house while he accompanied the two boys to the barn. Once the horses were brushed and secured in stalls, he looked around, noticing that the barn was neat and clean and that it held almost a dozen exceptional horses. It appeared that McBride was a fine judge of horseflesh. They were all prime animals, and Luke thought longingly of Pa's horses. When he and Maddie got to the Snake River country, he hoped he could begin a herd like Pa's.

The boys laughed and chattered with ease as they worked with Luke's horses, and he was pleased to see they'd been trained well. Their motions were smooth and sure as they brushed Prince, and they took care to arrange bridles and saddle blankets just so in a clean, orderly tack room. They plied him with questions and grew excited when he told them he'd come from Texas on Mr. Oscarson's cattle drive.

He didn't wish to leave Maddie alone for long, so he didn't linger over putting up the horses and in a short time was on his way to the house to join her. He paused to wipe his feet on a mat before entering the house. Once inside, he looked around curiously and was impressed by the solid wood furniture and elegant furnishings in the house. It was bigger than the Pattersons' home, but it had that same welcoming atmosphere.

He'd just removed his coat and seated himself beside Maddie in what he supposed was the parlor—though it was the biggest parlor he'd ever seen—when Ian McBride returned. His arrival was announced by a clamor of excited children's voices coming from the entry followed by the deep rumble of masculine laughter.

Luke rose to his feet when a tall, robust, red-haired man of about forty entered the room. He shed gloves as he entered and walked straight toward the fireplace, where a log burned brightly, keeping the chill out of the room. He held out his hands to the fire, and Luke stepped forward. He extended a hand to McBride and introduced both himself and Maddie.

McBride clasped his hand firmly and responded with an introduction of his own. "I see you've already met Mary." He nodded toward his wife.

"Reed Oscarson said we were to come here with two bulls he ordered from England," Luke began. "They've been delayed and won't arrive until spring. I received word yesterday that Oscarson wants us to remain here until they arrive, if that's all right with you."

"Yes, he spoke to me early last summer on his way to Texas about the pedigreed bulls he was sending for." They talked for a while about Oscarson's plans and the weather that was keeping the rancher and his herd in Colorado. In the course of the conversation, both men turned to the use of first names. Ian was charismatic and knowledgeable about raising stock, and Luke soon became absorbed in their discussion. He found himself sharing his own plans for starting a ranch, and Ian was eager to offer advice on both land and stock selection.

"Dinner is ready," Mary called from the next room. Luke hadn't even noticed when Ian's wife had left the parlor. Maddie walked close beside Luke as Ian ushered them toward the dining room. Luke gave her hand a gentle squeeze of encouragement. This room was large too, and the table that ran down the center of the room would easily seat twenty. It soon became apparent the McBrides didn't believe in feeding the children in the nursery or making them wait until after the adults had been served.

Amid the scramble for chairs, Luke noticed an older boy, one somewhere between his and Maddie's ages, slip quietly onto a chair beside Mary, who had taken the seat at the foot of the table. The boy's hair was dark, and he bore no resemblance to Ian or the bright-haired children seated along both sides of the table. Two more girls with strawberry-blonde hair arrived carrying large serving platters. Ian motioned for Luke and Maddie to sit on either side of him.

When everyone was seated, sudden silence filled the room as Ian bowed his head. Luke and Maddie followed suit as Ian offered a brief grace before they began to eat. Ian seemed perfectly at ease presiding over the large, noisy clan seated at his dinner table, but Luke felt more than a little overwhelmed. A chubby little girl of about four with sausage curls spilled her milk, and it ran off onto the floor, sending Mary scurrying to clean it up. A younger child cheerfully launched green beans at his siblings, which kept the boys who had helped Luke care for the horses giggling. Another child complained that someone had taken his cup. A shrill wail brought Luke's head up, and he watched as Mary lifted a toddler from a cradle pushed back against the wall, where he hadn't noticed it. She cradled the child in one arm and resumed her place at the table.

Luke had no experience with children, and one look at Maddie told him she too was overwhelmed. Neither Ian nor Mary seemed to find anything unusual as they dealt with each minor crisis and restored a kind of order.

Following slices of apple pie with rich cream, Mary and the two older girls cleared the table and sent the other children upstairs. The dark-haired boy remained seated at the table.

"Your wife looks as though she's fair ready to fall asleep." Ian chuckled before he continued. "We'd best be getting you settled in. 'Tis a noisy lot, my family, and takes some getting used to. Besides, with us not knowing a lady would be accompanying Oscarson's man, we thought it best to prepare the cottage. I've never known a bachelor to be comfortable with so many young ones. It's a wee house I built afore I wed Mary and had need of a larger house. It's ready and waiting for you."

Luke tried not to let his relief show. He thanked Mary for supper and stood. Maddie, echoing Luke's words of appreciation, rose to her feet beside him, and he took her arm.

"Young Brigham will show you the way," Ian announced, and they turned to follow the boy. The sturdy youth fetched a lantern, and Luke helped Maddie on with her cloak. When they stepped outside, they found that the light snowflakes had increased their tempo and a fine layer of white covered the ground. Luke held Maddie's arm to make certain she didn't slip as they followed Brigham along a narrow path to a cabin in the trees. A single step led from the path to the front door, and Maddie's face showed her delight in the small house as she looked around the three small rooms.

Settling in for an early night, Maddie sank into a thick feather bed that smelled sweet and fresh. In spite of her drooping eyelids and the weariness that found joy in a comfortable bed, she felt a measure of pleasure too in knowing that for the next six months the cabin would be her home. She didn't remember ever living in any one place so long. The prospect of staying here and creating a home for Luke and herself brought a smile to her face as she drifted off to sleep.

Luke was already awake but hadn't yet climbed out of bed when Maddie awoke at first light the next morning. He insisted she remain snuggled under the patchwork quilt until he had a fire going in the cookstove. She and Luke spent most of the day orienting themselves to the cabin and the McBride farm. It was the most peaceful day she remembered in all her life.

When Mary sought her out and invited her to spend time with her in the house, she felt a little bit the way she'd felt years ago when Catrin had invited her to be her friend. Memories of that pleasant association and the kind treatment she and Luke had received from the McBrides stilled her nervous reservations about the Mormons. The McBrides were just as kind and welcoming as the Prosser family had been. She should have known that men who spent their time in saloons, gambling with the likes of her father, couldn't be trusted to tell the truth. She smiled shyly and accepted Mary's invitation.

Brigham and Ian had left the farm on horseback before daylight, as they did most mornings during the winter months, to haul logs from a nearby canyon. In addition to the horses Luke had seen the day before, there were several milch cows, which were the responsibility of Jacob and Joseph, who treated every task as though it were a game. He couldn't help wondering, if he'd had a brother, if they would have enjoyed working side by side as much. A younger boy carried slops to a sow in a small enclosure attached to the cow barn, and some of the girls gathered eggs and fed the chickens in addition to their household tasks. He was pleased to discover that though the children teased and laughed a lot, they knew how to work.

Luke knew he couldn't be idle all winter without going crazy, and if he hoped to acquire land and build a house when they traveled north in the spring, they needed to save as much of their meager funds as possible. When Ian returned that night, Luke asked to speak with him. McBride seemed pleased with Luke's eagerness to work and soon made arrangements for Luke to help haul timber to a mill near the canyon in exchange for the supplies he and Maddie would use through the winter.

Most mornings found Luke, Ian, and Brigham riding toward the snow-covered mountains that towered to the east of the farm. The horses that pulled the log sledges were kept in a long stable near the mill, and two men lived in a cabin attached to a cook shack nearby. They seemed to be primarily responsible for caring for the horses and putting a hot meal on the table at midday. A dozen or more men arrived from nearby farms within half an hour of Luke and the McBrides each day. It soon became routine for Brigham and Luke each to hitch four horses to a wagon bed on runners and head up the canyon for logs, while Ian operated a steam-powered saw that turned the logs into boards. Most of the men returned to their homes each evening, but occasionally, when a storm became severe, they bedded down overnight in the cook shack.

At first Luke missed the open spaces of the prairie, but he came to appreciate the rugged beauty of the mountains. He hadn't seen a lot of snow in Texas, though there had been an occasional norther sweep down the prairie from the arctic north country. And even though his work was cold and slippery and challenged all of his skill with horses, he found a majestic beauty in the snow-covered mountains. Working beside Brigham and Ian helped to fill an ache for the companionship he'd once shared with his father, and he found the time a pleasant interlude, a time of waiting—for the birth of his child and the chance to acquire land of his own.

He didn't join in the casual talk between the other men, though he often listened to both their banter and the philosophy they frequently discussed. It wasn't because he was the only man not a Mormon on the logging crew—it was more that his years of trailing Blackwell had made him a loner. Sometimes he envied the easy way the other men and boys teased one another one minute, then turned to serious discussion the next. The easy relationship between Ian and Brigham both pleased and saddened him, reminding him of his own relationship with his father. It brought about a promise to his unborn son that he would be a father like Ian and his own father had been. He felt a glow of happiness each time he thought of the son who would be born in the spring, and his mind filled with plans for the family the three of them would make.

Luke was surprised one January morning to find Brigham alone in the barn when he went to saddle his horse. Mary was having pains, Brigham explained, and his father had decided to stay with her for the day. When they returned to the barn that night, a jubilant Ian met them with the announcement that he had another son. He insisted that Luke join Brigham in taking a peek at the new arrival. He found Maddie already at the big house along with several other women, smiling as though she'd had a hand in producing this new little McBride.

Luke drew closer to the cradle when Ian beckoned him. He stared in awe at the infant. He wasn't any bigger than one of the cats that lived in the barn, but far more delicate looking. He was red with a redder thatch of hair on the top of his head. Suddenly Luke felt afraid. The baby was completely helpless, and soon he and Maddie would be responsible for a tiny life like this one.

As though Ian could read his mind, he placed one hand on Luke's shoulder and, speaking in a quiet tone, as if he feared waking the baby, said, "You'll do fine. You and Maddie are young, but the Lord has a powerful lot of trust in you. And He'll be there for you when you need Him."

Luke wasn't too sure what Ian was telling him, but the words comforted him and restored his confidence somewhat.

Maddie felt a thrill as she looked at Mary's tiny new son. She'd been frightened when Mary asked her to stay with her through the baby's birth, but now she was grateful for her friend's insight in sharing this miracle with her. Without saying a word, Mary had helped to ease Maddie's fears.

Just yesterday, Mary had coaxed her to talk about the fear that had haunted her since childhood when she'd often heard her father bemoan the pain and horror of her mother's death. Papa had blamed himself, not Maddie, for her mother's passing, and she'd long known it was the only fault he'd ever admitted to. Still, he'd left his daughter with a terrible fear of childbirth.

Mary's explanation of all that would happen to her and the midwife's calm, efficient manner, coupled with sitting beside her friend as she rode out each pain, then laughed and chatted between contractions, went far to give Maddie courage. She knew now that giving birth would be hard work, but she was familiar with hard work, and having a beautiful baby like tiny Heber would surely be worth any amount of hard work and pain.

A few days later, as Luke ate his lunch, he was still thinking about the baby with his thatch of red hair. Looking up, he observed Ian's red hair and Brigham's dark locks close together as the two discussed a broken strap on the harness of the team Brigham drove and was struck with the oddity of a man with nearly a dozen children having only one who looked nothing like either himself or his wife. That night he mentioned his observation to Maddie. She was busy hemming a tiny garment for their baby, and Luke was sanding a piece of wood for the cradle he was making.

"I don't think Ian is Brigham's father," Maddie said, her voice sounding troubled. "I didn't mean to eavesdrop, but two ladies—I think they were Ian's sisters because Mary called them Sister Elsa and Sister Margaret—came to call at the house today. Mary had gone to the kitchen for refreshments, and I think they forgot I was there. One of them said it was a shame Ian treated Deborah's son as his firstborn when that honor rightly belonged to Jacob, especially since Deborah had no right to call herself a wife. The other lady said she'd always been proud of Ian for bringing that poor girl home and marrying her when she had no one else to turn to, and she thought it was wonderful the way Mary had always been a mother to the boy."

Luke thought about what Maddie had said. The snippet of gossip suggested a number of dark secrets, but it didn't seem right to pry into Ian's business, so he never questioned the man he'd come to count as a friend. If their relationship was something like his relationship with the Pattersons, he was fine with that.

It wasn't until the night his and Maddie's child was born that he learned about Brigham. It was spring, and Mr. Oscarson's bulls had arrived right on schedule the first of May. More than a month had passed since the men had made their last trip to the mountains for logs, and Luke had been helping Brigham work a couple of two-year-old colts when word arrived that Mr. Oscarson's bulls were in Ogden.

Maddie was close to her time, and he'd felt concern over leaving her to fetch them. Along with worrying about his wife, he worried too about how he would manage to drive the bulls from town to the farm by himself. As he rode along, he observed men working their fields, readying them for spring planting, and knew his employer would soon reach his ranch and be anxious for the bulls to join his herd. He didn't want the baby to be born while he was away from the farm getting Oscarson's bulls, but he was concerned that if the child didn't arrive soon, they would be expected to begin their trek north before Maddie and the little one were ready to travel.

On reaching the rail yard, he found that one of his worries had been for nothing. The task of moving the bulls to the McBride farm proved easier than expected because the bulls weren't anything like the longhorns he was familiar with. Not only were they shorter, stockier, and possessed of a better temperament than the longhorns, but their horn span was no more than that of Ian's dairy cows. They offered little resistance to being led by a rope behind the stallion.

He and the animals ignored the spring rain that burst upon them as they made their way from the main road to the lane leading to Ian McBride's cow barn. Ian and Brigham, followed by some of the younger boys, came out to admire the animals. Once the bulls were settled, Luke rushed to the little house in the trees to tell Maddie about them, only to find her sitting on the edge of their bed, holding her back and gasping as though she were having trouble breathing.

He ran to the house for Mary when Maddie doubled over with pain a few minutes later. Mary sent Brigham for the midwife, who lived but a few miles away. Mary picked up her baby and followed him to the little house, where she bustled about, preparing clean sheets and towels, all the while speaking in soothing tones to the anxious young couple. When the midwife arrived, she sent Luke splashing through rain puddles to the barn to wait until she sent Mary for him. What seemed like hours later, Ian found him there.

Ian alternately paced the floor with him and sat on a bucket, staring into space. They listened to rain spatter against the roof, and at increasingly frequent intervals, Luke strode to the door to peer out into the cloud-darkened night. He hadn't known having a baby took so long— and he hadn't known he'd heard so many stories of women dying in childbirth, tales that came back to haunt him now, especially since Maddie had shared with him the story of her own mother's death.

"There's a small group of settlers from Salt Lake headed for homesteads the other side of the Snake River in a couple of weeks. If you're interested, I could arrange for you to trail along with them," Ian offered, distracting Luke for a few minutes.

"Thank you. I'll likely accept your offer. I've been thinking it wouldn't be good to take Maddie and the babe so far without more protection." Indians were still a concern as far north as Idaho and Montana. Then too, there were always outlaws and wild animals to consider.

"I know you set great store by those horses of yours, but I've been thinking a team and wagon would be of more use to you in starting your homestead and in moving your family north. You've made a few pieces of furniture this winter you'll want to take along, and you'll need a lot of supplies to start your own place. Maddie won't be able to sit in a saddle for more than a month, and unless you plan to delay your trip until she can ride, I'd like to make an offer for your pair of horses. I've had my eye on that stallion of yours since you arrived. If you're of a mind to trade, I'll give you one of my wagons and the team you drove all winter, plus your pick of the stallion's first batch of colts."

Luke stopped pacing. He hadn't given a thought to how soon Maddie would be able to ride. Ian's offer made sense, but he wasn't certain he could part with his horses. The horses and Pa's watch were all he had left of his folks. Trading was the sensible thing to do, but he and the stallion had been through a lot, and Maddie had grown attached to Prince. He stood still, listening to the drumming of the rain on the roof, and knew it had to be. He was starting a new life, beginning a new family. He swallowed hard and nodded his acceptance of Ian's offer. It took a few minutes before he could mouth a verbal thank-you.

Silence prevailed again, except for the rustle of footsteps as Luke walked to the door and peered out once more. Rain was slanting down, forming puddles and small streams. A freshness filled the air with the promise of fertile fields, flowers, and new beginnings, but Luke was almost oblivious to it.

"'Tis the hardest part," Ian spoke into the silence. "The waiting and the worrying. 'Twould be far easier to be groaning and pushing ourselves than to let our minds run to picturing the awful pain the woman we're loving is suffering for the sake of the wee babe."

"It never gets easier?" Luke asked. "Maddie wanted me to stay and hold her hand, but the midwife insisted I'd only be in the way."

"My Mary tells me each new one is easier than the last. She said birthing little Heber was much easier than Jacob or Clara, our first two. But I never noticed it getting any easier for me," Ian remarked with a shake of his mop of unruly red hair. He coaxed Luke away from the door.

Luke sat on an upturned bucket and wished he'd stayed beside Maddie. She'd been afraid, and it seemed cowardly to wait in the barn while she worked and suffered. He found he'd voiced the words aloud.

"My first wife, Deborah, was frightened," Ian confided in a low voice.

Luke looked at Ian blankly, and Ian went on as though answering Luke's unasked questions. "Deborah was a young girl, not much older than your Maddie, when two missionaries knocked on her family's cabin door back in Tennessee. Her pa hadn't come back from the war. Her ma wasn't well, but the two of them listened to the missionaries preach, and they read the Book of Mormon the missionaries left with them. After a few weeks, they were baptized in the creek back of their cabin, and they started making plans to move west where most of the Saints had settled. Soldiers were still straggling home from the war, and some of those Missouri soldiers hated Mormons even worse than they hated Yankees. They killed Deborah's ma and burned down their house. They hurt Deborah and left her for dead, lying there in the dirt. The missionaries found her and took her away with them."

"You were one of the missionaries?" Luke sensed Ian was glossing over unbearable memories.

Ian nodded his head. "The wee poor lass. I took her home to me mother, and when it became clear she was to bear a child, I married her. There was little we could do to ease her pain, and when the time came, which was too soon for her babe, she suffered something fierce. All the pain she'd suffered was too much, and all the light and joy had gone out of her, but I couldn't give up, so I prayed like never before. When the tiny mite she birthed gave his first cry, she turned her face to the wall. She didn't want to even see him. I sat beside her for weeks, begging her to take a sip of broth or a bite of bread, but it was no use. Me mother cared for the babe at first and named him Brigham, though she never expected such a wee one to live. But he was a scrapper, and when I chose to settle here to raise horses, I brought him with me. It fell to me to rock him and soothe him with a rag twist in a bottle of goat's milk. Three long years we lived here by ourselves until I married my Mary."

Luke stepped to the door again. He didn't feel particularly surprised by Ian's story. Pieces of the tale he and Maddie had already surmised, and the night was the kind of night when confidences are shared. Ian joined Luke at the door, and together they peered through the rain, searching for a light, a sound, anything that would tell them Maddie's ordeal was over. The wind blew a gust of rain, drenching them where they stood, and Ian reached for the heavy doors to draw them shut. After a few minutes, Ian began speaking again as though there had been no interruption.

"Brigham is more my son than the child of some faceless mobber. He's a fine lad, and I feel a wee bit of pride, though I know pride is a sin, each time he calls me Pa."

Luke thought about the story Ian had told him. He felt sorrow for a woman who had been so badly hurt that she lost the will to live. In a strange way, the story gave him a small amount of assurance that all would be well with Maddie. After all Maddie had been through, she still loved life and would fight for both her and the baby's future.

He suspected Ian had told him about Deborah to take his mind off Maddie, but he was only partially successful. It had been so long since he'd been banished to the barn that he feared something had gone wrong. His mind filled with despair when he thought of going on without Maddie. It hadn't been a year since he'd first laid eyes on her, and now she was the most important part of his life. He found his eyes turning repeatedly to the door. He wished Ian hadn't closed it. Mary had promised to come for him the moment the child arrived, and he wanted to watch for her.

"You can trust Sister Porter to take care of your Maddie," Ian told him, once more attempting to offer reassurance. "Mary trusts her completely. She's been with her for each of our babes. I expect she's been with close to a hundred women for their lying-ins, and I never heard of her losing a mother or a babe."

"What about Mary?" Ian supposed Luke was asking how he came to marry his second wife, when in fact Luke was wondering why she hadn't come for him yet.

"Ah, sweet Mary. She's a feisty one. I knew her in Scotland when she was just a wee bairn. When she arrived here with the last of the handcart companies, she still wasn't more than a slip of a girl, but I knew right off I wanted her for my wife. It was my good fortune that her heart agreed with mine, and in time we managed to convince her mother to allow us to wed."

"You've been through this a dozen times." Luke turned to Ian in almost desperation. "How could you go through this again and again?"

"I won't lie to you," Ian said. "It's never easy watching someone I love suffer to bring new life into this world. Mary's courage humbles me. I'm thinkin' when God laid out his great plan whereby we'd come to earth and all be responsible for helpin' each other return to Him, He gave the bearing of children to women because he knew no man could match a good woman for sheer determination to get the job done."

Luke thought about Ian's words, and a long-ago promise he'd made to his mother came to mind. He'd been afraid of Mormons at first. Now he wondered if perhaps they had the truth Ma had wanted him to find. There were questions he needed to ask Ian.

Light footsteps caught Luke's attention and sent him racing toward the heavy barn door without waiting to hear more. He threw the door open, and there stood Mary, smiling in the rain-fresh dawn.

"You have a daughter." She clapped her hands and practically danced with excitement as she shared the news.

"And Maddie? Is Maddie all right?"

"She's doing fine and fair bursting to show you your daughter." Luke took off at a run. He was almost to the cabin before it registered in his mind that the baby was a girl, not the son he'd assumed it would be. He didn't miss a step. A daughter would be fine. A short time later, when he held the tiny girl in his arms as he sat beside Maddie, watching them both sleep, he figured having a daughter was more than fine.

CHAPTER FIFTEEN

Luke brought the wagon to a halt on a small hill, and Maddie stared in astonishment. She'd never seen anything like it. Rocks, looking like coal clinkers, stretched as far as she could see. Interspersed with the rock was an occasional twisted tree. When they'd stopped to deliver Oscarson's bulls to him, she'd heard the men talking about ancient volcanoes that had spewed melted rock from wide cracks in the earth near the section they planned to homestead. They'd called the rocks lava and assured her that they were nothing to fear, that the lava had cooled many years before explorers had discovered them.

"We're almost there." Luke's voice held an edge of excitement. She turned to look at him. Didn't he see? He couldn't raise cattle—or the horses he dreamed of—among the jagged rocks. It was all some kind of cruel joke.

"Over there, Maddie." He raised his stock whip to point. At first she saw only miles and miles of gray brush bordering the once-liquid rock, then she saw what Luke saw. In the distance, the brush gave way to green hills and, beyond them, purple mountains. Hope soared once more.

Luke slapped the reins across the backs of the team he'd acquired from Ian, and the big horses continued on. She missed Horse and Prince, but a glance at the wagon behind her assured her Luke had made the best choice in leaving the saddle horses behind in exchange for the team of sturdy workhorses. The wagon was piled high with furniture, tools, and enough supplies to last until the end of the year. The last of their cash had gone to the storekeeper at the Mormon village they'd passed through a couple of hours ago in return for a cookstove, to be delivered as soon as Luke finished building their house.

A thrill of excitement passed through her as she thought of the house she would help Luke build. It wouldn't be large, but Luke had promised it wouldn't be a soddie. And it would be their own. The bundle in her arms began to whimper, and she turned her attention to Krista. When she looked up again, she could see that Luke had angled the wagon away from the rocks and the horses were picking their way through thick brush. An occasional rock poked through the ground, causing the wagon to lurch, and she clutched the baby more tightly, but at last they reached a level spot, and Luke brought the horses to a stop in a patch of thick grass.

He stood, pulling a paper from his pocket. He studied the paper, then checked the landmarks. Finally he announced, "This is it. See that rock that towers over the others and is streaked with white? That's one corner, and over that way, there's a pile of rocks separating our homestead from the next one. We'll share a boundary all the way to that hill . . ." He continued talking, but she heard no more once she spotted the tree-covered hill in the distance. It wasn't a large hill— only a foothill to the mountains that towered behind it—but it reminded her of the hills and mountains behind the little house she'd loved in Ogden. Seeing it gave her a warm feeling.

"I think we should position the house with the lava beds behind it," Luke went on. "Oscarson said to watch for small bits of land reaching into the jagged edge of the lava flow. He said that with lava on three sides, there's only one side needing to be fenced to turn those coves into sheltered corrals for young stock. That will save time. Later we can build a barn and real corrals out of cedar."

They drove on, with Luke picking one spot and then another for their house. It became a game, until the wagon topped a small incline and they both knew they'd found the perfect place. A flat plateau rose a little higher than the rest of the section, and a trickle of water from a small spring filled a pool at the edge of the lava. Long grass and a few reeds surrounded the pool, and on either side, rocky, U-shaped fingers of grass stretched into the lava bed. There was plenty of room for a house and barn. Luke helped Maddie down from the wagon, taking care to avoid jostling the baby. He lifted the thin cloth Maddie had placed over Krista to protect her from the sun and softly kissed her cheek. Behind the wagon seat was a wooden crate that had served as a cradle while they traveled; he placed the baby inside it, then straightened, reaching for Maddie's hand.

Standing side by side, they feasted their eyes on the land. Maddie knew Luke wasn't seeing acres of rock and brush to be cleared, but horses galloping across lush grass. She didn't see the rocks and brush either. Soon on the spot where she stood would rise a little house where she would cook for Luke, and where Krista would learn to walk and grow into a young woman. Behind the house, she would try her hand at gardening.

There were still a few hours of daylight left, and Luke spent them unloading the wagon and setting up a small tent to shade Maddie and Krista from the sun while he traveled to the mountains for timber to build their house. Maddie tried not to think of the days he would be gone. As she cooked their supper over an open fire, she dreamed of the stove Luke had ordered and shut her mind to the time when she would be alone with only the tent for protection.

"Don't move." Luke's voice was quiet, but she sensed something deadly behind his words. She froze in place, fear tearing at her heart. Her baby! She'd left Krista in her cradle in the wagon. She started to turn toward her daughter just as a bullet landed near her feet. She screamed and looked down to see a huge snake writhing on the ground. Luke holstered his gun, then removed the snake with a shovel while she sank down weakly on the wagon tongue, waiting until her heart stopped pounding before continuing to prepare their meal.

Luke didn't leave for the mountains the next morning. Instead, he pounded stakes into the ground to mark where he would set the foundation, then he began the tedious task of hauling rocks to form that foundation. Luke wouldn't let her help with the rocks, insisting they were too heavy for her. Some of the rocks were too heavy even for him to move, and he had to use the horses to drag them into place. Occasionally she would hear gunfire and know Luke had shot another snake. Each time she shuddered.

Her dread of the day when Luke would leave to cut timber grew with each day he spent building the foundation. She kept herself busy planting the seedlings she'd brought from Utah and digging a small trench from the pond to carry water to them. In a few years they would be trees, providing both shade and fruit. She kept Krista in a sling much like the one Cookie had made for her, and she examined each patch of dirt for snakes before she stepped on it. But the morning finally dawned when Luke planned to leave.

She awoke early that morning and knelt on her blankets. *Please, Father,* she prayed. *Help me to be brave and to protect my baby. Keep Luke safe too. And keep the snakes away.* A sound interrupted her prayers. Her eyes flew open to see Luke fully dressed, reaching for his rifle. He motioned for her to get dressed before he lifted the blanket that formed a flap for their improvised tent.

A shout came from some distance away, and she hurriedly pulled her dress on. Fearing the baby might cry if Luke had to shoot, she swept Krista into her arms and sat in the middle of their quilts to nurse her. She fidgeted, straining to hear what was happening beyond the shelter. At first she heard nothing, then the jangle of harnesses and the steady rhythm of horses' hooves drew closer.

Several voices seemed to be talking at once, then she heard the higher pitch of a woman's voice. Moments later, the flap lifted once more and a woman crawled inside the tent. Startled, Maddie could only stare.

"Hello, neighbor." There was a sauciness to the woman's voice, and a smile curved her mouth into a bow. "You likely don't remember me, but I saw you a few times on the trek from Utah. I'm Zina Richards. My husband and I are homesteading the section next to yours. We figured you were about ready to go for logs, and since we are too, we thought our men could ride together, if that's all right with your man."

The woman was tall but as slender as a boy, and Maddie guessed she was a decade or more older than herself. She seemed vaguely familiar. Possibly she had seen the other woman around the wagon train she and Luke had followed. "I-I'm Maddie McCall," she stammered. Before she could say more, Luke called her name. Swiftly buttoning her dress, she and her visitor left the tent.

"Maddie, these folks are headed to get timber too." Luke sounded pleased. She looked around at half a dozen men, including three teenage boys. "Ian told them I logged last winter and helped at the mill with him. They proposed that with my experience and their manpower and tools, we should work together so we can be back sooner. And Mr. Richards offered to leave his wife and his oldest boy here to keep you company while we're gone."

He looked anxious, and she knew he understood far more than she had guessed how fearful she was of his planned absence. She smiled, letting him know she approved of the plan, then followed him to the makeshift corral he'd made for Duke and Dolly near the pond. He stooped to kiss her, and when he straightened, he removed his gun belt and strapped it around her waist.

"Just in case." He cut off her objection. "This morning when I awoke you were praying, and when the Richardses pulled in with their wagons, I figured God was answering your prayers. But I know how scared you are of snakes, and if one gets past God, I'll feel better knowin' you're armed. Just remember everything I taught you, and you'll be fine if you have to shoot."

* * *

The days passed far more quickly than Maddie expected while Luke was gone. Zina showed her how to lay out her garden, and William, her son, took over turning the soil. It was late in the season for planting some things, but Zina assured her there was plenty of time for corn and squash. She enjoyed having another woman to talk to, and Zina was generous with tips for keeping Krista clean and cool. Only at night, when she lay alone in her blankets, did she find herself worrying. What would she do if Luke didn't come back?

He would come back, she assured herself. He wasn't like Papa—Luke took responsibility seriously. Unless something bad happened to him, he would come back. The home they were building was his dream too. Still, at the back of her mind there was always the constant worry. She'd never been certain enough of Papa's love to feel confident he wouldn't abandon her one day. And though Luke was nothing like Papa, it was difficult to leave the old fears and insecurities behind, especially when she knew they faced long separations. In the fall, Luke would return to the Oscarson ranch to work until winter set in. And someday—she hated even thinking of it—Luke would return to Texas to keep the promise he'd made to his parents.

"They're coming!" William's shout brought her head up late one afternoon, and she watched four wagons piled high with rough-cut lumber coming toward them. Duke and Dolly had barely come to a halt when Luke leaped from the wagon and gathered her close, chasing away her fears.

Luke taught her to plane and sand boards for a smooth floor, and she helped him erect a frame for their house. Her days were filled with the sound of hammering as she tended her garden and played with Krista. Gradually the house took shape, and the Richards men came again to help Luke raise the roof before they journeyed to the mountains again for more logs. This time they arrived with a surprise for Maddie. In one of the wagons was her long-awaited stove. Zina brought her a lump of sourdough starter and, while they waited, taught her to bake bread.

When the men returned this time, the first ears of sweet corn from Maddie's garden were ripe, and there was fresh bread to complete the feast she prepared. Luke surprised her with a dozen small trees from the mountains to plant for both shade and a wind-break for their house.

Luke worked at a feverish pace on the house, fashioning shingles from logs, building steps, and dismantling their packing crates to build cupboards. He started on the barn but only had time to build a shed, which he would enlarge later. The days were growing shorter, and he frequently glanced toward the sky. He would be leaving soon for the Oscarson ranch. At last the day came when Luke carried their furniture inside, and Maddie followed him with Krista. She set the baby on the sweet-smelling pine floor and looked around in awe. This was their home—her and Luke's. Tears came to her eyes. She'd waited so long for a home she could claim as her own. Luke's arms came around her, and though no words were spoken, she sensed he shared all that was in her heart.

Too soon, she stood on the step of their new house with Krista in her arms, waving good-bye to Luke. She watched until the wagon was completely out of sight, then, squaring her shoulders, she marched inside to scrub the floor. While Krista slept, she stitched curtains. Before the week was over, she'd finished nearly every task she'd planned to keep herself busy while Luke was away.

With him gone, the days were long and lonely and the nights worse. Inside her house she felt a measure of security, but each time she went outside to garden or to water the trees, she watched apprehensively for snakes and felt the loneliness crushing in. One October morning, she awoke to a layer of frost covering the ground. Remembering that Zina had warned her to gather her squash right after the first frost, she bundled Krista in warm clothes and took her to the garden with her.

Krista had outgrown the box, and she wiggled and scooted so much Maddie feared she'd tip it over and injure herself, so she spread a quilt on the ground and placed Krista on it. Leaving the baby happily chewing on a rag doll one of Mary McBride's daughters had made for her, she began picking squash. She carried two small squash to the house and four larger ones to the barn, then returned with a hoe to chop down the cornstalks to cover them and to save for feed for the calves Luke would be bringing back with him.

Looking up from her task to check on Krista, she noticed that the baby had scooted to the edge of the quilt and would soon be in the dirt. With the hoe still in her hand, she hurried toward Krista, only to catch herself up short at the sight of a rattler weaving its way toward her baby. Lifting her hoe, she smashed it down hard on the snake's head. Over and over she struck. When the snake lay still, she snatched up her baby in trembling arms and ran to the house.

It took two more days for her to gain the courage to finish chopping the corn. This time, while Krista slept in her cradle inside the house, she strapped on Luke's six-shooter and eyed with suspicion each bit of brush the fall wind scattered across her garden plot. She was glad when the last of her garden was harvested and she no longer needed to go outside longer than it took to visit the privy or bring in an armful of wood from the pile Luke had left beside the door.

Zina rode over one afternoon to visit. One of the younger boys came with her since William had hired himself out to one of the big ranches a few days' ride away. Maddie enjoyed visiting with the woman, and when Zina left, she tucked a small volume of poetry into Maddie's hands. Maddie thanked her and promised to take good care of the book.

"I don't read very well." Zina laughed. "And I never did get the hang of poems, but a friend of my mother wrote the poems and gave a copy to her, and she passed it on to me. My husband likes to read, and he thought with Mr. McCall being gone and all, you might like a book to keep you company."

Maddie loved the book and spent hours reading the poems and marveling that a woman Zina knew had made them up. Some of the poems were sad and talked about hardship and sacrifice, but they all ended on a hopeful note and were full of praise to God. She read a few of the poems every day and frequently ran her fingers over the name stamped into the leather cover—Eliza R. Snow. When she saw Mr. Richards again, she would thank him for the book that not only helped her pass the time, but gave her so much hope and strengthened her courage.

The days grew colder, and Krista began to crawl. She was soon pulling herself up against the furniture, and Maddie had to guard against her touching the stove. Caring for the baby was the greatest joy in her life, though sometimes she wondered if she was equal to the task. With the chubby baby in her lap, Maddie marveled at the perfection of her child, and often her thoughts turned to her own mother, wondering if she had loved Maddie the way Maddie loved Krista. She wondered too who, if anyone, had watched her learn to crawl, then to walk. Had someone marveled at each new task she learned? She felt certain Papa hadn't. Long ago, Catrin had said mothers keep on loving their children even in heaven, and she'd always hoped that was true. At the worst times in her life, she'd felt comforted by a quiet feeling that her mother was close by. She'd meant to ask Mary if what Catrin had said was true, but the time never seemed right. Perhaps Zina would know. She seemed to know an awful lot of things.

Krista fell asleep, and Maddie carried her to her cradle. She stood watching for a long time, then turned to supper preparation. The bread she'd mixed earlier had risen to the top of the pans and was ready to go into the oven. A restlessness filled her, and several times she walked to the window, pushed the curtain aside and stared out. The ground was cold and hard, but there had been no snow yet. The sky was blue, but it looked cold and hard too, and a sharp wind whistled around the house, shaking the precious glass windows they had hauled from Utah. Luke had been gone almost three months, and even the wind sounded lonely.

She watched tumbleweeds roll across the ground. A rabbit darted from one clump of brush to another. Farther out something moved, and she wondered if it was the small herd of antelope she and Luke had seen a couple of times.

The wind blew the door open. She heard it crash against the side of the house and felt the cold wind rush in. She turned to close it and stopped in shock. An Indian stood in the doorway. All the stories she'd ever heard of savages preying on isolated settlers flashed through her mind. She wondered if she could reach the cupboard where she kept Luke's gun in time to save Krista and herself.

She began to edge toward the cupboard, but the cry of a baby stopped her before she reached the weapon she kept there. She glanced toward the curtain she'd hung to separate the cooking area from the bedroom. The cry hadn't come from her daughter. She looked back at the Indian, noticing he looked ill. Perhaps she could help him, though she didn't know a lot about medicine, and he'd go on his way without hurting her or even knowing Krista slept in the next room.

Forgetting the gun, she took a step toward him. That was when she discovered he wasn't alone. A woman, clutching a bundle in her arms, hovered on the step behind him. Maddie assumed the cry she'd heard was the woman's baby. Something softened inside her, and she felt a desire to help.

The Indian stepped into the house, and Maddie backed up a step. The woman balanced in the doorway like one of the elusive antelope, set to run at the first threat. Maddie's fear began to lessen, seeing the woman's fear of her.

"Is he sick?" She motioned toward the Indian woman's baby. After a moment, the father made a grunting sound, then motioned with his hands as though he were trying to tell her something. Finally she understood. They were hungry.

She reached for the kettle of beans that she'd let simmer on the back of the stove all day. She poured some into a bowl, but before she could fill a second bowl, the Indian took the kettle from her. Unsure what to do next, she remembered the bread baking in her oven. She opened the oven and pulled out two beautifully browned loaves. The Indian reached past her to snatch one of the loaves. He tore off a chunk and placed it beside the bowl of beans. Keeping the remainder of the loaf tucked under one arm, he reached for the other loaf. With both hands full, he turned toward the door.

She watched as the Indian woman scurried down the steps. The man stepped past her, carrying the kettle of beans and both loaves of bread. She fell in step behind her man, and they were out of sight before Maddie could collect herself sufficiently to slam the door shut and drop the bar in place. It was the following morning before she gathered the courage to peek out her door again. Her empty kettle was sitting on the bottom step.

* * *

Luke noticed something different about Maddie when he returned home. He first noticed that her hair was long enough again to wrap around his hands as he pulled her to him. She greeted him with tears and laughter, along with a good hot supper. Tears came to his eyes when he lifted Krista in his arms and saw how much she'd grown. Maddie patted the horses' noses and exclaimed over the half-grown calves. Most of all, she expressed enthusiasm for the milch cow that trailed behind his wagon. But she seemed a little older, and there was new confidence in her steps. Only a shadow remained of the frightened, insecure girl he'd first known.

He'd missed Maddie and Krista, but until he returned, he hadn't realized how much. He'd missed the homestead too and was filled with plans for the future. But for now, it was enough to know it was home. It had been a long time since he'd claimed any place as home. Leaving next fall would be harder—and harder still would be the day when he'd have to return to Texas.

CHAPTER 16

December 24, 1885

Giving his boots an extra stomp, more to give his vision an opportunity to clear than to remove the snow from his worn footgear, Luke raised a knuckle to his hat brim, lifting it slightly. He was nearly blind from the brilliant whiteness outside, and it took a moment for the dark shapes in front of him to become barrels and dry goods. To his right he could make out a long counter piled with various household items. Behind the counter stood a tall, thin man wearing a worn leather apron, his bald head rivaling the bright snow outside for sheer shine.

The sun was brilliant now, but there was a bigger snowstorm pushing in from the north, and if Luke was going to beat it to the homestead, he had to get a move on. He'd only stopped at the store to pick up flour and a few necessities. Reed Oscarson had paid him for nearly four months' work with the sweetest little bay mare, the promise that in the spring he could have his pick of six new calves sired by one of the bulls he himself had trailed from Utah to the Oscarson ranch, and twenty silver dollars. On an impulse, Luke had decided to spend one of those dollars on Christmas presents for Maddie and the little ones. The rest of his wages would pay for the flour and other supplies they would need to survive until spring.

Stepping up to the counter, Luke fished a slip of paper out of his shirt pocket and set it in front of the man. He looked at it briefly. "It'll be a few minutes."

"That's fine. I'll look around." Luke let his eyes scan the dark depths of the store, resting briefly on the well-padded matron piling items on the other end of the counter, then drifting to a man and his wife standing in front of a bright red, boy-sized sled with gleaming silver runners. He'd seen them all before, but he didn't recall their names. Most people in town had been part of the wagon train he and Maddie had trailed while bringing Oscarson's bulls north. He didn't know any of them well because he and Maddie had mostly stayed to themselves on that journey. He looked at the sled again. Someday, when the ranch was paying its own way, he'd make a sled like that for his boy. Little Luke wasn't big enough for a sled yet, but when he was . . .

The woman walked away from her husband's side to touch the yellow hair of a doll with a china head. He'd heard Maddie talk about dolls like that, and he knew she dreamed of giving one to Krista. Maddie had never had anything so nice, but she shared Luke's fierce determination to give their little ones a better life than either of them had known.

The yellow-haired doll looked a bit like Krista, and he wished he could tuck it into his saddlebag to take home to her for a Christmas morning surprise. He couldn't spend money needed for winter supplies on a doll now, but someday . . .

Pushing aside the wistful thought, he picked up a couple cans of peaches. Maddie would be happy to see them. She never complained, but he knew that after growing up in the South, she sometimes got tired of the dried apples and berries she spent all summer putting away for the winter months in Idaho. Her garden hadn't produced as much last summer as she had hoped, but with the birth of Little Luke, she hadn't had a lot of time to lavish on it. They'd only been on their place three years, but it was starting to take shape, and if all went well next year, he wouldn't have to leave Maddie and the children while he worked for Mr. Oscarson again. Next year he'd have a few head of beef of his own to sell, and the trees they'd planted that first year would begin to bear fruit. He remembered the delight on Maddie's face when Mary had tucked the four trees with their heavily wrapped root balls into the wagon beside her and Krista the morning they'd left Ogden. She had given her a dozen handmade nappies and a hatbox full of tiny clothes for Krista too. Maddie's eyes had filled with tears, and she'd continued to twist her head and wave farewell until they were out of sight.

"Will that be all?" Luke heard the clerk ask the woman at the counter.

"Oh, I suppose I'd better have a nickel's worth of peppermints for George." The woman's laughter floated across the room. "He has a worse sweet tooth than our grandbabies do." Maybe he'd get a stick of candy for Krista— and one for Maddie too.

The clerk joined a hearty chuckle to the woman's laughter as he scooped the peppermint drops into a paper for the woman and tucked them into the box he'd packed for her.

"You want me to hold this for George to come get?" the man asked.

"No, no, Brother Barnes." The woman continued to laugh. "I can't wait for him to get around to it." She hefted the wooden crate into her arms and headed for the door. Before Luke could open it for her, it was pushed wide by two men entering the store. The woman with the crate sailed through the doorway before it could close.

As Luke had done, the two men stood squinting their eyes, giving them time to adjust to the general store's dim interior. He noticed that they both wore guns, strapped low on their thighs, just where a man's hand would easily come to rest. The older man wore a poncho cut from buffalo hide, his beard was thick and full, completely covering the gap between a beaver pelt cap and the poncho. The younger man wore a wool coat and a cowboy hat tied in place with a long scarf that trailed over one shoulder. His beard was full too, but lighter in both color and thickness. The pair were trouble, the kind Luke had seen from Texas to Idaho, the kind he took care to avoid now that he had Maddie and the little ones to think about. Gunfighters or bounty hunters—they were the same to him, and he didn't need either one. He moved deeper into the shadows. He'd get the few things Maddie wanted and be on his way.

A bolt of blue cloth caught his attention. Maddie had been wearing blue the first time he'd seen her.

He'd never know what prompted him to take her along, or why she'd agreed to go with him, a complete stranger, but he'd never regretted having Maddie accompany him on his flight from Texas. He'd never regretted either the impulse that had led him to stand beside her in front of a preacher in the Pattersons' parlor. He picked up the bolt of cloth.

The couple who had been in the store when he'd arrived moved to the counter and finished their order. They weren't laughing or whispering anymore but seemed anxious to leave. The wife stammered a request for a handful of peppermint sticks as though only the disappointment on her children's faces if they found no sweets Christmas morning frightened her more than the two men who stood between her and the door.

The younger of the two men began wandering through the narrow aisles while the older one moved closer to the counter. The woman, clearly holding her breath, swept her skirt back so it wouldn't brush the man's boot as she practically ran from the store. Her husband, carrying a bulky burlap bag, hurried after her.

The older man stepped to the counter, and Luke listened as he greeted the clerk with an order for beans, a jug of molasses, a pound of coffee, and a slab of bacon. The clerk gathered the items quickly and handed them over in exchange for a few coins. The man was stuffing his supplies into a canvas bag he'd produced from under his poncho when he asked, "You seen any strangers 'round here lately?" He shoved a folded piece of paper Luke suspected was a wanted poster toward the storekeeper. The clerk barely glanced at it.

"Not that I recall." Brother Barnes didn't miss a beat. "Most folks around here are homesteaders. The close ones show up at church on Sundays. The ones buildin' ranches further out only make it to town once or twice a year, but they aren't strangers." He pushed the paper back toward the bounty hunter.

"You know the man hidin' back of the canned goods?" He jerked a thumb toward Luke, and Luke started. He'd let his attention wander to the younger bounty hunter, who stood uncomfortably close with his hand resting low on his hip, his fingers inches from his gun.

"Sure. That's Luke McCall. Come on over here, son, and meet these folks," Barnes called out as though they were old friends. Luke hadn't known the storekeeper even knew his name. The few times he'd been in the store, they hadn't spoken beyond what was necessary to outfit him for the winter. He wouldn't have known the store-keeper's name if the woman who had been in earlier hadn't called him Brother Barnes. When he thought about it, he vaguely remembered the storekeeper from the wagon train of folks he'd followed north with Oscarson's bulls three years ago last spring.

Luke moved carefully toward the older man. He didn't want to appear nervous or reluctant to meet the newcomers. It had been four years since he'd left Texas, and there wasn't much chance anyone would recognize him now, but he'd taught himself caution.

"Afternoon." He touched the brim of his hat and turned halfway, addressing his words to the man behind the counter. "I don't want to rush you, but if you're ready to load my barrels of flour, I'll bring my team up. I'd like to be home before the snow sets in." He saw a flicker of disappointment on the gunman's face.

"Soon's I finish with these gentlemen." He turned back to the other man. "Will that be all? I still have a few sweets, if you're of a mind to celebrate the season."

The younger man snorted his derision, and Luke figured that if the pair did any celebrating, they'd do it with a jug rather than a paper of horehound drops. So he was surprised when the man wearing the smelly buffalo poncho smiled, showing a row of yellow, decaying teeth.

"Sure, mister," he said. "Give me some of them hard candies. You got any chocolate creams?"

"Sure do." The storekeeper beamed approvingly as he swept the last of his supply of candy into papers. Luke watched as the peppermint sticks disappeared and regretted there were none left to take home to Maddie and Krista.

"Haven't I seen you before?" Luke jumped. He'd let his attention wander again. The younger gunman had moved to within a few feet of him. It was one of the few times he regretted no longer carrying a gun.

"Not likely," Brother Barnes answered for him with an air of familiarity before Luke could respond. "Not unless you've been down in the Utah Territory. The McCalls settled up here the same time as me 'n Bishop Samuels. That was a hard trip. We got caught in a spring squall along the Bear River and nigh froze to death. You might want thread and a bit of lace to go with the dress goods." He alternated speaking to Luke and the strangers as he took the bolt of blue cloth from Luke's hands, and Luke struggled not to appear surprised by the man's words. It was true he and Maddie, with little Krista, had arrived in the area the same time as a wagon train of Mormons, but they hadn't really traveled together. He and Maddie had merely followed behind the Mormons' wagons. Of course, Brother Barnes hadn't exactly said they had been together.

"That little gal of yours is getting big enough to be wanting a shiny ribbon for her hair too," the storekeeper went on. "You go get your wagon backed up next to the alley door, and I'll just get your grub box packed." He reached for one of the wood crates stacked on the floor behind him.

Luke touched his hat brim once more and began walking toward the front door. It seemed to take about a thousand more steps than he'd taken coming in. When he reached the boardwalk, he resisted an urge to break into a run. But even walking, he lost no time heading for the stable.

The old man currying his mare looked up as Luke slipped through the open door and headed for the horses, which were up to their noses in oats. He checked to make certain his rifle was under the wagon seat before beginning to tighten buckles on Duke and Dolly's harnesses.

"I'd like to beat that storm." He ducked his head toward the open door, where deep clouds showing dark underbellies had replaced the brilliant afternoon sun. He also wanted to ride straight out of town without returning to the general store, but he couldn't leave without the supplies. Maddie was counting on him. He quickly backed first one horse, then the other on either side of the wagon tongue.

"I'll just finish brushing this purty girl while you load the wagon," the old man offered. "I'll have 'er ready when you come back by this way." He continued to run a brush over the sleek coat of Luke's new mare.

"Much obliged," Luke thanked him before climbing on the wagon seat. He noticed the bags of oats the old man had propped beside one wheel and climbed back down to boost the sacks into the wagon. He paused to hand the man one of his silver dollars, then, with a nervous glance toward the darkening sky, he leaped back on the wagon seat, picked up the reins with one hand, and released the brake with the other. Five minutes later he was pounding on Brother Barnes's back door.

Barnes was waiting and moved quickly to load Luke's wagon. Then he helped Luke fasten a tarp over the contents. Luke paid him and noted he had few coins left. He couldn't spare any to get something special for Maddie. There was no time anyway.

"You best be on your way," Barnes told him, giving the last knot a twist to ensure it stayed firmly tucked in the back of the wagon. "Those two strangers are lookin' for someone. The picture on their poster is so poorly drawn it could be 'most anybody. I never heard of anybody around these parts by the name writ on it, but I didn't like the way the younger one was eyeing you. Best to avoid trouble if you can."

"Thanks." Luke hunched into his coat. "I appreciate what you said in there."

"Think nothing of it. Folks settling this land together got to stick together." He jumped back to the ground. "Better get a move on. Those two gents went to the saloon for a little Christmas cheer. You should be halfway home by the time they give you another thought. Merry Christmas, and God bless you."

Luke slapped the reins against the horses' rumps, and the wagon began to roll. He stopped briefly at the livery stable to tie the mare's lead rope to the back of the wagon, then he was on his way. The first sting of wind-blown ice struck his cheeks as he topped the hill, leaving the handful of buildings struggling to become a town behind him. He pulled his wool scarf higher to protect his face.

* * *

Frank Haladen held a cup of steaming coffee, peering into its murky depths, while Grif swallowed a shot of whiskey. The dingy room where they sat wasn't much of a saloon—no girls, not even a piano, nothing like the Golden Garter. But he'd done all right since pairing up with old Grif. The law wasn't looking for him—he was the one doing the looking—and he and the old man were never short of spending money. Stretching his long legs toward the potbellied stove, he basked in the heat.

"Can't figure where we lost him." Grif brought him back to the problem they were facing. "Tracks were clear all the way to the ferry, then that skiff of snow turned the trail to a pig wallow all the way to that big spread. Figure he rode right through the corrals, mixing with the Bar O stock, then lit out for the hills."

"He came this way. I know he did." Frank scowled at his drink. It tasted like mud and had little appeal. "Those tracks we cut south of town were his." They'd been scouring the hills north of the ranch when the rancher paid off his men and the temporary ranch hands took to the road, several of them driving teams pulling heavy wagons. Frank and Grif's quarry had taken advantage of the traffic, riding ahead, secure in the knowledge that the other riders and teams would obliterate his tracks. The ploy had worked until, two miles out of town, they'd found a clear print with a five-point star cut into the mud beside the road, the distinctive shoe mark used to identify the horses of the Colorado rancher who had been killed for his horse and the ranch's payroll almost a month ago.

They'd learned that when the rancher sold a horse, his blacksmith removed the Colorado Star shoes and replaced them with plain shoes. Any horse this far north, wearing the star shoes, was a stolen horse. Two days after the man's body had been found, the rancher's sons had placed a thousand-dollar bounty on the murderer's head. Frank and Grif planned to collect that reward.

"Finish up yer drink, and let's git a move on." Grif set his own glass on the table, wiped his mouth with the back of his hand, then rose to his feet. "There's a storm brewin', and if we don't cut his tracks before the snow comes, we're gonna lose 'im."

With a sigh, Frank gulped the contents of his cup and stood beside his partner. He didn't relish stepping outside. The temperature was dropping fast, and he hadn't slept in a bed for more than a month, but bringing in Cole Walker would set him up for a long time.

"You expect that cowboy over at the store might be Walker?" Frank asked just loud enough for Grif to hear.

"Possible," the old man muttered, "but not likely. I never hear'd of Walker settlin' down, and that young man was lookin' at woman and kid fixin's. Drivin' a team too."

Shards of ice were blowing in the air when they stepped onto the boardwalk that lined both sides of the narrow street. Trailing their horses behind them, they walked the length of the short Main Street, passing the general store and stable, paying particular attention to the horseshoe prints around the blacksmith shop. They passed a church and half a dozen homes sporting cedar wreaths on their doors before Grif suddenly knelt beside the road heading north out of town.

A broad smile spread across Frank's face as he too gazed down at a clear set of tracks. Cole Walker would soon be theirs.

"Looks like he's trailin' that horse behind a wagon." Grif narrowed his eyes and glared toward the approaching storm. "The wagon will slow him down some." Without another word, both men swung into their saddles and pointed their horses north. The storm was coming on fast, and they wanted to catch up to their quarry before snow wiped out his trail.

* * *

Sleet changed to snow before Luke reached the old lava flow. He wished he could drive his team right across the mass of twisted black rock, but even the most sure-footed horse couldn't cross lava rocks without breaking a leg. He'd kept an eye on the road behind him since leaving town and hadn't seen anyone following. The snow had shortened visibility and was quickly filling in the tracks left by his wagon. It would take an awfully good tracker to follow him after he left the road and headed through the sagebrush toward the lava beds, which he would circle until he reached his homestead on the other side.

As he thought about the homestead and Maddie, his heartbeat accelerated, and he urged the horses to a faster pace. Looking back once more, he noticed that the snow was sticking to the dark coat of the mare he'd tied to the tailgate of the wagon. She was a beauty. He hadn't had a saddle horse since he and Maddie had traded both the chestnut stallion and the gray gelding for a team and wagon before they left Utah. He and Maddie sometimes rode the workhorses now pulling his wagon. Though they were good horses, they weren't saddle horses and they weren't agile enough to work his fledgling herd. He'd been lucky to get the mare.

If everything went well next summer, he'd write to Ian McBride and make arrangements to collect one of the young stallions that had been part of the first batch of colts Pa's stallion had sired for McBride. With McBride's colt and Oscarson's mare, he'd have the beginnings of the horse breeding and training operation he had dreamed of all his life.

Keeping the mound of lava rock to his right, he looked for the familiar stand of twisted cedar trees. When he spotted the first of the gnarled shapes through the curtain of snow, he began watching for a small mound tucked up close to the rocks he'd picked out last September when he left the homestead for Oscarson's ranch. He'd decided that day his children were going to have something he hadn't had since he was a small boy—something his ma had considered important. In the shelter of the bushlike trees, the wind didn't feel quite as fierce, and he could see more clearly. It didn't take long before he saw a cluster of rocks and a snow-covered shape that looked familiar.

"Whoa!" He pulled back on the reins, and when the team halted in the shelter of a large cedar tree, he set the brake and reached under the seat for the ax that lay beside his rifle. The snow reached to his ankles when he stepped down from the wagon. He trudged up a small incline to the tree he'd selected. The first swing of the ax shook a layer of snow onto his hat brim, and some slithered down the back of his coat collar. He swung again. It took only a few minutes to chop the tree down and drag it back to his wagon, where he tied it to the top of his load.

Lifting his eyes to the swirling mass of white around him, he felt a slight uneasiness—as though he weren't alone. He wondered for just a moment if stopping had been the wise thing to do, but climbing back onto the wagon seat, he patted the spot over his shirt pocket, feeling the familiar metal shape he'd placed there before leaving the Oscarson ranch early yesterday morning. With a smile of anticipation, he slapped the reins across his team's backs. The horses strained against their collars and, after a slight hesitation, the wheels began to turn. He wouldn't stop again until he reached home.

* * *

Maddie brushed the curtain aside to check once more. There was still no sign of Luke, and it was beginning to snow hard. She could scarcely see across the yard to the barn. She would have to secure the stock in case the storm grew in intensity and she couldn't get back out in the morning.

"Krista, Mama has to go check on the cow." She reached for her warm outerwear and picked up a thick woollen scarf. "Little Luke is asleep, so you must play quietly. You can watch for Papa through the window if you like." She wrapped the scarf about her head and headed for the door. The wind nearly ripped it from her hands when she opened it. As she struggled to close it, she noticed the end of a coil of rope Luke had attached to the rail he'd built beside the two steps leading to the door. Perhaps she should take it with her.

The wind snatched at her clothes as she struggled toward the dark shape she could faintly see through the driving snow. When she reached it, she looped the end of the rope through the metal ring Luke used as a door handle and tied it securely.

It didn't take long to milk the cow, though she seemed a little startled by the early milking. Maddie still had plenty of milk in the house, and she didn't think she could manage a bucket on the trip back, so she gave the milk to the pigs, then fed her few chickens. She was glad she'd gathered eggs earlier and wouldn't have to find a way to get them safely back to the house.

While she worked, she listened for the jingle of Duke and Dolly's harnesses, but by the time she was ready to return to the house, they still hadn't arrived. Tomorrow was Christmas, and it seemed she and the children would be alone, as they had been for the past four months. She didn't complain about the time Luke was away, but she hated for them to be apart. Unlike the times when her father had left her, she knew he would be back. But she missed him, and with two small children, caring for the stock and harvesting the garden had proved difficult.

She slid the door open and stared out into a curtain of white. The only thing she liked about winter, she decided, was that she didn't have to worry about rattlers. She'd killed two last fall with her garden hoe, one of which was only a few feet from where Krista sat on a quilt watching Little Luke while Maddie picked the last of her beans.

Hand over hand, she clung to the rope as she made her way back to the house. She slipped inside and discovered that Little Luke had awakened from his nap. Krista bent over his cradle making silly noises, and she could hear the baby's happy giggle. She made up her mind. Even if Luke didn't come, she'd make Christmas special for the children. She'd roast a chicken and make a pudding—and she and Krista would make the sugar cookies Luke loved.

* * *

Where the trees grew more sparsely, the snow was beginning to drift, and even the heavy draft horses were struggling to pull the wagon through the deepening snow. Luke knew it had been no later than two in the afternoon when he'd left Brother Barnes's store. That had only been a couple of hours ago, but night came early in the north, and with the pounding storm, it felt more like night than late afternoon.

Between the early darkness and the thick snowfall, he found he could see no farther than the broad rumps of his horses. Knowing how easily a man could become disoriented under such circumstances, he relaxed the reins, giving the horses their heads. Though he might become lost, the horses could find their way home. It wasn't long before he began to feel the strain of the horses attempting to pull the heavy wagon through the deepening snow. They were reaching the point where the team wouldn't be able to pull the wagon anymore, and he had no idea how much further they needed to travel. The snow had wiped out landmarks and distorted time, leaving him uncertain of his exact location, though he knew he was within a mile or two of home.

He was just beginning to think he'd have to abandon his wagon and ride one of the draft animals the rest of the way when the team stopped of their own accord. No amount of urging would convince them to go farther. Since the horses would neither stop nor prove so obstinate without cause, Luke climbed down from the wagon and felt his way to the front of the team. As he ran his hand up one of the horse's deep chests toward its head, his hand encountered a rope stretched in front of it.

Maddie! A wave of relief swept over him. She'd stretched the rope from the house to the barn just as he'd instructed her to do at the first sign of snow. He made his way to the tail of the wagon to loose the mare's lead, then, hand over hand, he followed Maddie's rope to the barn. Duke and Dolly strained to start the wagon rolling again, then followed Luke, plodding wearily through the deep snow. Fortunately they had stopped only a few steps from the barn. Once inside, he found the lantern hanging on a nail near the door.

By the faint glow of the lantern, he looked around in appreciation. Maddie's cow was bedded down in a warm stall, and from the far corner, he heard the grunt of the sow he'd acquired a year ago, followed by the squeal of one of her remaining offspring. Fresh straw covered Duke and Dolly's box stalls. It didn't take long to prepare another stall for the new mare.

After securing the horses and making certain they had feed, he lifted the tarp covering his wagon and transferred the contents of the box Brother Barnes had set beside his barrels of flour and bags of feed to a burlap bag. With a short piece of rope, he tied the small tree to his back and attached the burlap bag to his belt. He was ready to make his way to the house.

The wind and driving snow combined with the awkward burdens he carried to make the trip to the house arduous. Several times he staggered in the knee-deep snow. He was grateful for the rope to guide him and help him stay on his feet as he worked his way toward the light shining dimly in Maddie's kitchen window.

At last his boot bumped against the broad step he'd built beside the cabin door. He and Maddie had built the cabin their first summer while living beneath a piece of canvas stretched from the side of the wagon. Krista had slept or played quietly in a wooden box nearby while they'd worked.

Luke found it hard to keep the moisture that burned his eyes from falling when he flung open the door and saw Maddie standing beside the stove with a long wooden spoon in her hand, the lantern on the table making a halo of her pale golden hair that once more reached below her shoulders. It had grown back long ago, thick and long and a little darker than the silvery lock he still carried in Pa's watch case.

"Luke!" Maddie dropped the spoon and flew across the room, her arms open to welcome him.

"Papa!" a second voice shrieked, and he had to put out a hand to stop his small daughter from flinging herself at his snow-caked pant leg. Maddie stopped too, practically dancing along with Krista in her excitement.

"Wait a minute." Dropping the bag he carried and lowering the little tree to the floor, he fumbled to remove his gloves, finally resorting to using his teeth to strip first one and then the other from his numb fingers. Maddie reached for the buttons on his coat. Krista ran for the broom and returned to brush his pants and boots with an excess of enthusiasm. In minutes his coat and boots were off and drying beside the stove, and both Maddie and Krista were wrapped in his arms.

"Your dinner is probably scorched." Maddie drew back at last, smiling through her tears. She wiped her eyes with the corner of her apron before returning to the kettle she'd been stirring. "Krista, set Papa a place at the table."

The little girl hurried to the sideboard and began pulling plates from a shelf. She stopped and Luke followed her gaze to the things he'd dropped on the floor when he'd burst through the door minutes earlier.

"Papa, why did you bring a tree into the house?" Krista stared in puzzlement at the cedar tree lying where he'd dropped it on the floor.

"It's a Christmas tree!" Seeing her puzzled expression deepen, he drew a chair out from the table to sit on and pulled her onto his knee. "When I was a little boy, my mama always found a little tree to be my Christmas tree. She told me about the beautiful fir trees her mama and papa brought into the house each Christmas in far-off Norway to be covered with pretty balls and little, bitty candles. Then when I started working for Mr. Oscarson, I noticed that every year he fixes up a Christmas tree for his children, and I got thinking you and Little Luke ought to have a Christmas tree of your own this year."

"Thank you, Papa." She still looked uncertain, but he noticed that Maddie's eyes were glowing.

"It'll be wonderful, Krista. You'll see." Maddie deftly picked hot biscuits from the pan she held and placed them on a plate, which she carried to the table. Before she could say more, a howl erupted from behind the curtain that separated the main room from the bedroom.

"I'll get him." Luke grinned with excitement as he hurried behind the curtain to fetch his son. He returned moments later with the wide-eyed baby in his arms. "Look how big he is!" He lifted the child high in the air and was rewarded with a wide grin that revealed two tiny teeth.

"Here, I'll take him so you can eat your dinner." Maddie reached for the baby, only to have Luke insist on keeping him.

"You need to eat too," he told her. "Me 'n Little Luke have some getting reacquainted to do." Holding the baby with one hand, he pulled out a chair to sit on. With the child in the crook of one arm, he held his spoon with the other. Maddie buttered a thick slice of hot bread and set it in front of him. She bowed her head and waited expectantly. He didn't disappoint her. As he bowed his head, he figured he had a lot to be grateful for.

The stew was rich and satisfying, the bread fresh; he was home at last on his own place with Maddie and their little ones—and tomorrow it would be Christmas. He couldn't remember a time in his life when he'd felt more content, not even when his parents were alive and they were together in the house his father had built to replace the soddie they'd first lived in. A moment's sadness touched him as he thought of his parents. They should be here to see Krista and Little Luke.

He didn't think about his parents and their senseless deaths every day anymore. It wasn't that he didn't love them or miss them just as much, but now he had Maddie and the children giving him more reason to think about life than death.

"Mama, do we have any little candles to go on the Christmas tree?" Krista turned on her chair to look at the tree again.

"No," Maddie told her. "We don't have the right kind of candles or any of the little holders to keep the candles from setting the tree on fire, but we can decorate it with other things. We have dry berries and popcorn. After we finish eating, I'll wash the dishes while Papa makes a tree stand, then I'll show you how to sew the popcorn and berries into pretty ropes for the tree."

The baby reached for Luke's bowl, and when Luke stopped him from dumping the stew in his lap, Little Luke objected loudly.

"He's hungry." Maddie started to rise from her chair.

"Finish your dinner," Luke told her while fishing a chunk of potato out of his stew and mashing it before offering it to the baby. "It's time this little man learned some manners."

"Look at Lukie's face!" Krista's laughter rang out.

"But he wants more." Luke offered his son a second spoonful of mashed potato. The child opened his mouth eagerly this time.

When the meal was finished and the dishes washed, Luke and Krista popped enough corn to fill Maddie's dishpan while Maddie nursed Little Luke. Once the baby was settled in the cradle that Luke had dragged closer to the stove and to where Maddie and Krista were making ornaments for the tree, Luke bowed out of stringing the popcorn. Instead, he volunteered to put away the supplies he'd brought from town.

As he transferred the staples and the cans of peaches he'd purchased to the cupboard shelf, he wished he'd been able to buy more. The bolt of blue cloth would be all he'd have to give Maddie and Krista on Christmas morning. He was pleased to see the end of a bit of lace poking out from the folds of cloth and was glad Brother Barnes had added it to his order. When he spotted the piece of satin ribbon for Krista's hair, a slow smile covered his face. Carefully he pushed the cloth and ribbon to the bottom of the bag, where it would stay until Christmas morning. Knowing how clever Maddie was with a needle—something she'd learned from Mary McBride—she'd probably manage a shirt for Little Luke out of the scraps as well.

His fingers touched a twisted piece of paper, and he paused, not certain what the paper held. He opened it to find two peppermint sticks. He didn't know how the storekeeper had known he'd wanted the candy for Krista and Maddie or when he'd sneaked them from the jar and added them to Luke's order. He felt a lump form in his throat. Thanks to Brother Barnes, this was going to be a real Christmas.

While he put away the supplies he'd brought, Luke listened to Maddie tell Krista a story about a wonderful Christmas tree she had seen once in New Orleans in a big house where her papa took her when she was a little girl. She and the little girl who lived in that house had played with dolls and sung songs beneath its huge boughs. From a wistful note in Maddie's voice, he suspected Maddie had longed to stay at the big house with the little girl, but that hadn't happened.

Seeing his wife and daughter's heads close together as they bent over the rapidly growing string of popcorn, Luke felt a sense of amazement. How did Maddie know so much about being a mother when she'd been raised without one? He'd at least had a ma when he was a boy, but Maddie hadn't. A twinge of sadness filled his heart. Ma had made Christmas special when he was a boy. She'd always made a pudding, and there had been a few sweets for him. She'd read the Christmas story from the big Bible her grandmother had brought with her from Norway, then from the English one that had belonged to Pa's family. He wished he'd been able to save those books so he could read the story to Krista. Next time he went to town, he'd see if Brother Barnes had a Bible for sale in his store. He'd see about one of those Mormon bibles too. It seemed to him it was about time he made good on his promise to Ma to look for the truth about religion. He didn't know if the Mormons had the truth, but he'd had ample example of their goodness, and it seemed to him that goodness and truth often traveled the same road.

"All right, this string is ready to place on the tree." Maddie held up a long chain of popcorn, interspersed with dried berries. Luke took one end of the chain, and together they wound it around the tree, with Maddie checking to make certain each loop draped just right. When they finished, she got out her sewing bag and dug from its depths tiny scraps of cloth and bits of yarn to tie to the tree's boughs. Soon the little tree looked bright and festive.

Luke produced the star from his pocket that he'd cut from a piece of tin one lonely evening after his work was done at the Oscarson ranch in anticipation of this moment. He carefully placed it on top of the tree as Krista clapped her small hands. Luke stepped back beside Maddie and his daughter to admire their handiwork.

As they stood there, a faint sound reached Luke's ears over the wail of the wind. Moments later the cabin door burst open, and two snow-shrouded figures stumbled into the room.

CHAPTER SEVENTEEN

Krista let out a cry and buried her face in Maddie's skirt. Instinctively Luke stepped in front of his wife and daughter. Even with a thick coat of snow covering them, he recognized the two bounty hunters he'd seen in Brother Barnes's store. A sick sense of dread replaced the happiness of a moment before. If they'd come for him, he'd have to find a way to protect his family.

When the pair made no move toward him, he recognized that they were in bad shape, especially the younger man. Perhaps they'd only stumbled onto his ranch, looking for a haven from the storm. No matter who they were or what their intent might be, he had to help them. He took a step toward them.

* * *

But for his hold on Grif's buffalo coat, Frank would have collapsed. He was cold beyond feeling, and he couldn't make his eyes focus. He knew they were in some kind of building, but it could be a house, a barn, or a line shack, and he wouldn't know or care. His only sense that seemed to be working was that of smell, and along with the air he struggled to breathe came the aroma of stew—not the sorry mess old Grif sometimes stirred up, but stew like Ma used to fix for supper. Along with the stew smell, he breathed in the sharp scent of cedar and something else he couldn't quite place. Then he remembered—popcorn! An ache for the times when he was young brought more pain and confusion to his already befuddled mind.

"Come sit by the fire. You look near froze to death." A woman's voice penetrated the white fog around him. For a moment he wondered if he had frozen to death and the voice was his angel ma. But no, that wasn't Ma's voice. Besides, he was pretty sure that if he were dead, he'd be feeling the opposite of all this ice and snow.

Hands shoved him onto a chair and he heard someone—Grif, he thought—say something about the horses. Shapes and sounds whirled around him. He had no idea how much time passed before the burning sensation in his hands and on his face made him conscious that the woman was bathing them.

"Too hot." He tried to draw back.

"No, the water's barely got the chill taken off it," the woman said. "Really, it's quite cool, but if you can feel it, that's a good sign." She continued to bathe his face and hands, and after a while it didn't feel so bad. He began to shiver, and he doubted he'd ever be warm again.

Gradually, he became aware that the woman had removed his boots and that his bare feet were resting in a basin of scalding water. He tried to pull them free but couldn't. A tingling sensation ran upward from his burning feet, then somehow his feet were out of the water and someone was drying them, only it seemed that someone was doing more than drying them. He suspected that he wouldn't have an inch of hide left when the woman got through scraping them.

A massive shudder shook his body, and he gritted his teeth to keep them from shaking too. He felt hands too big to be the woman's help him to a pallet on the floor, but hers were the hands that covered his shaking shoulders with a thick quilt. Then he knew no more.

* * *

Maddie had learned a great deal about cold and frostbite since she and Luke had arrived in Idaho, and she knew that no matter how gentle she was, the man suffered each time she touched him. Pain or no pain, she had to bathe and warm him or he'd likely lose fingers and toes.

In spite of her preoccupation with the stranger's needs, she sensed that something about the men troubled Luke. She'd noticed the guns strapped low on both men's thighs and remembered what Luke had told her about gunfighters who kept their guns at the ready. But perhaps it was only that this was Luke's first night home after almost four months of being apart and he was disappointed that their reunion had been interrupted.

She was disappointed too. Luke had left for the Oscarson ranch as soon as his fall work was completed—just as he had done the previous three winters—leaving her to milk the cow, feed the pigs and chickens, bring in her squash and pumpkins, and dig the root vegetables while caring for two small children. It had been easier in most respects this time than the first years had been.

She was aware of the big man, Grif, and Luke returning from the barn. They helped her get the younger man into a bed she had made for him on the floor. The men's exhaustion was evident, and she urged them both to turn in for the night while she banked the fire and settled the children.

When she at last stepped behind the curtain that concealed her family from the men sleeping on the floor, she changed into her nightgown, knelt briefly, as was her habit, then lifted the quilt only enough to slide in beside Luke. His arm settled around her and he mumbled something sleepily into her ear.

She lay still for some time, reveling in the feel of her husband's warm body beside her. She heard Krista sigh in her sleep and listened to the faint smacking noises Little Luke made and thought of the words to a song she'd first heard drifting on the night air from the Mormon encampment she and Luke had followed from Ogden. She liked the song, and it gave her courage and hope when she was tired and lonely. Tonight she mentally sang the chorus, "All is well, all is well," as she drifted asleep.

* * *

It was no longer dark when Frank opened his eyes. He lay still, adjusting to his surroundings. A lantern burned near the large, black cookstove, and he could see the swirl of a woman's skirt. By moving his head slightly, he could see a window with small, frosted glass panes. Snow was still falling, but the blackness of night had gone.

Turning his head slightly, he discovered Grif lying on a bedroll not far away. The old bounty hunter was stretched out on his back, snoring. His stinking buffalo robe hung over a chair a short distance away. Frank breathed a bit easier. Hazy memories of the day before came back, and he recalled how they had found the prints of the stolen horse on the hill just outside of town and followed them until they'd lost the tracks in the snow and rocks of a badland like he'd never run across before. Even coated with a fresh layer of snow, the jagged rocks had stretched before them in broken waves as though the devil had used the land as a dumping place for great cauldrons of burning brimstone.

By that time the snow had been coming fast and hard, convincing them they should look for shelter. Grif had led the way, skirting the frozen lava flow, looking for a sheltered spot in the rocks and cedars. They'd found a few caves, but they were too narrow for the two of them to squeeze inside, and Grif had said they were likely full of rattlers hibernating through the winter anyway. Frank had no love for snakes and figured he'd rather take his chances in the snow, even if the snakes were sleeping.

The smells and sounds of the small house brought back memories Frank had avoided for a long time. He recalled the mouthwatering aroma of stew when he and Grif had stumbled into the house. The memory caused him to suffer a dull ache like a wound that never healed; it reminded him of Amelia and the pot of stew she'd kept simmering on the stove in the back of her newspaper shop. Grif frequently made stew too, but thinking of Grif's stew caused Frank's nose to wrinkle in disgust.

The stew seemed to start a flood of unbidden memories. He tried not to think of the time before he and the old man had become partners, but the memories wouldn't stay buried.

He saw Amelia with ink smudges on her face, Amelia struggling with the big lever of the printing press, Amelia scrambling across town with her notepad and pen clutched in her hands, the challenging expression in her eyes when she stood up for what she deemed right, Amelia jumping into his lap when he asked her to be his wife, and Amelia's blood seeping through his shirt and pants as her life ebbed away. The picture of Amelia he dreaded most crowded into his mind—Amelia looking sad and accusing. He suffered guilt, knowing he'd let her memory down.

A deep shudder shook his body, and Frank thought how he had arrived in Colorado from Texas that spring after Amelia's death. Instead of pursuing the man who had shot Amelia, or even taking up her newspaper to continue her fight for equality and justice, he'd turned to drink and tried to leave it all behind. Too drunk to defend himself, he'd been ambushed on a lonely trail within days of leaving Texas.

The only good thing that had come from his flight from Texas and the encounter with thieves was meeting Grif. The two had been chasing outlaws in the Arizona territory by winter. They had drifted throughout the Southwest until last summer when they'd again returned to Colorado and begun working their way north. The farther north they traveled, the more his thoughts had started straying to his childhood, and he began seeing his actions in those years following the loss of his mother and sister in a different light. His father hadn't turned his back on him; he'd been consumed by grief. He'd come to see that Pa had loved Frank's mother as Frank had loved Amelia, and her loss was just as devastating to Pa as losing Amelia had been for him.

The wind howling around the eaves of the little house made him burrow deeper into the quilt that covered him. He'd seen snow before, but nothing like the never-ending frozen nightmare they'd ridden through yesterday. Grif had shown him how to wrap his extra set of clothes around his hands and feet to hold in the little heat his body produced, and he'd tied a bandanna across his face to protect his mouth and nose. He understood now why the old man grew his hair and beard long. Draping his blanket around his shoulders, he'd envied his partner's thick buffalo cape. He'd shivered with the cold until a kind of numbness had set in.

Frank had a vague recollection of their horses stumbling into a fence, but he had no idea how the old man had been able to follow it as far as he had. He'd been too cold and tired to care when Grif had fumed and sworn because he'd lost the fence. They'd stumbled around for some time in the blowing snow, unable to see because the thick clouds and raging storm hid any sign of moon or stars. It had been sheer dumb luck when their horses had been brought up short by a rope strung across their path. Grif had dismounted, then pulled Frank from his saddle. He remembered that much. Leaving the horses, they'd clutched the rope in their frozen fingers as they'd waded through snow that brushed the holster strapped to his leg. At last they'd seen the faint glow of light coming through a cabin window and followed it to its source.

Frank turned his head a few inches so he could watch the woman. He faintly recalled her ministrations of the night before and figured she'd likely saved his life. He remembered Grif telling the woman their names, but he didn't recall hearing hers. He noticed she was pretty, with a thick rope of yellow hair hanging over one shoulder. She was young and slender too, really more girl than woman and not yet hardened by the harsh life of a frontier woman. He wondered about her man and if he was the one they'd been trailing.

The cabin was slowly filling with the aroma of baking biscuits, and Frank's mouth watered. It would be good to have a home-cooked meal. It had been a long time since he'd sat down to a real, woman-cooked breakfast. He hadn't done so since he'd boarded at Mrs. Bronson's house. Long before that, Ma had insisted he eat a big breakfast each morning until she took sick and died when he was just a half-grown boy. He'd eaten breakfast with Amelia the mornings they delivered papers, but those breakfasts were seldom more than a loaf of Mrs. Bronson's bread and hot coffee—though he'd give anything if he could sit across that rickety table from Amelia again. He wouldn't care what they ate.

A sound caught his attention, and he turned to see a little girl enter the room through a curtain that likely hid a doorway leading to the cabin's only bedroom. She had pale hair too—lighter than her ma's—and round, pink cheeks. His breath caught; he'd had a little sister like that until a fever had taken her and his ma away. The girl walked to a juniper tree that appeared to be growing out of the floor at the other end of the room. Here in this part of the west it was probably called a cedar, though it looked the same to him as the junipers found farther south. It was a strange-looking, bushlike tree with some kind of white rope wrapped around and around it and a big tin star sitting on the top branch.

It was the star that brought back memories of the Christmas trees his ma had set up in the parlor when he was a boy. Those trees had been pines, nothing like the scrubby juniper the girl was admiring. From the awe on the child's face, she probably thought it was every bit as wonderful as his own Christmas trees had been. A wave of nostalgia swept over him, which he immediately dampened. Christmas trees, parlors, and little girls with golden hair belonged to that time before he'd struck out on his own. They belonged to that time before he'd picked up a gun and begun riding with Blackwell. He turned his head away from the tree, away from his memories.

A man carrying a baby moved into his range of view, and he recognized the man from the store. He thought he recognized him from a wanted poster too. He fit Cole Walker's general description, except he appeared to be younger. If this was the man he and Grif were looking for, he hoped he'd come peaceably; he didn't want to shoot him in front of the woman and little girl.

Frank watched the other man approach the woman and hand her something. He heard her soft murmurs of delight when she looked at a bolt of blue cloth. A happy giggle turned his attention to the little girl. She was holding up a long, shiny hair ribbon.

"This is for you too." The young father handed the child a peppermint stick. Her eyes grew round as she reached for it.

"Put it in your pocket until after breakfast." Her mother's words brought a brief frown to the girl's face, but she obediently tucked the candy into her pocket.

"And here's one for Little Luke." The young man held another stick of candy out to the woman.

"He's too little for sweets." Laughter accompanied the woman's protest.

"I don't suppose a lick or two will hurt him any, and his mama might help him with the rest." The laughing words brought a pain to Frank's chest. It was Christmas morning, and he had no one to share a Christmas sweet with. If the storm hadn't landed him here, he wouldn't have even remembered it was Christmas. And if the woman hadn't treated his frostbite, he'd not be alive to celebrate this Christmas or any other. He hoped the woman's husband wasn't Cole Walker.

* * *

By hanging onto the rope, Luke made his way to the barn to check on the stock and milk Maddie's cow. Snow was still coming down, thick and heavy, but the storm didn't feel as fierce as it had been the day before. After completing his chores, he placed blocks beneath his wagon's axles, removed the wheels, then mounted runners in their place. He wanted to be prepared so that when the snow stopped, he could harness Duke and Dolly to take a load of hay to his herd. The cattle foraged well on the long grass beneath the snow through most of the winter, but when the snow became as deep as it was now, they needed a few extra feedings.

As he worked, he thought about the two men sleeping in bedrolls on the cabin floor. He couldn't refuse them shelter, but they made him uneasy. His fingers moved faster; he didn't like leaving Maddie and the children alone with those men in the house.

When he finished turning the wagon into a sled, he searched in the wooden boxes Maddie had set in the chickens' shelter, finding half a dozen eggs, which he cocooned in a thick layer of straw in his pockets. Using a clean piece of cloth, he strained the milk into a jug he could cover to carry to the house.

It wasn't a sound, but the absence of sound, that made him pause before leaving the barn. The wind had died down. When he looked out, he could see across the distance that separated the house from the barn, and a glance at the sky showed him specks of blue through the thinning clouds. Deep drifts needed the attention of a shovel. A few lazy flakes were still falling, but the brunt of the storm had passed. The prickle of uneasiness that had followed him to the barn remained. It was like feeling strange eyes watching him. He hoped the two men who had sheltered in his home would move on now.

When he entered the warm kitchen a few minutes later, he found Maddie standing at the stove, stirring a large pot of mush. Krista was across the room beside their Christmas tree playing with Little Luke and showing him the tree, which he was trying to reach with his chubby fists. The bounty hunters both sat at the table, their eyes following his every move as he divested himself of his coat and pulled off his snow-caked boots.

"'Mornin'." He sensed it wouldn't be in his best interest to allow the two bounty hunters to know how much they unnerved him. They brought back memories and fears he'd spent years trying to block from his mind.

Luke figured the two men who had stumbled into his cabin the night before were bounty hunters rather than gunfighters, but he had reason to be as wary of bounty hunters as gunfighters. Wanted posters across Texas bore his name, and it had been only four years since he'd had to flee that state for his life. Not for one day had he regretted taking Maddie with him when he left Texas, but now he feared she and their children would share his fate if the bounty hunters recognized him.

"More biscuits?" Maddie asked the older man, bringing Luke's attention back to the table. Grif helped himself to one of the hot, flaky biscuits from the bowl she extended toward him. She turned toward the other stranger, the one the older man called Frank. He shook his head at the biscuits she offered before returning to his squinting perusal of Luke.

"Mighty fine breakfast, ma'am." Grif slathered butter on the hot bread, followed by a liberal helping of blackberry jam.

"I helped Mama make the jam," Krista said. Luke noticed how the younger man's eyes followed his daughter, causing his own gut to tighten with fear. The gunman could watch Luke all he wanted, but he didn't want the man's attention turning to his family.

"A mighty fine job you done." The old man's praise brought a smile that produced dimples in the little girl's cheeks.

"Are you a grandpa?" Krista slid off her chair to stand beside Grif.

"Krista!" Maddie admonished.

The older man chuckled as though she'd handed him a compliment. "No one's ever called me grandpa." A touch of sadness flickered across his face. "I had me a couple of young'uns once, a long time ago though."

"Did they go away?" If Luke hadn't been worried about the man's reason for being in his home, he would have sympathized with his discomfort.

"Fever," Grif mumbled. "If they'd lived, I'd likely be a grandpa by now."

"I don't have a grandpa. Do you want to be my grandpa?" Round blue eyes widened with excitement as Krista made her generous offer.

"Krista, don't bother . . ."

"Now, now, Mrs. McCall. Yer little gal ain't botherin' me none." Turning his attention back to the child, he added, "I'd plumb enjoy bein' your grandpa fer a spell."

"Come see my Christmas tree." She urged the man to his feet, and together they stepped closer to the decorated cedar tree.

"Well now, that's a mighty fine Christmas tree." Grif smiled down at Krista. "I never had me a Christmas tree, but my ma used to set me down every Christmas and read to me all about Jesus bein' a baby what was born in a barn, and how his ma made him a place to sleep in a feed box."

Krista leaned her head to one side and looked up at the old man. "Babies don't sleep in barns. They might get hurt, and the barn is too cold."

"This Baby slept in a barn," Grif repeated.

Krista turned trusting eyes to Luke for confirmation or denial of the old man's story. His heart swelled with pleasure at her innocent trust that he held all the answers.

"He's right." Luke moved across the room to pick up his daughter. Bringing her back to the table, he sat, settling her on his lap. He'd pretty much dismissed religion from his life after his parents' deaths, but Maddie and then Ian McBride had got him thinking about it again. He even found himself praying once in a while. Now he wished he'd taken the time to tell Krista the stories Ma had read to him from her big black Bible. Suddenly it seemed important for his children to know the stories as well as Ian's children had known them. They'd talked about Bible folks as though they were close neighbors. He wanted Krista and Little Luke to be able to climb onto a chair to look at a large black book and trace with their small fingers the names of their parents and grandparents inside it, as he had done when he was a boy.

"One night, a long time ago," Luke began, trying to recall the details of the story, "a little baby was born in a stable because the baby's mama was a long way from home when it was time for the baby to be born. This was a special baby God sent to the world to tell people to love each other. He sent angels to tell people His son had been born. When the sheepherders out on the hills heard the angels, they hurried to the barn to see the Baby, and kings came from far away to bring Him presents."

"He got presents? Like my blue dress Mama is going to make for me?"

"Yes, your grandma told me we give presents on Christmas to help us remember that Christmas is that Baby's birthday and that He was a present from God to all of us. The kings knew that, and that is why they brought gifts to Him."

"What was the baby's name?" Krista looked up at him with wide eyes.

"Jesus."

"I know about Jesus!" She clapped her hands and looked toward her mother. "Mama said Jesus makes sick people better and that He 'specially likes little children. He told some people who wanted the children to go away that if they were mean to children they should be dropped in a river."

Luke turned his attention to Maddie, who was suddenly busy gathering up dishes. He hadn't known she'd ever heard any Bible stories. They'd never discussed religion much, other than her friendship with a little Mormon girl a long time ago and her firm commitment to praying every day. He'd assumed her drunken father had never taken her to church. Ian McBride's wife might have talked religion to her, just as Ian had shared some of his beliefs and views with him. She'd spent a lot of time around Mary McBride when he and Maddie had stayed in the little cabin behind the main house that winter in Utah.

Maddie lifted her eyes at last, and he saw the crimson flush on her cheeks. She sounded defensive when she spoke. "A woman stayed with Pa once for several months. She said she'd been a preacher's daughter—sometimes she told me stories." She took a deep breath, then added, "While you were gone, Sister Barnes and Sister Richards came to see how I was doing several times. They talked about Jesus, so I asked them if the stories I remembered were true, and they said they were."

"'Course they're true. They're in the Bible, ain't they?" Grif spoke up. He'd resumed his chair at the table.

"They're true," Luke confirmed. He'd never given much thought to whether the Bible stories were true or not, but Ma had believed in them, and something deep inside told him he should have listened more closely to them when he was a boy. Before another Christmas—if the bounty hunters didn't shoot him or haul him back to Texas—he'd make certain there was a big black Bible to take down from the shelf. Come spring, he'd encourage Maddie to ride the mare over to the Richardses' ranch, their closest neighbor, to visit with the missus there. And he'd take her and the young ones into town to thank the Barneses for their kindness too. Maybe they'd even go to church some Sunday.

Luke wasn't sure he wanted his daughter making friends with the bounty hunter, but the talk of Christmas seemed to soften the old man a bit. Luke might be worrying for nothing anyway. The two were following someone, but that didn't mean they were after him. He wasn't worth enough to bring two Texas bounty hunters all this distance. Besides, he didn't resemble the boy on that poster much anymore. He leaned back in his chair, his eyes narrowing to a sleepy slant. It was good to be home.

* * *

Frank had seen that pose before—a man almost asleep, tilted back on a wooden chair with one hand hidden beneath the table, his eyes appearing almost closed, but in reality seeing more than most men saw with both eyes wide open. He had a vague recollection of seeing this man looking much the way he looked now the night before Amelia had died. He'd been in the Golden Garter! The man's identity hit him with the force of a sledgehammer. Kid Calloway! He'd heard it had been Calloway's bullet that had killed Amelia. Slowly his hand began to inch toward the holster resting flat against his thigh.

CHAPTER EIGHTEEN

"For me?" The little girl's voice reminded Frank of his surroundings. Grif was holding out one of the creams he'd purchased at the store the day before, and the child was staring at the sweet with an expression of delight on her face. He winced, reminded of his sister once again.

"Shore," the old man chuckled, popping a piece of the candy into his own mouth and chewing it with obvious relish. "I'm kinda new to this grandpa'n business, but my own grandpappy uster keep a sweet or two in his pocket fer me when I was a lad." The child looked at her mother, who nodded, then she reached out hesitantly to accept the cream.

Frank relaxed his hand. Calloway didn't have any idea who he was. There was plenty of time to think this through. He'd have to get Grif aside—let him know McCall was really Kid Calloway and he was worth two Cole Walkers. He'd learned while perusing a stack of wanted posters in Denver a few months back that Harrison Duncan, a shady figure from his own past, had raised the ante for the Kid. A reward that had been a couple of hundred was now several thousand. He'd learned too that Duncan was set to make another run for governor. His cynical side wondered for just a moment if there was a connection between Calloway and Duncan's political ambitions.

"The snow has stopped." He turned to face his partner, glad for an excuse to get Grif outside, where he could share his discovery. "We should check on the horses."

"The cattle will be needing feed. I'd best be getting it to them." Luke rose to his feet, and Frank noticed the look of concern the other man directed toward his wife. He sensed McCall's reluctance to leave her side as long as he and Grif were in the house. An urge to assure the man that he and Grif didn't harm women or children caught him by surprise. He'd never felt concern before for the families of any of the men they'd captured.

The older man rose reluctantly to his feet too and reached for his buffalo-hide poncho. Seeing Krista wrinkle her nose, he chuckled and patted her head. "This old buffler has kept me warm for many a winter. It's a little hard on the nose if you ain't used to it, but it suits me fine."

When the men reached the barn, Luke turned to harnessing his team and hitching them to a wagon on runners. Grif drifted from stall to stall until he saw the mare. Lifting a hoof, he found the star and merely grunted, as though confirming the end of their search.

"He ain't Walker," Frank said in a soft whisper.

"I know that." Grif didn't sound disappointed. "Last night whilst the woman was treatin' your frostbite, McCall told her about the mare Oscarson gave him for wages and how he plans to get a young stallion from Utah and use the pair to start a herd of fancy horses. Walker tricked us. He traded the mare for one of Oscarson's horses, but we'll catch up to him sooner or later."

"We don't need Walker." Frank paced with growing excitement in front of the mare's stall, still talking in a low voice while casting furtive glances toward Luke, who was just outside the barn now, forking hay onto the wagon. "I remember McCall from Texas. He's worth a lot more to us than Walker." He began outlining his plan to take Kid Calloway.

"Wal, I don't know." Grif scratched his beard. "We slept in his house and et his bread. It's Christmas too."

"Aren't you the one who taught me there's no place for sentiment in this business?" Frank turned to glare at his partner. He couldn't let sentiment stand in the way. If Calloway was the man who shot Amelia, he wanted him to pay.

"It just don't seem right."

"You let the little girl get to you," Frank accused. "You like her calling you grandpa."

"That might be true," the old man conceded. "It's been a lot of years since a little child spoke to me, and it's got me thinkin' 'bout things, 'specially with today bein' Christmas 'n all."

"You saying you don't want that reward money?"

"No, I'm just sayin' it ain't right. McCall and his woman have been square with us. 'Sides, I don't hold with hurtin' children." He had a faraway look in his eyes that made Frank wary.

"Look, he's getting ready to take hay to some stock out by the lava beds. We can be ready when he comes back. There'll be no chance for his woman and kids to get hurt." Frank let his eyes follow Luke's movements as he pitched hay onto the wagon bed.

"Oh, they'll be hurt," the old man muttered, so Frank wasn't quite sure he'd heard the words. It annoyed him that he couldn't quite put the woman and kids out of his mind either.

The snow crunched loudly as Luke clucked to his team and the draft horses leaned into their harnesses. The two bounty hunters watched the wagon carrying McCall move slowly through the deep snow, the cold sending a squeaking sound into the bright, cold air.

"What if he just keeps going?" Frank asked.

"He won't," Grif said with finality. "Men like that'n always come home."

Returning to the warmth of the cabin, Frank felt a tug of conscience when Maddie insisted on checking his spots of frostbite she'd treated the night before. It wasn't relief as much as guilt that he felt when she said he wouldn't be losing any toes or patches of hide. She'd been kind to him, and he was repaying her by leaving her without a man to provide for her. *She won't be alone long,* he comforted himself. *A looker like her with a bit of land and stock—she'll find another man by spring.*

Across the room, Grif knelt on the floor beside McCall's little girl, absorbed in some game the child was playing that involved the bits of colored cloth attached to the limbs of the cedar Christmas tree. The scents of some kind of fowl roasting in the oven filled the air, along with that of apples and cinnamon, bringing memories of before Ma died when the same odors had wafted through the air of his childhood home. Melancholy filled his heart, bringing a longing for home he hadn't experienced for many years. Perhaps he'd head east for a bit after he collected that reward money. It would be good to know if Pa was still alive.

Feeling a tug at his leg, he looked down to see the baby use his pant leg to pull himself to a standing position. A wide, wet mouth showing two small teeth grinned up at him. Something inside him recoiled, filling him with a panicky need to free himself from the small fists clutching at his knee. He reached forward to unclasp the baby's hands, only to find one of his fingers firmly clutched by the child's small hand.

The baby continued to smile his near-toothless grin. His eyes were wide and bright, and Frank found himself almost returning the smile. There was something about the smile and the light dancing in the baby's eyes that brought back a time when he'd followed Pa about, basking in his presence and striving to do everything he did. Frank felt a lump in his throat.

"It's time for us to leave." He spoke with a gruffness in his voice. When he stood, the baby sat abruptly on his well-padded bottom and began to wail. The baby's cries sent guilt slamming straight to his heart.

Maddie turned her head at the sound of the baby's cry, then hurried toward him. She picked him up, rocking and shushing him before she turned to Frank. "Won't you stay for dinner? I have two plump hens in the oven." From the safety of his mother's shoulder, the baby peeked through his chubby fingers to smile broadly at Frank once again.

When Frank shook his head in refusal, Maddie carried the baby to his cradle, where he fussed for a few minutes before falling asleep. While she rocked the cradle, Frank and Grif pulled on their coats. As Frank looked back at the woman bending over the cradle, pain resurfaced, unexpectedly taking his breath. *That woman could be Amelia. We could have had a son like that, and I would have built her a house behind the shop. Our children would have spent Christmas . . .* He stopped himself. Remembering the past was futile. Collecting that reward money was all that mattered now.

As soon as the baby was asleep, Maddie hurried to the sideboard for bread, which she sliced into thick chunks while the men were still preparing for their departure. To the bread she added slabs of roasted meat, then wrapped the sandwiches in strips of cloth and placed them in a sugar sack. Two generous slices of pie joined the sandwiches before Maddie extended the bag toward Frank.

He hesitated. It didn't feel right to accept the bag when she didn't know they would be taking her husband away from her, but to refuse the offer might look suspicious. Finally he accepted the bag, tucked it beneath his coat, and reached for the door. Grif followed him out with only one last sorrowful look at the little girl, who was crying as she waved farewell.

Neither one spoke until they had their horses and the stolen mare saddled and returned to their stalls, where they would remain out of sight until needed. He hoped they wouldn't have to shoot McCall. At first he'd wanted nothing more than to see him dead, but he didn't want another death on his conscience. He'd rather turn him over to the sheriff in the first town they came to, collect a bank voucher, and be on their way, knowing the mare would be returned to Maddie. He could see no reason to tell the sheriff the mare was stolen.

By silent consent, he and Grif hid in the tack room, leaving the door open a crack, to wait for Luke McCall, or Kid Calloway, to return. Cold seeped into Frank's boots, and he remembered the agonizing pain of Maddie working to restore circulation to his feet and save him from losing his toes. He curled them several times and promised himself that when this was over, he would be on his way to Texas, away from the snow and cold. But a picture of Maddie stayed in his mind. She was a good woman, a lot like his ma had been. It was almost as if he could see her watching through her kitchen window in the hours to come for Luke to return while the untended fire in her stove slowly went out. He could see the little girl too, standing beside her Christmas tree, crying endlessly until her tears turned to long streaks of ice, and the baby holding out his chubby hands toward him, staring with those huge, round eyes, first in entreaty, then with a coldness more deadly than ice. He shifted position, hoping a more comfortable stance would bring more comfortable thoughts.

"You know what Christmas will always mean to that little girl?" Grif broke the silence with a whispered question.

"Yeah," Frank admitted. He almost wished he hadn't remembered Kid Calloway and the five-thousand-dollar bounty that double-dealing, would-be governor had placed on the man's head.

The jingle of harnesses sounded on the frozen air. The man they'd set out to ambush was returning. Frank tensed, one hand gripping the handle of his weapon. The sooner they got this over with and collected their money, the better.

McCall didn't release the team from the sled and bring the horses inside as they'd expected. Instead he stepped inside the barn's dim interior without his team. He walked stiffly with his hands awkwardly extended away from his body, like a blind man feeling his way.

McCall is snow-blind! This is going to be easy. Frank opened his mouth to call for Luke to surrender, but Grif clapped a hand over his mouth. Startled, he jerked to free himself, and that's when he saw the man with a gun pointed at McCall's back. Frank's grip on his own gun tightened until his knuckles turned white. He shifted his weight, turning slightly, until his own gun was pointing toward the newcomer.

McCall opened the mare's box stall, then seemed to stumble. Frank knew McCall was surprised to find the mare already saddled. The man with McCall stepped forward, then began to swear and wave his gun about. The intruder's anger caught Frank by surprise, then as the angry man waved toward the mare, he understood what had upset him. Cole Walker was attempting to steal the same horse he'd stolen once before. If he and Grif could capture both men, they'd be sitting pretty for a long time.

"I went to a lot of trouble to get rid of that horse," Walker said. "Get another one."

"She's the only saddle horse I own." McCall's voice was calm, though Frank knew he had to be shaking in his boots.

"Don't give me that!" There was a sneer in Walker's voice. "I ought to plug you right here. That would bring those bounty hunters who've been trailing me running. I warned you that if they interfere, expecting to collect a share of the price old Duncan put on your hide, I'll kill them both and put a bullet through your woman's head too. She ain't worth nothin'. Her pa's dead, so he ain't lookin' for her no more. That horse will do." He pointed toward Grif's Appaloosa.

Frank felt Grif tense. The old man was touchy about his horse. He'd raised it from a colt back when he was living with the Indians. Frank considered shooting Walker and taking McCall, but Walker's next words stopped him.

"It was considerate of Frank Haladen to follow you here—saves me tracking him down. It's taken far too long locating you. Duncan promised five thousand dollars to the man who silenced you for good and double money if I got Blackwell and Haladen too. I almost had all three of you back in Wallace Creek, but some two-bit sheriff got Blackwell, and that old drunk Brannigan scared Haladen into running. He had two chances at Haladen and missed both times, thanks to that stupid newspaper woman who got in the way. Now it's my turn, and nothing's going to keep me from collecting on both you and Haladen this time." Frank rocked back in shock. Calloway hadn't killed Amelia. Some old drunk following Duncan's orders to kill him had killed Amelia instead.

"What makes you think Duncan will let you live after you get Haladen and me?" McCall didn't sound scared, but his question didn't please Walker. McCall had managed to plant a valid concern in the outlaw's mind.

Frank seethed. He'd been stupid not to guess Duncan was behind his own quick exodus from Texas. The only question was whether the Wallace Creek sheriff had been Duncan's stooge or whether the lawman had saved his life by getting him out of town. He raised his gun, sighting it toward Walker, then stifled a curse. McCall was in his line of fire. Feeling a slight tug on his trousers, he turned, half-expecting to see round blue eyes and a near-toothless smile, but he'd only caught his pants on a nail. This time he recognized the corresponding tug at his heart. He didn't want that little boy growing up without a pa. Truth was, he no longer wanted Calloway—only Walker.

Calloway moved, taking a step toward the Appaloosa's stall. He lifted the loop of wire holding the enclosure, then gave the gate a shove, sending it flying straight into Walker's gut. Taken by surprise, Walker sprawled in the dirt, and Calloway was on top of him.

While Frank was still shifting his gun back and forth, looking for a clear shot, Grif dived from their hiding place into the melee. Frank hesitated a moment longer before following his partner. It didn't take long for the three men to subdue Walker.

Moments later, Luke stood beside Frank and Grif. Walker lay at their feet, trussed like a turkey. Luke held a gun, concealed from the other two men by the folds of his coat. He'd slipped the Colt into his coat pocket before leaving the house with the two bounty hunters earlier that morning. Walker had caught him off balance, and he'd been unable to reach the gun. He'd been expecting trouble from

Frank and Grif, but he hadn't guessed a third man had waited out the storm in one of the nearby lava rock caves.

Luke figured the bounty hunters had heard everything Walker said and knew about the bounty Duncan had placed on his head. He suspected they were only toying with him now, waiting their chance to catch him off guard. He'd guessed they were waiting to ambush him the moment he'd seen the saddled horses. Walker had merely delayed their plan.

He could shoot them, but he knew he wouldn't. He'd not only promised Maddie he wouldn't take up a gun again except to protect her and the children, but he'd been thinking a lot about all the times he might have shot Duncan or Blackwell or even one of the gunfighters out to build a reputation, and he hadn't. It seemed almost as if a will stronger than his own had kept him from killing those men. Whether it was Ma's and Maddie's praying that had stayed his hand or his own growing trust in a merciful God that stopped him now, he didn't know. He only knew he wasn't going to kill the bounty hunters. There had been enough killing. He let his gun slide soundlessly into the deep straw filling the stall where he stood. He wondered if they would let him kiss his children and tell Maddie good-bye.

"We'll send you your share of the reward." Frank made no attempt to conceal his contempt for the man lying at their feet. He saw the question in Grif's eyes and the startled expression on Calloway's face. Something in the slant of the sun shining through the barn doors—or perhaps it was the expression on Calloway's face—gave him pause.

The memory of a boy lying in his own blood on a hillside over-looking his home merged into that of a frightened youth hiding in an alley. Suddenly Frank knew why Duncan wanted Calloway dead. His own heart beat faster, and a load lifted from his shoulders. At last he was free of the past—no, perhaps not quite. There was much he could do to see justice served. He could fight for the principles Amelia believed in, and he could make certain Duncan never sat in the governor's seat in Austin.

Frank shook his head, and Luke didn't know if the former outlaw was telling his partner to wait or if he'd changed his mind about trying to capture Luke. His next words surprised Luke again as much as they did Grif. "I'll be heading back to Texas as soon as we drop Walker off with the closest sheriff. When I get there, I plan to have a talk with my uncle. He owns a good-sized newspaper in the town where I grew up, and he has a friend who writes for that big Austin newspaper. I think they would be interested in hearing all about a certain would-be governor's past dealings. I just might manage to mention how the kid who survived the massacre of his family a few years back was shot and killed by some outlaw along the Arizona strip a couple of years ago."

Frank stooped. When he rose to his feet, he was carrying Walker, whom he draped none too gently over the rump of one of the saddled horses. A few twists of a rope, and Walker was settled for a long, cold, uncomfortable ride. Frank stepped into his stirrup, settled himself in the saddle, gave a curt nod toward Luke, then started toward the barn door. Grif followed him.

"I don't want the reward money," Luke shouted to the departing men's backs.

Frank turned to give him one long, appraising look, then nodded as though he understood before facing forward and riding on.

"Here!" The old man, now wrapped in his buffalo robe, tossed something toward Luke, which he instinctively caught. "Give this to the little girl. Tell her Grandpa said she should have it."

Luke glanced down at the paper in his hand and knew it held the last of the old man's candy. When he looked up, the two men were mere specks on the snowy landscape. The sun shone brighter than a thousand rain-washed mornings as he turned toward the house where Maddie and the children waited for him.

* * *

Maddie lifted one corner of the gingham curtain to see a world of brilliant whiteness. The snow spread toward the lava flow in drifts that brought to mind the undulating waves of grass on the great prairie. She narrowed her attention to the barn. Luke's team and wagon stood in front of the doors, but there was no sign of Luke. A prickle of dread gripped her heart, telling her something was wrong.

Chiding herself for being fanciful, she continued to watch. After a few minutes, her vigilance was rewarded with the sight of two men on horseback leaving the barn. She recognized Grif and his partner. Right from the start, something about the two men had disturbed Luke, and though he hadn't said anything to her about the men, she'd noticed that his six-shooter was missing from the cupboard where he'd left it before he'd ridden off to the Oscarson ranch last fall.

As she followed the men with her eyes, she became aware of the bundle draped behind Frank's saddle. It looked like a body. Icy fingers of fear ran along her spine. It couldn't be Luke! There was no reason . . . Despair crept into her heart. She'd always known Luke was wanted in Texas, and she should have guessed Grif and Frank were bounty hunters.

Heedless of the snow, she flung open the door and raced toward the barn. Then she saw him. Dizzy with joy, her skirts billowed around her and she ran faster. Luke was running too—straight toward her—and he was smiling. He held out his arms, and she knew he would always be there for her. As Luke's arms caught her to him, the snow seemed to fade away, replaced by a carpet of spring grass, and Maddie had the distinct impression that somewhere an angel smiled.

ABOUT THE AUTHOR

Jennie Hansen graduated from Ricks College in Idaho and Westminster College in Utah. She has been a newspaper reporter, editor, and librarian. She reviews LDS fiction in a monthly column for *Meridian* magazine.

Her Church service has included teaching in all auxiliaries and serving in stake and ward Primary presidencies. She has also served as a den mother, stake public affairs coordinator, ward chorister, education counselor in the Relief Society, and teacher improvement coordinator. She currently teaches the seven- and eight-year-olds in Primary.

Jennie and her husband, Boyd, live in Salt Lake County. Their five children are all married and have so far provided them with eight grandchildren.

Jennie enjoys hearing from her readers, who can write to her in care of Covenant Communications, P.O. Box 416, American Fork, UT 84003-0416 or e-mail her at info@covenant-lds.com.

THE FOLLOWING IS AN EXCERPT FROM

FOUL PLAY

a novel by

BETSY BRANNON GREEN

The guard waved as she started her car and headed toward her apartment. She stopped at an all-night drive-through for a hamburger and ate it as she drove, saving a few scraps for her overgrown, red fish, even though it wasn't strictly part of Fred's recommended diet. She parked her car in her assigned spot, and after unlocking the front door to her apartment, dropped the sandwich crumbs into Fred's tank, then put up her purse and turned on the computer.

She knew she should go to bed but couldn't resist checking her e-mail one last time. By the time she got connected to her Internet server, there were two messages waiting for her. Her mother had sent one informing her it was now eleven forty-five, still cold and dark, and instructing Billie to turn off the computer and go to sleep. Billie smiled as she opened the other e-mail from her friend Cowboy, a computer programmer for the newly formed Global Football League. The e-mail read:

To the famous authoress Miss Regina St. Claire—

Sorry I didn't write yesterday. I've been installing state-of-the-art computers round the clock with barely enough time to eat and sleep! And I'm having so much fun it hardly seems fair to cash my paychecks (but I still do!). I'm spending the night in Atlanta but didn't bother to call since I'm headed to Cincinnati in the morning. But I'll be back here for the big game in a couple of weeks. I've heard it's a sellout, but I think I could finagle a couple of tickets. Do you want to go with me? Maybe Camille could come too?

Cowboy

P.S. I'll even buy you both a hot dog.

Billie smirked at the words on the computer screen. Even fifty-something computer nerds couldn't resist Camille, although Billie knew Camille wouldn't give someone like Cowboy the time of day. Billie hit the reply button and settled back in her chair.

Dear Cowboy,

A lucky computer genius shouldn't brag about his dream job to poor, hardworking people like me. And I hate football, but the offer of a free hot dog does tempt me. I'll check out the holiday schedule with my mother and let you know about the GFL game.

In other news, my career with LoveSwift Books may be coming to an end. I'm running behind schedule on my new novel. (I know that shocks you.) The manuscript was supposed to be submitted a week ago, and I'm only on chapter 7. My proposal for the next one was due yesterday (and I don't have any idea what it will be about). Oh well. Maybe when LoveSwift cancels my contract, I'll take a course on computer programming and join you with the GFL.

Regina/Billie (something less than famous—but still hopeful)

Billie turned off the computer and bumped the thermostat up a notch. Then she put on pajamas and climbed into bed. After closing her eyes, she thought of playing shuffleboard with young single adults from South Carolina and tanning on white sand beaches until she fell asleep.

* * *

When Billie returned home from church on Sunday, she made herself a peanut butter and jelly sandwich and fed the scraps to Fred, then spent an hour straightening up her apartment. Afterward, she turned on her computer and scanned through a mildly threatening missive from her editor at LoveSwift Books demanding the overdue manuscript. Then she opened an e-mail from Cowboy.

Dear Ms. St. Claire,

It was snowing in Denver when I left there a couple of days ago, but the sun's shining in Cincinnati. Can't enjoy the weather though. Too busy. Worked so late last night I fell asleep on a computer that cost more than some people earn in a year. Have you thought of a brilliant idea for your next book yet? And have you decided about the GFL exhibition game? Did you ask Camille?

Cowboy

Billie sighed, then typed a quick reply.

Dear Cowboy,

I don't have an idea for my next book yet, brilliant or otherwise. But I am going on a five-day cruise to the Bahamas, and surely I can get some work done then (assuming that I don't get seasick). I'm taking my laptop and cell phone, so you can reach me any time of the day or night—voice, text, or e-mail. If you think of a good plot for my next book, I'm open to suggestions!

I haven't had a chance to ask my mother about the GFL game, but pencil me in. Camille is already going with someone else. Sorry.

Next time I write you, I'll be tan.
Regina/Billie

Billie typed in her cell phone number, then pushed Send.

Once she had finished packing, Billie set her alarm for six o'clock in the morning, settled under the thick covers on her bed, and read until she fell asleep.

Billie awakened from a deep sleep with an uneasy feeling that something was not right. The apartment was very dark and quiet, so she knew it was late. Then a loud pounding startled a scream from her throat. She jumped out of bed and ran to the front door. Through the peephole, she could see Camille's magnified face. Reluctantly she opened the door and stepped aside.

Camille entered quickly, followed by a man with a huge neck. "You sleep like the dead," she told Billie. "This is Jeff Burdick," she added as if Billie wouldn't recognize him. His face had been on magazine covers and cereal boxes ever since he had announced his intention to leave the NFL and play in the new Global Football League.

"Hey." The quarterback flashed her one of his famous smiles.

Billie nodded, struggling to keep both her bathrobe and mouth from gaping open.

Camille moved into the living room and looked around, then shook her head. "I can't believe how small this place is. I've seen closets with more square footage," she exclaimed as she dropped her suede jacket across the back of a chair.

"Everyone doesn't have a rich uncle to finance spacious and expensive apartments," Billie replied with an edge to her voice as the quarterback sat down. His long legs pressed against the coffee table, and his knees were almost touching his nose.

"I think it's cozy," Mr. Burdick tried, and Camille laughed.

"Right, sugar." She gave him a complacent smile then sat beside him. "Just like a coffin."

Mr. Burdick had obviously been taught some manners, since he blushed at Camille's rude remark. He pointed to Fred, who was swimming furiously around the tank. "What's his name?"

"Fred, but it's a her," Billie provided.

"*Her* name is Fred?" Mr. Burdick clarified.

Billie nodded. "I didn't find out she was female until after she was already named, and then it didn't seem right to change."

Camille kicked off her expensive pumps and settled her nylon-encased feet on a needlepoint pillow.

"My mother made that." Billie pointed at the pillow.

"It's cute," Camille said but didn't move her feet. Then she squinted at the brightly colored clothing draped over a kitchen chair. "For your trip to the Bahamas?" she asked, and Billie nodded. "My cruise wardrobe is much nicer." She turned around. "The Competitors are taking a week off from training."

Billie looked back and forth between her guests. "That's good, I guess."

"It's the perfect opportunity for Jeff and me to spend some time together," Camille explained. "But the press hounds Jeff, and now his ex-wife has hired a private investigator."

Jeff Burdick spread his hands. "Everywhere I go, it's like a parade."

Billie shook her head in confusion. "Even if nobody was following him, I don't see how the two of you can spend the week together since you'll be touring southern Georgia with the Blalock Industries representatives."

Camille scooted forward. "There were obstacles, but I overcame them!"

Billie was immediately on guard. "How?"

"We'll take the honeymoon suite on your cruise, and no one will know it's us!"

Billie shook her head in exasperation. "How many times will I have to tell you that you can't have my cruise?"

"Jeff will buy you another one," Camille replied.

"I want *this* cruise!" Billie's tone was adamant.

"Jeff has *this* week off," Camille repeated as if she were talking to a dimwit. "It's our only chance."

Billie was unimpressed. "Wait until after the football season. By then his divorce should be final and his ex-wife won't care what you do."

Jeff Burdick finally felt compelled to make a comment. "Camille, baby, if she doesn't want to sell us the cruise . . ."

Camille stroked the football player's cheek before turning to Billie. "I'm really not here to negotiate, just to inform you of the changes in your situation. Your vacation has been revoked, and you have been assigned to take the Blalock trip. You can either sell us the cruise or let it go to waste. The choice is up to you."

Jeff Burdick blushed again, but Billie was too upset to feel sorry for him. "Frieda wouldn't do that to me," she whispered.

Camille shrugged. "It's nothing against you personally. She's just doing a favor for Uncle Conrad. And don't you think you're being rather shortsighted? Jeff can help me get a job with the GFL, and once I leave the Chamber, all the good assignments will come to you."

Billie very much wanted a chance to prove herself and to be rid of Camille, but sacrificing her cruise was asking too much. She shook her head firmly. "No, I won't do it."

Camille's eyes narrowed. "If you refuse, I'll ask Uncle Conrad to have you fired."

Billie's breath started coming in quick, little gasps. "I don't believe you would really go that far."

Camille moved closer, her expression menacing. "Actually, I'm prepared to go much further. Be glad all I want is your cruise."

Billie flinched as Camille ran her fingers through her hair, then moderated her tone slightly as she continued. "If you'll be reasonable and take care of the Blalock Industries folks next week—life will be better for both of us. And I'm not asking you to give up your vacation, just to postpone it."

Billie wanted to call Camille's bluff, but she couldn't afford to lose her job at the Chamber until she had a contract with Randall House. There was no doubt in her mind that Camille would carry out her threat to have Billie fired if she didn't cooperate. So, feeling like a coward, Billie surrendered.

"I guess I don't have much choice. I'll call my mother . . ."

Camille shook her head. "I've already called her. Everything's arranged. She said the tickets would be waiting for us on the ship."

Billie nodded. "If my mother doesn't receive payment for this cruise by the end of the week, I'll call the press myself and make sure Mr. Burdick's ex-wife is waiting for you when you disembark."

Camille gave her an exasperated look. "For heaven's sake, Billie. I said Jeff will pay for it."

"Full price," Billie added, feeling a measure of satisfaction. "And I want him to start using my mother's agency for all his travel needs."

Camille waved impatiently. "Okay, okay."

"I want Mr. Burdick to give me his word," Billie said. "Yours doesn't mean much."

Jeff Burdick nodded. "I'll tell my personal assistant to use your mother's agency from now on. And I'm sorry about all this . . ."

Camille stood and looked at Billie through narrowed eyes. "Your mother said you had a map and information about the cruise."

"In my purse . . ." Billie's voice trailed off as Camille walked over and studied the contents of Billie's handbag.

Camille removed an envelope from the handbag. She turned and smiled, all sweetness again now that she'd gotten her way. "Do you have one of your mother's business cards you could give Jeff? He'll need her address to mail the check. And now that she's going to be his travel agent, he'll need her phone numbers."

Billie walked stiffly into her bedroom and took a business card from a drawer in her dresser. When she returned to the living room, Camille and Jeff were standing by the front door.

Billie extended the card, and Camille tucked it into her purse. "I couldn't find my itinerary for the Blalock trip, but Edgar will have an extra when you meet him at the airport."

"Edgar?"

"Uncle Conrad's chauffeur," Camille clarified. "He's going to be driving you and the Blalock people around. You'll need to be at the airport by four o'clock. Call if you need me." Camille stepped forward and whispered into Billie's ear. "But only if you *really* need me." Then she turned to Jeff Burdick. "Come on, sugar." She took the quarterback by the hand and led him outside.

Billie locked the door behind them, then took several deep breaths, refusing to cry. It wasn't that big a deal, she told herself. She needed time to work on her book, but she figured she could do it in her hotel room at night during the Blalock trip. The only reason she had to believe that a week spent on the cruise ship might be significant was the nose-itching theory of her crazy great-grandma.

Since it was only five-thirty in the morning and the Blalock reps didn't need to be picked up until later that afternoon, Billie retreated to her room to get some more sleep. She fell back into bed and burrowed under the covers. Then, once her head was buried deep into the pillow, she allowed a few tears to slip from her eyes.

Billie was awakened fifteen minutes later by a phone call from her mother. "I can't believe the Chamber canceled your vacation!" was Nan Murphy's first comment. "But it did work out nicely that Camille and her cousin could use your ticket."

Billie realized immediately that Camille had given Nan a fictionalized version of the situation, but in order to set the record straight she knew she would have to upset her mother, so she sighed and answered, "Yeah, that was a real stroke of luck."

"And I'm sure the LDS businessmen will appreciate the fact that a member of the Church will be showing them around."

Billie murmured a noncommittal, "Hmm."

"I've already booked another cruise for you that can be taken anytime during the next twelve months. Since Camille said money was no object, I put you in a stateroom with a balcony."

"Thanks, Mama," Billie said softly.

"Are you all right, sweetheart?" Nan asked. "You sound kind of stuffy."

"I told you my nose was itching. Maybe I'm catching a cold," Billie replied. "And let me know if you don't get a check from Camille's *cousin*."

"Camille said he was a very responsible sort of person. I'm sure he'll pay me promptly. She also said that he'll be giving me a lot of business in the future."

As Billie ended the call, she marveled that her mother could be so shrewd in business and yet such a bad judge of character. Billie took the last Pop-Tart from the box, then sat in front of the computer and worked on chapter 8 of *Breathless* until two-thirty. At that point, she turned off her computer and stared at her luggage.

She didn't have the heart to repack, even though she would be going on a tour of southern Georgia in December instead of a cruise to the Bahamas. Hoping she could adapt her wardrobe, she stepped into the shower. As the water sluiced down her, she realized that Camille and Jeff Burdick were probably just getting settled in to what should have been her luxurious honeymoon suite.

Billie let the water run until it started to get cold. After drying her hair, she put on a business suit and sensible shoes. As she covered the sprinkling of freckles across her nose with makeup, she wondered if she *should* cut her hair. It hung almost to her waist, and though she'd always thought it was her best feature, Camille's remark about updating her appearance still stung.

Once she was ready, she slipped on her red, down-filled coat, gave Fred a generous helping of fish food, and picked up her purse. She reached inside and felt for her keys but couldn't find them. After several fruitless seconds of searching, she walked over to the kitchen counter and dumped the contents out for closer examination. There were still no keys.

Grinding her teeth in frustration, Billie stalked to her room and opened the jewelry box she had inherited from Grandma Murphy. As she grabbed the extra set of keys she kept there, she saw her emergency hundred-dollar bill. Since the Chamber would pay expenses on the trip and taking her own money might tempt her to spend it unnecessarily, she started to close the jewelry box. Then, she had the overwhelming feeling that she should take the money with her. Whether it was Grandma Murphy or the Holy Ghost or her own imagination, she didn't dare ignore the prompting. So she tucked the bill into her purse and rushed outside into the cold winter afternoon.

Billie made it halfway down the sidewalk before she realized that her car was not in its regular parking space. Dumbfounded, she stared around the crowded lot. Her Taurus, while dependable, was certainly not enviable, and she doubted that a thief would choose to steal it over the other cars in the apartment complex. Then her eyes settled on a silver Volvo, which looked very much like Camille's, parked where her Taurus should have been. Closer inspection proved that it *was* Camille's car. Furious, Billie pulled out her cell phone and dialed quickly.

She had to call three times before Camille finally answered. "Billie!" She sounded delighted to hear from her coworker. "This suite is incredible! It has a huge hot tub and a skylight and a big screen television—"

"You stole my car!" Billie interrupted.

"I didn't steal it," Camille said with a laugh. "I just traded so that the private investigator wouldn't follow us. When you leave my car in the long-term parking lot at Hartsfield International, he'll assume I've gone on my business trip as planned."

Billie took a deep breath. "You could have at least asked me."

"You would have said no," Camille replied blithely. There was a noise in the background, then Camille giggled. "Just a second, sugar! Billie, I've got to go. The keys to my car are under the front passenger seat." The line went dead.

Billie stared at the cell phone for a few seconds, then turned it off and got into the Volvo. Once she got the car started, she noticed that the gas gauge was below empty, so she had to stop at the nearest gas station. Then, with evil thoughts of Camille thrashing around in her mind, Billie finally headed to the airport.